DAWN LEE MCKENNA & AXEL BLACKWELL

DEAD RECKONING

A STILL WATERS SUSPENSE NOVEL— BOOK 1

A SWEET TEA PRESS PUBLICATION

First published in the United States by Sweet Tea Press

Edited by Debbie Maxwell Allen

Cover by Shayne Rutherford
wickedgoodbookcovers.com

Interior Design by Colleen Sheehan
wdrbookdesign.com

ISBN: 978-0-99866669-1-4

For Plutes
who is without peer among his species,
whichever species that might be

&

In loving memory of Vi Hartigan
—Dawn Lee

For Jo, the light of my life
—Axel

ONE

PEOPLE WHO DREAM about quiet country nights have never been in the country after dark.

Even after their dogs had shut up, Mooney White and Grant Woodburn were surrounded by nothing but noise. The crickets and the frogs were screaming at each other, and there was a decent summer breeze moving through the trees that had been bothersome to the men before they'd finally bagged their fill.

It was just past three in the morning, and dark-dark. The men were in the ass end of Gulf County, FL, in the woods just north of Wewahitchka and near the Dead Lakes Recreation Area. The low, thick cloud cover made the moon pointless.

Mooney was a black man in his late forties. He was dressed in an old pair of his blue work pants and a navy windbreaker. The many spots of white in his close-cropped hair looked like a little patch of fireflies in the night. He used his flashlight to guide their steps over rocks and fallen limbs. His .22 rifle was slung over his shoulder, and he held his dog's leash in the other hand.

Grant Woodburn, a redheaded man just a bit younger than his best friend, held his dog's leash in one hand, and a .410 single shot in the other. Their bag of coons was slung around his neck.

The men's boots crunched softly atop the thick carpet of pine needles. Ahead of them, the two dogs were almost soundless in their passage.

It was Mooney who first spotted the dim lights. They rounded a thick copse of shrubs and old cypress, and the two circles of light were just visible through the trees, about a hundred yards ahead.

"Hey, Woodburn," he said. "You left the lights on in my truck, I'm gonna kill you."

Woodburn stopped and looked at the lights. "Man, I didn't leave your lights on," he said. There was a high-pitched buzzing near his right ear, and he brushed at it with the sleeve of his Carharrt jacket. "We ain't even over there." He lifted his arm again and pointed off to the right. "We're over there."

Mooney's dog, a fawn-colored Ladner Black Mouth cur, went to tugging on his leash. Mooney tensed up on the leash and made a sound almost like he was getting something out of his teeth. The dog stopped, and the leash got some slack to it again. Mooney stopped, too.

"Those lights is about out," he said. "Somebody's gonna be pissed when they get back to their vehicle."

Woodburn looked over at him as he jerked slightly on his own leash. His brown and white Beagle stood stiffly where he was, looking toward the truck.

"Reckon we should go shut his lights off for him?" Woodburn asked.

"If the fool left his doors unlocked," Mooney answered.

"Man, this is right around where we heard that shot a while back," Woodburn said, his voice slightly hushed.

Mooney stopped walking. His dog and then his friend followed suit.

"That don't necessarily mean nothin'," Mooney said quietly.

"Maybe we should just go to your truck and call the police or somethin'," Woodburn whispered.

"Man, we got two guns," Mooney said. "Besides, what are we gonna tell 'em? Haul y'all asses out here to shut this fool's lights off? You watch too much TV."

He made a clicking noise with his tongue, and men and dogs veered off their intended path and headed for the lights. When they were about fifty feet out, Mooney squinted at the pickup that sat silently in the clearing. From where they were standing, they were looking at the truck head on. The driver's side door was standing open. The interior light either didn't work or had already burned out.

"I know that truck," Mooney said quietly.

It was a black Ford F-150, which in Gulf County was like saying its name was John. But the Gators antenna topper was ringing a bell for Mooney.

"Whose is it?" Woodburn asked.

"Hold on, I'm thinking," Mooney answered. He was quiet for a moment. "That's Sheriff Hutchins' truck."

"Are you sure?" his friend asked him.

"Yeah, man, I put a new tranny in it last year," Mooney answered.

"Aw, man, I don't like it," Woodburn said. His beagle, Trot, had set to whining.

"I'm not real excited, either," Mooney said. "But maybe he needs help or somethin'."

"Not from us, man," Grant said. "Maybe from the cops."

"Man, pull your pants up," Mooney said. "Norman, let's go," he said to his dog, and started following him slowly into the clearing.

Mooney and Norman were in the lead, Woodburn and Trot lagging a bit behind, which was definitely Woodburn's choice and not the dog's. The beagle strained at his leash.

As Mooney got closer, he realized that the weird shininess on the driver's side window wasn't some trick of the light. It was something on the window, all over it. He stopped walking. A sheen of moisture had suddenly appeared on his onyx skin, and he swiped at it with one huge, calloused hand.

"Sheriff?" he called out, flicking his flashlight on and off against the windshield. The flashlight wasn't a particularly powerful one. Its light bounced off the glass, revealing nothing. "Hey, Sheriff? It's Mooney White!"

The crickets and frogs went silent. For a few moments, there was just the wind in the trees and the quiet keening of the dogs.

"Shut up, Norman!" Mooney snapped, and both dogs quieted. A new sound, a faint one, reached Mooney's ears. "You hear that?"

Both men listened for a moment. "Radio," Woodburn whispered finally.

"Hell's up in here?" Mooney asked himself mostly.

He flicked the flashlight on again, trained it at the open door. In the edge of the light, he saw something, and dropped the beam lower. Beneath the door, he saw pants. Knees of pants. And one hand just hanging there.

"Aw hell, man," Woodburn whispered. "This ain't right at all."

Mooney slid his rifle down his arm, released the safety with his flashlight hand. The light bobbed off to the side of the truck.

"Sheriff?" Mooney called again. "Scarin' Mooney just a little bit here."

There was no answer. Norman gave out a couple of barks, higher-pitched than some people would expect from such a sturdy dog. Mooney gave him his lead, and followed Norman as he pulled toward the truck. Mooney tugged him off to the side, made him circle wide, about eight or ten feet from the old Ford. He could hear Woodburn several yards behind him, whispering to himself.

When Mooney had gotten round to the back side of the open door, he pointed the flashlight at it.

"Oh, hellfire," Mooney said to himself.

Sheriff Hutchins was slumped forward on his knees, his upper body hung up on the open door. Closer up, the black on the window wasn't black at all, but a deep red, and there was a lot more of it on the inside of the door.

Mooney stood there staring, barely hearing his best friend gagging behind him, or Lynyrd Skynrd on the Sheriff's truck radio, singing about going home.

TWO

THE CELL PHONE BLEATED, vibrated, and did a little jig on the built-in teak nightstand. Evan Caldwell reached over and thumbed the answer button without looking at it.

"This is Vi," a deep voice intoned before he had a chance to speak.

"So it would seem," Evan answered. She always said it like that, deliberately and with brevity, like a newscaster introducing himself.

"You need to get out to Wewa," she said. "It's very serious."

"I'm off today, Vi," he said.

"Not anymore," she said, her voice like gravel that had been soaked in lye. "We need you to get out there immediately."

"I don't think that I actually know where it is," he said.

"You may not know how to pronounce Wewahitchka, but certainly you can recognize it on a map," she replied. "Take 71 straight to Wewa. Go to the Shell station at the intersection of 71 and 22. You'll be met by Chief Beckett."

"Is he an Indian chief?"

He heard Vi try to sigh quietly. She was Sheriff Hutchins' assistant, and had apparently been with the Sheriff's Office since law enforcement was invented. Evan had only been there a few weeks, and had yet to make a good impression on her. Granted, he hadn't put forth much effort. It seemed rather pointless, considering he was from "out of town" and would probably be gone again before she could decide if she liked him.

"He is the Chief of Police in Wewa," she said. "Lt. Caldwell, this is a very grave matter, which I don't want to explain over the phone. Chief Beckett will fill you in, then lead you to the scene."

Evan was mostly awake at this point, and her voice told him that his sarcasm would be unappreciated and possibly inappropriate.

"Did the Sheriff ask you to call me?" he asked her as he sat up.

There was silence on her end for a moment. When she finally spoke, he thought maybe her voice cracked just a little. "Please just go, as quickly as possible," she said, and hung up.

Evan looked at his phone for a moment, then checked the time. It was just after four in the morning. He swung his legs over the side of the bed and rubbed at his face as the teak sole of the master stateroom chilled his feet.

Evan was just shy of forty-two, and starting to collect tiny lines at the corners of his eyes and crease lines along the sides of his mouth. His eyes were a bright, clear green that was surprising beneath his black hair and thick eyelashes. The very narrow, white scar that ran from the left corner of his mouth down to his chin kept him from being too pretty, or so his wife Hannah liked to say.

He stood up, took two steps over to the hanging locker beside his bed. One of the many reasons he'd chosen the 1986 Chris-Craft Corinthian over some of the other boats he'd seen was that it had a master stateroom with an actual bed and some halfway decent storage. Evan hadn't kept much when he'd emptied the Cocoa Beach house and moved aboard the boat, but he liked everything to have a place, and to be there when he expected it to be.

He opened the locker, pulled a pair of black trousers from their hanger and slipped them on. Three identical pairs remained in the locker, next to five identical white button-down shirts. As he bent to step into his pants, he swore he could smell cat urine. His upper lip twitched as he leaned into the locker and sniffed. The only light in the room came from the lights on the dock, shining vague and gray through the curtains over the portholes.

His shoes, two pairs of black dress shoes, one pair of Docksiders, and a pair of running shoes, were lined up neatly on a shelf at the bottom of the locker. He bent lower, and the scent magnified. He picked up a shoe from the middle, a left dress shoe. The inside was shinier than it ought to be. He brought it to his nose and jerked back.

He managed to stop himself from throwing the shoe across the room, distributing cat pee throughout his cabin, but just barely. Instead, he carefully set it down on the floor, and pulled a shirt from the locker.

Once he had dressed, he walked in his sock feet into the boat's one head, which the previous owner had fortuitously remodeled just before he got divorced and had to sell. The guy had expanded it into the space that had been a closet, which gave him room to put in a real shower, and a space for a stacking washer and dryer. It only fit the type that people used in RVs, but it was enough for Evan, who had trouble using public appliances and would prefer buying new clothes every week to going to a laundromat.

Evan grabbed his cleaning tote from the top of the small dryer, wet a cloth with a mixture of warm water and the expensive wood soap, and thoroughly cleaned and dried the small, sloped shelf on which he kept his shoes. Then he carried the wet shoe up to the galley, tied it up in a trash bag, and set the trash bag just outside the French door to the large sun deck.

When he came back inside, he spotted the cat sitting on the built-in teak cabinet between the steps down to the V-berth Evan used for storage and the steps down to the galley. Plutes was as black as ebony, and weighed at least fifteen pounds. Hannah had brought him home just a few weeks before her accident, and said she'd named him Pluto. Plutes for short.

Evan had thought she'd named him after the idiot dog from Disney. In fact, she'd taken the name from a Poe story. Evan didn't read Poe's stories, although he liked *The Raven* quite a bit, so he could never remember which story it was, but he thought the name was probably appropriate anyway.

The cat had never made a sound in all the time Evan had been burdened with him; at least none that Evan had been there to hear. He was a shiny, black statue of seething disdain and discontent. He turned away from one of the windows that wrapped around the entire salon and stared at Evan over his shoulder, his eyes narrowed and dismissive.

"Was that you?" Evan asked the cat, then cringed at the realization that he had become one of those people who asked cats questions. It was also a stupid question, since Plutes was the only cat aboard.

Plutes blinked at Evan, just once, slowly. Then he looked back out the window. If he could sigh, he clearly would have.

"Do it again and you'll go to the pound," Evan said, then went down the three steps that led to the eat-in galley. It was small, but got good light from the windows in the salon, and it suited Evan's needs. To one side was the U-shaped galley itself, with fairly new stainless appliances and two feet of gray Corian countertop that was just enough. On the other side, a built-in dinette booth with blue striped upholstery and a small window.

Evan poured a cup of milk two thirds full and set it in the microwave to heat, then loaded up his espresso machine and turned it on. Vi had sounded distressed, and no doubt the call was urgent, but Evan had only had three hours of sleep. He wouldn't get to We-whatever any faster by crashing.

While the espresso brewed, Evan walked back to his stateroom and retrieved the undefiled dress shoes from the locker. He slipped these on, then opened a side table drawer, and pulled out his holster, his badge and his Sheriff's Office ID. He dropped the ID wallet into his pocket, clipped the holster over his belt on the right side, and fastened his badge to the front of his belt on the left.

There was a decent breeze coming through the open windows, and the air smelled briny and clean simultaneously. Evan took a deep lungful of it and mourned the day out on the water that he'd had planned. Then he went back to the galley, poured the milk and espresso into his travel mug, and took three swallows before he headed back up to the salon.

He returned Plutes' look of disgust as he crossed the salon, then stepped out onto the sun deck. It was Evan's favorite part of the boat, large enough for a rattan table and chairs and a decent stainless BBQ. He picked up the trash bag containing the stinking shoe and walked it out to a garbage can on the dock. Then he headed down the long dock toward the main marina building, now mostly dark, and the lights of Port St. Joe, FL. It was mostly dark, too.

Aside from the creaking of fenders against the dock and the clinking of mast rigging on the few sailboats nearby, the sound of Evan's footfalls was the only noise that disturbed the infant morning.

Evan's tires hummed over course asphalt, rolling through the predawn haze. The air thickened as he moved inland, humid and heavy with the fragrance of cypress, brackish water and silt. Evan counted eighty-seven bug strikes on his windshield during the twenty-three-mile drive, mostly small white moths drawn into his path by yesterday's heat slowly rising from the blacktop.

As he neared the intersection of State Highways 71 and 22, the first blush of dawn added a pinkish tint to the thickening fog. Light too artificially white to be anything but the fluorescents of a gas station bloomed and spread just past the intersection, where a traffic light seemed to hover untethered over the street. High above the service station and the slowly dissipating fog, the gas station's sign's illuminated letters blazed bright red: H-E-L-L.

"Perfect," Evan muttered.

He slowed as he approached the intersection. His light was green, but this was Florida cracker country, and cracker logic dictated that dense fog was a license to speed - it's harder for the cops to write you a ticket if they can't see you coming. A vehicle travelling highway speed would barely have time to stop for a light in this fog. One travelling at cracker speed probably wouldn't even have time to wave at a cop car as it passed.

After checking for oncoming headlights, and ascertaining that his odds of making it through the intersection without being t-boned were better than a coin toss, he passed under the hovering traffic lights and pulled into the Shell station.

A 1987 Monte Carlo, black with thin gold accents above the wheels and along the sides, idled beside the ice machine. The single blue dome on the roof, just above its driver's side window, suggested this was Chief Beckett's car.

The man himself, trim and tall, leaned against his car, legs crossed at the ankles, deep in conversation with a young, female station attendant. He was in his late fifties Evan thought, and wore heavy boots, dark blue jeans, and a uniform shirt pressed to the point of crispiness. Evan guessed he used glue rather than starch to hold those creases against this humidity. A hint of closely cut silver hair showed beneath his hat.

Evan parked next to the Monte Carlo and got out of his car. The attendant held a Styrofoam cup of coffee in her hands. As Evan drew closer, he saw she wasn't half as young as she was trying to be, though the bleached blond mass of curls had been fairly convincing.

She lounged against the Monte Carlo, a bit more casually than the chief, batting her eyelids so emphatically that Evan feared she'd wear a hole through her corneas. The smile playing on her lips was rehearsed to near perfection, but it dropped away the second her eyes fell on Evan. Evan wasn't sure if it was interest he saw in her eyes or just curiosity. He was used to both, and cared about neither.

"Looks like your boy made it," the woman said to Beckett. She perused Evan from his face to his shoes and back again, then popped her gum and rolled her eyes back to the chief. "Here you go, Beck," she sighed, sliding the coffee across the roof of his car. "Swing by later when it's just you. Maybe I'll have some pie or somethin' for ya."

She headed toward the front door of the station, her hips twitching like a compass between two magnets.

"Thanks, Billie," Beckett said. "I'll see what I can do,"

"Well, don't break your neck on my account," she called over her shoulder. Bells jangled as she pushed through the door into the station.

Beckett had been admiring the view as she walked away. After the door closed he turned to Evan. "I'm Nathan Beckett, Wewa Chief of Police. You must be the Brevard County boy they hired over at the Sheriff's Office."

"Evan Caldwell," Evan said, holding out a hand. "Practically a man."

The humor Beckett had faked in his banter with Billie now twinkled somewhat more authentically in his eyes. "You don't say," he said as he shook Evan's hand. He squinted just a bit, as if taking his measure over again. "Looks like your new boss finally pissed off the wrong bad guy. Couple ol' boys found your sheriff shot dead in his truck a few of miles from here."

"Sheriff Hutchins?" Evan asked.

"Yep."

Fog hung over and around them like a wet, gray tent. Beyond the glow of the station's fluorescents, Evan heard a couple of vehicles zipping past and wondered if they were on their way to the scene. Above, the bright red HELL still blazed, the burnt-out "S" now visible in silhouette against the slowly brightening sky.

"We haven't had a law enforcement officer murdered here in over twenty years," Beckett said. This is going to be one hell of a mess." He clapped Evan on the shoulder. "Glad this ain't my jurisdiction."

"Chief," Evan said, meeting the older man's eyes, "I hope it won't hurt your feelings if I tell you I feel the same way."

Beckett's smile vanished, or blinked, rather. It was gone and then back again in an instant, but the new smile was more in his teeth and less in his eyes. "Don't worry, son. I recover quick enough."

Evan frowned down at his shoes, now covered in condensation from the fog. He wondered, not for the first time, why he even bothered polishing the things. He let out a slow breath as he looked back up at Beckett. "So, are we about to embark on some kind of country boy/city boy conflict that I should prepare for?"

Beckett's mouth twitched with the ghost of a grin. "I couldn't care less where you're from, Caldwell," he said.

"So what's the problem?"

Beckett sighed and glanced at the sound of a passing car before he answered. "Let me explain it this way: about four years ago, one of my officers and I came across a human hand over not too far from where we're headed this morning. Right on the jurisdictional line." He paused to take a sip of his coffee, then winced as he swallowed. Apparently, the coffee wasn't what Beckett came there for. "I call the ME, and he tells me I have to call the Sheriff's Office to have them verify what we found before he can come out. So I wait in the hot sun and a cloud of love bugs for a full hour until the Sheriff comes out, looks at the damn thing, and confirms for me that it's a human hand. On account of I might have confused it with something else that has thumbs. Then we were allowed to call the M.E. so that he could take the hand away and I could take my happy ass on home."

Beckett tossed the undrunk coffee into the trash can by the pump and opened the door of the Monte Carlo.

"Y'all are as bad as the Feds, is what I'm saying," he added.

"Well, I'll try not to insult you unnecessarily," Evan said simply.

"Alrighty then, Big Time. How would you like to proceed?"

"I guess you'd better take me to the body."

"Well I guess I'd better," Beckett said, climbing into his vehicle. "I was going to offer you a ride, but I think maybe you ought to take your own car. I don't plan on lingering. Although, if you're gonna be working much back in here, you might want to trade that Pilot in for something a little less Japanese."

"Thanks for the suggestion," Evan said with a tight smile. "I'll try not to keep you too long at the scene."

Beckett cranked the engine on the Monte Carlo. It roared to life, the aftermarket exhaust amplifying rather than muffling. He rolled down his window. "You're fine," he said. "I'll just stay long enough to take some notes on how it's done."

THREE

COUNTY ROAD 22 CUT arrow-straight through the pines and scrub brush, with an occasional ranch house or double-wide punctuating the neighborhood. Evan half expected Beckett to roar through the early morning fog, just to make Evan earn his place at the crime scene, but the Wewahitchka police chief kept it under sixty for most of the trip. Evan was glad for the time. Aside from the fact that he dreaded working the scene of his own boss's murder, the ride gave him a chance to drink his *café con leche* and smoke several cigarettes in quick succession.

The fog was retreating quickly from the rising sun. Pink gave way to a creamy yellow, which gave way to a radiant blue that was as hard and stark as it was beautiful.

About ten minutes outside of town, a low bridge broke the monotony of the woods. Beckett slowed as he reached it, then turned right onto a gravel road just over the other side. Evan rolled to a stop halfway across, intrigued by the surreal vista.

The flat expanse of water seemed to be stamped into the earth. Ancient cypress stumps, weathered to a stone gray, rose out of the lake's mirror-smooth surface. The stumps and their reflections appeared to be suspended in the clear blue firmament, making Evan think of hundreds of dead, rising from watery graves. After a moment, he slid his foot onto the gas again and followed Beckett's car. He found it parked in a clearing about a hundred yards back. It was one of several vehicles.

Evan parked behind Beckett as the other man got out of his car. Evan met him halfway.

"First time to the Dead Lakes, Sheriff?" Beckett asked.

"It is," Evan affirmed.

"Well, as the new lawman in town, you're going to want to familiarize yourself real quick. Folks get up to all sorts of shenanigans out here, now and again."

Evan's eyes narrowed at Beckett's use of the word *shenanigans*. Beckett might be backwoods, but Evan was pretty sure he was no aw-shucks country boy. He wondered if this was an act he played for everybody, or just people who needed to be jerked around.

The Chief nodded at Evan and started walking toward the center of the clearing. "Let me show you what you've got here."

Two Wewa squad cars sat side by side about twenty-five feet away. Just behind them was a Sheriff's Office cruiser. Another twenty-five feet beyond them was a pickup that Evan recognized as his boss's. Two Wewa cops and a sergeant Evan recognized as Ruben Goff were huddled together not far from the truck.

Goff was holding a .22 rifle in one hand and a shotgun in the other. Both hung at his sides. Several yards back from the truck, two civilians sat on the grass, looking up at another Wewa cop who was speaking to them in low tones.

As they approached the scene, Beckett continued, "This is a good place to meet up with folks you don't want anyone knowing you met up with, if you catch my meaning. Only, Hutch's meeting didn't go so well for him. Looks like an execution to me. On his knees with a single large caliber bullet to the back of the head."

"How much scene contamination?" Evan asked, pulling a pair of latex gloves from his pants pocket.

Beckett stopped at the yellow crime scene tape that encircled the truck and its immediate environs, and narrowed his eyes at Evan. "Just the two ol' boys that found him. Might be one of them left a little puddle of vomit near your scene, but that'll be all. They said they didn't touch anything, and I made my observations from outside the perimeter."

"You have any early guesses as to who he might have been meeting out here?" Evan asked.

"Could have been just about anybody, I suppose," Beckett said. "He might even have interrupted someone

DAWN LEE MCKENNA & AXEL BLACKWELL

else's meeting, if drugs were changing hands, or if he rolled up on the wrong man copulating with the wrong woman. 'Bout the only thing I'd say for sure is your shooter is going to be a man."

"What makes you say that?" Evan asked, as he stopped at the line of yellow tape.

"Court wouldn't call it a fact, but looking at the damage, I'd say the shooter used a magnum, .357 or maybe even a .44. There's a few women I know can handle a cannon like that, but it certainly wouldn't be their weapon of choice, not for this kind of work."

"You can tell the caliber used from outside the perimeter?" Evan asked.

"This ain't my first homicide, Big Time," Beckett said.

The other officers watched Evan warily as he and Beckett circled around the tape until Sheriff Hutchins's body came into view.

The sheriff was on his knees, slumped against his open door, one hand in the cab, the other dangling. A swarm of red droplets spread across the window and door panel, the lower ones elongating into drips rather than drops. From beneath the sheriff's face, where it rested against the door, ran a wide swath of blood. It had coagulated but not dried. The grass and sand around his knees was a darkening red. Evan had to agree with Beckett; no small automatic had done this.

"I'm going to wager it'll be a closed casket," Beckett said under his breath. "What do you think?"

Evan turned his gaze from the dead sheriff to the chief of police. "I think you seem a bit too chipper for the hour and circumstance."

"You should have picked up a cup of coffee at the Shell," Beckett said. "Nothing else the day throws at you will seem quite so bad by comparison."

Evan stared at Beckett, letting his eyes convey his intense lack of amusement.

"Let me explain something to you, my bright new colleague," Beckett said. "I didn't have much affection for your boss. Even so, the killing of any law enforcement officer makes me sick. I'll deal with this the same way I deal with any other unpleasant scene, which would be any way I see fit. I'd say you'll deal with it however you, please, too."

"Okay," Evan said, which conveyed little and meant even less.

Beckett cleared his throat, and looked away. "Look, I never want to see a cop gunned down." His eyes came back to meet Evan's. "But as far as Sheriff "Randy" Randall Hutchins is concerned, there's quite a few folks in Gulf County who won't be mourning his passing. I happen to be one of them, but that doesn't mean I won't help you run his killer to ground."

"Understood," Evan said, more to end the conversation than for anything else.

Beckett stared over at the Sheriff's body for a moment, and Evan wondered who would tell him why the bad blood between him and Beckett seemed to be personal.

"Hutchins and his wife live just about three miles from here, in the Wewa city limits," Beckett said after a moment. "You want me to notify Marlene for you?" He tilted his head just a bit. "It might be better coming from someone she knows."

Evan shook his head slightly. "Thank you, but I'll do it. I'll need to talk to her anyway."

"Your show," Beckett said. "Medical examiner should be here any minute, I reckon. Vi said she'd call your crime scene team as soon as she got off the phone with you. I'll let you have my guys as long as you need them. Just make sure to sign for their hours so I'll know how much to bill the Sheriff's Office." He took a hand out of his pocket to point across the grass. "That's Pete Wilcox over there with your two witnesses. John Sharp's the one talking to your guy. Should be just about everything you need from me."

"If I can think of anything else I need from you, I'll be sure to call," Evan said, looking at Wilcox and the two coon hunters.

Beckett winked at him. "I'm sure you've got this in the bag, Big Time. I'll be looking to see it solved by the evening news. So, if you don't mind, I think I'll leave you to it, maybe go get me a taste of Gina's peach pie."

"I don't mind at all," Evan said, "but I thought her name was Billie."

"Billie's at the Shell," Beckett said, "Gina's at the Chevron."

"The gas stations around here serve a lot of pie," Evan said as the man walked away. "Or is that a euphemism for something?"

Beckett looked over his shoulder and winked. "I don't know. I'm gonna have to run home and look that word up."

FOUR

RUBEN GOFF, THE OLDEST member of the Gulf County Sheriff's Office, could have been described as scrawny, if he put on twenty pounds. Some of the other deputies called him Frost – though whether that was due to his temperament or his blue eyes and silver hair, Evan didn't know. Local legend suggested Frost was lightning fast with a pistol, a skill that had come in handy more than once. Evan and he had probably exchanged fifty words in the several weeks that Evan had been with the SO.

Goff slipped up beside Evan, quiet as a rat pissing on cotton. They watched Beckett get into his car. "He's only an ass ninety-percent of the time," Goff said, his voice soft but resonant. "Wants you to think he's Burt Reynolds. But he's sly. Knows his trade and he knows the folks around here. You'll want to take any help he offers."

"Maybe I should appoint you as liaison," Evan said.

Goff made a *pfftt* sound through his mustache, "I can't stand the man." He turned and walked alongside the crime scene tape to the back of the truck. "Something you need to see before the sun burns it away."

Evan followed him under the tape. Goff hunkered on his heels behind the truck and Evan squatted down next to him. Goff leaned forward until his face was only inches from the ground. He turned his head sideways, looking under the truck. Evan watched, then did likewise.

"Do you see it?" Goff asked.

Evan saw nothing but sand and gravel and short grass.

"Folks coming and going from here, probably a hundred different sets of tire tracks on this little patch," Goff said in his perpetually conversational murmur.

Then Evan saw what he was looking at, a variation in color among the dry nubs of grass, so slight as to be almost imperceptible except at this extreme angle.

"But there are only three sets," Goff continued, "that disturbed last night's dew." Goff rose to his feet. "The sheriff's truck, Mooney's truck, back over yonder about fifty yards, and the truck that was parked right here."

Goff walked about three paces to the passenger side of the sheriff's truck and crouched down again. Evan joined him, following the line of his gaze. That slight variation of color showed again in the grass. The tracks pulled up right alongside Hutchins's truck.

"Well, I'll be..." Evan said. "That's going to be our shooter's truck."

"Yep," Goff said, "I reckon."

The two men stood.

"Why didn't they ever make you sheriff?" Evan asked

"Too many skeletons."

"In your closet?"

Goff placed hands at the base of his spine and stretched. "Them. Plus the ones under my back porch."

Before Evan could follow up on that, two additional Sheriff's Office vehicles pulled up. Deputies Jimmy Crenshaw and Paula Trigg parked beside the two cruisers already blocking access to the scene, then jogged up the gravel road toward Evan.

Crenshaw had been employed as a deputy with Gulf County Sheriff's Office for over three years. Evan had met him several times in the month he'd been with the Sheriff's Office, but he hadn't worked with him yet. Crenshaw was about thirty, and Evan had heard he'd done two tours in Afghanistan and then joined the sheriff's office the minute he got back. With his hard physique and close-cut blond hair, he looked like he was still in the Army.

Paula Trigg was Gulf County's crime scene investigator. She had come to the Sheriff's Office after fifteen years as a Miami police officer. She didn't talk about Miami much. Evan knew she and her K-9 partner had been involved in a shooting, an ambush apparently. They had both been shot, and the dog had lost a leg. The three Columbians who'd jumped them had not been wearing body armor, and thus none were arrested for the attack. The tiny little woman and her dog had taken them down.

Upon recovering from her injuries, Paula had adopted her retired partner, who got around just fine on the three legs he had left. She had accepted a lateral transfer to Gulf County, which was closer to her parents and far enough away from Miami. When Evan had asked Trigg about a small notch he noticed in her left ear, she'd said that one of the bullets had grazed her. He'd asked her why she hadn't let the doctors take care of it.

"The department didn't want to pay for a matching notch in my other ear," she'd said with a straight face, and Evan had decided then that he could work with her.

Evan called to the two newcomers, "Camera?"

Trigg already carried an oversized duffle. Crenshaw wheeled around and jogged back to his cruiser, retrieved a large black case from the trunk and sprinted to catch up with Trigg. The two reached Evan and Goff together.

"Is it really Hutch?" Crenshaw asked, eyes wide.

Evan nodded and began to speak, but Goff beat him to it, speaking matter-of-fact and smooth. "Somebody shot Hutch, killed him. But you are on the job and this is a crime scene, just like any other you ever worked. So for now, that's not Hutch, that's a body to be processed. Keep that straight in your heads. Understand?"

Crenshaw nodded.

Trigg looked over Evan's shoulder at Hutchins's truck. "Has anybody been in there?"

"No, we just came in. Prior to it being taped off, I guess one of the witnesses vomited, but they said neither of them touched anything," Evan said.

"I'm going to want to get DNA, shoe prints and fingerprints from them," Trigg said.

"Yeah, I'll have them come see you when I'm done interviewing them," Evan said, "But before you move inside the perimeter, I need you to work with Goff on these tire tracks. There's not much left to go on, but get me wheel track, tread description if you can find any clear bit, tire width...anything at all."

"Tire tracks?" she said, doubtfully.

"I'll show you." Goff said.

To Crenshaw Evan said, "You're my doorman, Jimmy. Move those cruisers when the M.E. arrives so he can roll his van up here, but don't let anybody else in without clearing it with me first. And do not tell anyone what is going on back here. I don't want his next of kin reading about this on Facebook"

"Right," Crenshaw said.

Evan, Trigg and Goff handed him their keys. The young deputy passed the camera case over to Trigg, then sprinted back to the road block.

Evan approached Mooney and Grant. The two men looked up at him from the ground. A canvas bag sat next to the white man with the pale orange hair. Evan introduced himself.

"Man," Mooney said, "this is not what I was planning on doin' with my morning."

"I imagine Sheriff Hutchins would be saying the same thing," Evan said. "You two were our here all night?"

"Well, not all night. Got into the woods around midnight. Grant got a 'coon right off and we figured with luck like that we'd be back before the engine cooled," Mooney said. "Turned out we didn't see another one for over an hour. Finally filled our bag just before three."

"Filled your bag?" Evan asked, distracted by the large lump of canvas on the grass. "What exactly do you have planned for those raccoons?"

"You ain't never eat coon?" Mooney asked. He was polite about it, but clearly didn't understand.

"I can't say I have," Evan answered.

"My wife cooks 'em up in a meat pie with some celery an' onions," Grant said.

"They go real good with sweet potatoes, too," Mooney said. "It's like dark meat from a turkey, only a bit greasier."

"And more tender," Grant added.

"Young folks these days won't touch it if you tell 'em what it is," Mooney said. "They think fairies drop food off to the grocery store."

"That's what's wrong with these kids, man," said Grant. "They'll kill each other all day long, but you bleed a chicken and they look at you like you're the devil."

"Huh," Evan said, pulling his eyes away from the bag. After a moment to refocus, he said, "So, sometime between midnight and three o'clock you heard a gunshot? Can you be any more specific?"

Mooney said, "I reckon it was closer to two o'clock..."

"Maybe two-thirty," Grant said, "Or thereabouts."

"Did you hear anything else? Truck door slamming? Raised voices?"

"Nah, man," Mooney said, "We were a ways back in there. The shot sounded far off. Didn't pick up nothing else."

"Yeah, me neither," Grant said.

"Do you think you'd know the difference at that distance between a pistol, rifle, or shotgun?"

Grant shook his head.

Mooney said, "Bigger than a .22, smaller than a 12 gauge. Can't be too much more specific than that."

"Was the sheriff's truck here when you arrived? Or any other vehicle?"

"Nah. We'd have seen 'em," Grant said.

"We're parked about fifty yards further down the road," Mooney put in. "But if someone was backed into one of them little nooks over there with their lights out, we might not have noticed, I suppose."

Grant nodded his agreement. "Yeah, we only noticed the sheriff's truck because we saw his lights dimming. Otherwise we'd have just passed on by, minding our own."

Evan nodded and pursed his lips. He surveyed the scene, then looked back to the two men. "Anything else you can remember? Anything stand out to you as unusual?"

"You mean other than finding a dead guy in his truck?" Grant asked, starting to sound exasperated.

"Skynrd was playing," Mooney said, "When we walked up the battery was dying, but it had enough juice for the radio, and Skynrd was playing."

"Skynrd, huh?" Evan said, making a note of this. It might help him nail down the exact time the body was discovered, if the radio station kept a record of when they played what.

"Man," Grant said, shaking his head, "Who would do this? Everybody loved Hutch."

Evan thought that odd, considering that Beckett had said something fairly opposite.

"Yeah," Mooney said, "He was a good guy. Did a good job. Whoever gets his job's got some shoes to fill."

"I would imagine," Evan said, looking down at his own shoes. The toes were scuffed from when he had knelt to examine the tire tracks. Maybe he'd just give them to Plutes to piss in.

When he looked up, Mooney was eyeing him skeptically. "How long you gonna have to keep our guns?" the older man asked.

"Just a couple of days, I would think," Evan answered politely.

"Y'all don't think we did that, do you?" the redhead asked.

"It's just procedure," Evan answered. "We've got a man dead from gunshot, a law enforcement officer no less, and you're at the scene with a gun. I'll have Paula run a couple rounds through them, then we'll give you a call when you can pick up your weapons. Okay?"

"Yeah, I guess. Whatever we can do to help," Grant sighed, then shook his head and added, "This sure is some kind of messed up."

Evan looked over his note pad for a moment. "Officer Wilcox took down your contact information for me, so I can get hold of you if I have any more questions later. Here's my card. You call me right away if you think of anything else."

"Will do," Mooney said.

Grant nodded, "Mm-hm."

"I'd appreciate your patience just a little bit longer," Evan said. "Deputy Trigg needs to collect some prints from you guys, then you'll be on your way ," Evan said. "Thank you for cooperating with us this morning, I know this isn't easy for anyone."

"I just hope you find whoever did this, man," Mooney said, standing and stretching his back. Grant just nodded, looking miserable.

"That's my plan," Evan said quietly.

·•✳•·

Goff met up with Evan as he was on his way back to the truck.

"We got a couple measurements off those tracks. The wheel track is between seventy and eighty inches. Could be just about any Ford or Chevy pick-up. Looks like the tires are probably after-market, some fat off-road jobs. Probably an open tread."

"So that eliminates about a third of the vehicles in Gulf County?" Evan asked.

"Thereabouts," Goff said. "The one saving grace of old Gulf County Fords and Chevys, at least as far as we're concerned, they all leak oil."

"Oh, yeah?"

"Our shooter left a softball size puddle. I've got it marked for Paula to sample once she's done over there." Goff scratched at the side of his moustache. "Not sure if it'll amount to much, but it's better than a poke in the stick with a sharp eye."

Evan was looking at the black stain in the sand, about to comment on the value of spilled oil, but lost his thought trying to process Goff's last phrase. He glanced up at the older man, but Goff had turned slightly and was scribbling in his note pad, apparently done with the conversation.

Evan figured "Right," was the best response, so that's what he said, then continued on his way to see Trigg. The oil wouldn't get them any closer to finding the killer's truck than the generic tire track measurements would. But if they did find the truck, a matching chemical analysis of the dripped oil and the oil in the truck's crank case would provide fairly convincing evidence that the truck they found was indeed the truck used in the murder.

When he arrived at the truck, Paula Trigg was kneeling behind Hutchins' body, taking photographs of the door and window.

The largest blood splatter on the door was similar in shape to an inverted teardrop; a large bulbous top, with several drips at the bottom that stretched for a few inches before they'd begun to get tacky enough to be halted.

Evan stood behind Trigg. "That primary blood splatter there, looks like the shot came from a pretty steep angle."

She looked over her shoulder for just a moment. "Yeah, looks like."

"I'm guessing the Sheriff was on his knees and the shooter stood behind him," Evan said. "That sound probable to you?"

She took another shot of the door, then looked back at Evan again. He thought maybe he saw a little bit of surprise on her face, like she'd just remembered that he was new to Gulf County, but not new to the job. "I'd say that'll turn out to be the case, yeah," she said.

She stood up and checked a silver-toned watch on her wrist. Evan noted that it was an analog, and a smaller, man's watch rather than a woman's timepiece.

"I wish the M.E. would get here already," she said, looking around like he might appear from thin air. "I need to get on with it."

"I'm a little surprised he's not here already," Evan said. "Seem weird to you, what with this being a murdered law enforcement officer?"

She hesitated a moment, then shrugged. "He doesn't even attend half the scenes we call him on. Sends one of his interns usually."

"What does *he* do?"

"He does most of the actual autopsies," she answered. "But crime scene work seems too inconvenient for him most of the time."

"I don't think we want an intern on this one," Evan said, feeling a bias against the M.E. coming on. "Do you?"

She shrugged again, then started taking pictures of the ground in Hutchins' immediate vicinity. "Some of them seem sharper, you want the truth."

Evan sighed, looked around, and then walked over to the crime scene tape. Jimmy Crenshaw was standing just outside it, talking to one of the Wewa PD officers.

"Hey, Crenshaw?" Evan called over. "Can you check on the progress of the M.E. for me?"

"Just hung up with them," Crenshaw answered. "They said fifteen, twenty minutes."

"Call them back and mention to them that the highest-ranking law enforcement officer in the county is missing most of the front of his head," Evan said evenly. "See if they can divide that ETA by the factor of my foot in their ass."

"Will do," Crenshaw answered, and Evan thought he might have grinned if the circumstances were different.

Evan turned away and walked around the truck to the passenger side, keeping to the edge of the crime scene tape. The ground on that side was almost entirely gravel and rock. He doubted they would find any footprints, should they have had reason to exist. He stepped closer to the truck, then stood on tiptoe so that he could see the front seat.

"Hey, Trigg?" he called out. "You see the Sheriff's service weapon—or any weapon—over there?"

"No," she called back.

Evan supposed it might be on the floorboard, in the console, inside the glove compartment. Hutchins was wearing his holster, so clearly, he'd been armed. They might find it in the truck, or somewhere nearby, possibly knocked out of Hutchins' hand. If they didn't find it, then it was likely kept or disposed of by the killer.

But why would he willingly get down on his knees and allow himself to be shot? That bothered Evan somewhat. Actually, it bothered him quite a bit. Every cop he knew would rather take a bullet fighting than die on his knees. "Kneel to be shot or I'll shoot you," wasn't a very compelling command.

Evan needed somebody to tell him why the man was out here in the middle of the night, and what could have motivated him to allow himself to be executed. Perhaps there was more than one assailant – the person the Sheriff was meeting, and someone else who took the man by surprise. Or maybe there'd been someone there to threaten, someone Hutch was willing to die for. Evan had met Hutch's wife once, and he knew they had a grown daughter, though whether she lived locally or not, he couldn't remember.

He didn't want to give the crime scene short shrift, but he needed to get to the Sheriff's house soon. Not only to notify his next of kin, but to make sure she wasn't a victim as well. He considered having one of the deputies go to the house, but there really wasn't any way to accomplish that without telling her what they weren't saying yet. He would have to hurry up and get over there.

"Caldwell," Trigg said, "I've got all the photos I need from the truck and surrounding area. You can go ahead and send someone in to run the metal detector and collect trash. The slug is going to be a few inches past that hole," she pointed to a small divot two feet in front of the open truck door. "Probably not going to find the shell, but there's a couple bottle tops, a wad of chewing gum and a few cigarette butts scattered around. Most are old, but the gum looks pretty fresh."

"Goff?" Evan asked, turning to find him.

"On it," Goff replied, stooping to retrieve evidence bags and the collapsed metal detector from Trigg's duffle.

Evan's shirt was already thinking about clinging to his back. Once the sun had fully risen, it promised to be a heartbreakingly humid morning. The smell of drying blood thickened the air around the people working the scene. A large black fly droned past Evan's head and lighted on the puddle between the dead sheriff's knees. As he watched, two more joined it. Soon, there would be a swarm. Evan loathed flies. If one landed on his food, he'd throw it away. He'd seen too many of them covering corpses and buzzing out of their eye sockets.

They watched Trigg slip plastic bags over each of the sheriff's hands, securing them with rubber bands. She then swabbed his hair around the entry wound for smoke or powder residue. "Not much else I can do before the M.E. arrives. The passenger door is locked, and I can't access the cab from this side until we move the body."

At that moment, out on the highway, brakes shrieked. Evan cringed internally, expecting to hear the crunching, grinding impact of vehicles colliding. Instead, the shrieking was followed by the rattle of sprayed gravel. Evan saw Crenshaw slap his phone closed, mutter something inappropriate, and sprint toward the parked patrol cars.

A plume of dust billowed up at the turnoff to the scene, then a white van appeared, skewing sideways just a bit to make the turn. Again, Evan expected to hear crumpling metal and shattering glass, but the driver managed to keep all four tires under the van, though two of them left the road for several seconds. As soon as it righted itself, the driver gunned the engine, barreling towards the crime scene.

Jimmy Crenshaw stood in the van's path, holding up his hand, which became just a middle finger as the van slid to a stop only a few feet from hitting him. Evan admired his conviction, but wanted to slap him for the risk.

Dust billowed up around the van and drifted forward, encroaching on the taped off area. As it threatened to cross the tape, the light breeze pulled it to the side and it floated off toward the water.

The van's engine cut off. Evan and Paula stared at the windshield, trying to see through the glare of the early morning sun. The driver's door opened, and a young man pretty much flung himself out. He looked like an underfed kid, though he was fairly tall. He had thick black hair and thick black glasses. Without the green scrubs, he'd look more at home developing something for Apple or playing in a hipster band.

He closed the door and stood beside the van for a second, as if trying to get his bearings, then straightened his scrubs and stepped forward.

"I'm looking for the sheriff," the young man said. When no one answered, he added, "The dead one."

"I assume you're the medical examiner's intern?" Evan asked, noting crumbles of sleep in the corner of the young man's eyes, and a substantial cowlick on the side of his head. "I hope we didn't wake you."

"Well, I'm not on duty. I mean, I wasn't. I am now," the young man said in a single burst of words. "It's Kim's turn on midnights this week but she got called to a twofer out at Sunset Bay – those old folks like to drop off in their sleep and the staff finds them on morning rounds."

Evan's gut clenched. He worked at neither cringing nor yanking out his phone. He'd call Sunset Bay from the car as soon as he got done here.

"Usually they go in threes, not twos," the kid was saying, "but number three turned out to be all the way out here and it would have taken Kim an extra couple of hours to finish up there before she could get out here. Also, somewhat incidentally, that drill sergeant you got working the phones for you didn't sound like he wanted to wait that long, so Kim called me and here I am."

Evan was too distracted by trying to speed up his hearing to figure out whether the kid's use of the term "drill sergeant" referred to Vi or Crenshaw. Paula Trigg cleared her throat and Evan realized he had been staring at the intern for several seconds, and that everyone else was staring at *him*.

Paula said, "Lieutenant Caldwell, this is Danny Coyle, one of the medical examiner's assistants. I've worked a few cases with him. I think you'll find him as competent on a scene as Dr. Grundy would be. If he were here."

Danny smiled, might even have blushed just a tad, then stepped forward and extended a hand to Evan.

Evan found his internal balance, centered by Paula's professionalism and his own distaste for M.E. Mitch

Grundy's lack of it. He pushed all thoughts of Sunset Bay out of his mind and refocused.

"Mr. Coyle," Evan said, accepting the young man's hand. "This case is going to receive a lot of attention in the media. That means everything we do here will be scrutinized more than usual. Thank you for getting here quickly. But, now that you are here, I need you to take all the time you should. Dot all your I's and cross all your T's."

"Yeah, of course," Danny said. "That's the sheriff. No way am I going to miss anything on this one."

Evan grimaced at the implication that the kid might be in the habit of missing things on less important cases, but decided this was not the time, nor was it his place, to address that. The day was moving forward, fast, and Evan felt compelled to do the same. An initial survey of a murder scene was as much about collecting questions as it was about collecting evidence. Evan had just about bagged his limit of questions. It was time to get some answers, and to go speak to his boss's widow.

As Coyle returned to his van to gather his gear, Evan leaned close to Paula and said in a low voice, "Keep an eye on this kid., just help him out a little, okay? I've got to get back to Wewa and do next of kin before Mrs. Hutchins hears about this from someone else."

"I got it, Evan. Do what you need to do," she said. "But don't worry about Danny. He's pretty sharp."

"A little heavy-handed with the 5-Hour Energy, maybe," Evan said.

"Probably," Trigg answered. "Med school does that to you."

He patted her shoulder, then looked over at Goff. The sergeant wore enormous headphones connected by a black spiral cord to the metal detector. Evan got an image of Goff blasting old Hank Williams songs through the phones, and the thought would have made him smile under other circumstances. He did wonder just how he had gotten here, as far from Cocoa Beach and Miami as was culturally possible. An impossibly convoluted trajectory had brought him across the state, but it felt like he'd crossed the planet, and he wondered how long he'd have to stay. Then he felt guilty for wondering.

Paula saw Evan looking at Goff and said, "I'll let him know."

"Thanks," Evan said, bringing his mind back to the task at hand. "I'll talk to Crenshaw on my way out."

"You need to come back here after?"

"No, I think I have all I need to get started. Just please make sure the body and anything remotely like evidence gets processed properly. Once he's been transported to the hospital, see what you can get off the truck, then have it towed back to the station. I'll ask Crenshaw to stick around until the truck has been towed."

"Got it," Paula said.

Evan thought about his phrasing for a moment before he spoke again. "Listen, I know this is a small town, in a close-knit county, but we need to do everything we can to make sure this doesn't get out before we want it to, okay? Nobody on their cells, nobody running back to the Shell station to grab a Mello Yello, nothing. Okay?"

"Got it," Trigg said, and Evan was grateful she didn't look offended. "We're really more of an RC Cola/Mountain Dew crowd around here, anyway."

Evan nodded to her, then headed for his car. Danny Coyle passed him, hurrying the other way. He had a duffle slung over one shoulder that looked like it weighed more than he did. Evan cringed at the gleaming, twelve-inch long needle he carried, the thermometer probe he'd use to take the temperature of Sheriff Hutchins's liver.

As Evan walked in the direction of Deputy Crenshaw and his car, he again wondered about the paths people's lives take. He would never have imagined himself investigating an execution in backwater Florida, where the M.E. was too hungover to show up for a murdered sheriff so he sent a spazzed out intern instead. He wondered if Hutchins had ever imagined his own end in this way. He doubted it had crossed his mind when he'd hired Evan.

FIVE

EVAN HAD A CIGARETTE in his mouth before he reached his car, and had it smoked a disturbingly short time later. He was barely back on the county road before he pulled out his cell and called Sunset Bay to make sure everything was okay. Once he knew it was, he smoked two more cigarettes out of relief. And a fair amount of dread.

He'd made his share of notifications to next of kin, and every one of them had made him anxious, uncomfortable, and slightly nauseous. Once he introduced himself, he always looked into the person's eyes and wished he could delay for just a minute the unwinding of their world. But no one wanted to talk about the weather when a cop showed up on their doorstep.

The further Evan went into Wewa, the less he understood its existence. There were several residential neighborhoods, some working class and some not as fortunate.

Homes ranged from modest but well-kept brick ranch houses to dilapidated trailers to shotgun cabins, enough to fill at least a few square miles, so clearly plenty of people lived in Wewa. Evan just couldn't figure out why.

Aside from a few gas stations, a school, a fire department and a couple of forlorn-looking stores, Evan saw no real business district. He wondered if most of Wewa's residents worked in Port St. Joe or even Mexico Beach. But then why on earth were they living back here? He got claustrophobic once he couldn't smell the water, and he never understood why anyone lived in inland Florida.

Evan passed the Wewa Police Department on his way. It was a low-slung, clay-colored structure with a laundromat on one side and a lawnmower repair place on the other. Two patrol cars were parked in the small lot. Beckett's Monte Carlo wasn't in attendance.

Sheriff Hutchins' home was off of Red Bull Island Drive. Evan wondered momentarily if the founder of the drink was from Wewa, or if the residents just admired it so much they named a street after it. He had Google Maps up on his phone, and he could see that the Chipola River ran in something of a "U" shape around Red Bull Island Drive. The side streets on both sides of the road all ended at one bend of the river or the other.

Sheriff Hutchins' house turned out to be a pale-yellow ranch at the end of Palm Street, which made it waterfront property. There were only half a dozen houses on the street, all of them at least as modest as Hutchins'. These included two well-kept trailers. He caught a glimpse of the river just past the Sheriff's property. Evan didn't understand or trust fresh water, but he figured a river was better than nothing.

As he pulled into the sand and gravel driveway between two huge azaleas, he noted that there were lights on in the windows. He didn't have to wonder why; Chief Beckett's Monte Carlo was parked right in front of him. Evan's eyes narrowed through the smoke as he took one last drag, then doused the butt in the Coke can full of water he used as an ashtray.

He was halfway to the front door when it opened. Beckett stood there holding it like he was the one who paid the mortgage. He didn't look defiant about being there, but he didn't bother looking apologetic, either. He came down the two front steps from the porch and met Evan on the walkway.

"What the hell are you doing, Beckett?" Evan asked quietly.

"Look, I went all through school with Marlene," Beckett answered, his voice low. "She didn't need to hear this from someone she's never even met."

"You know as well as I do that seeing a spouse's first reaction is crucial to an investigator."

"Listen, it's not my case, so I don't give a crap about your investigation," Beckett said. "But since you're curious, her first reaction was to throw up on the carport. She didn't have anything to do with this, Caldwell."

"Because she threw up, or because you went to school with her? Which I appreciate you mentioning a long time ago, by the way."

"Mainly because she's got six Girl Scouts in her den," Beckett answered. "They had a sleepover, only nobody slept. They stayed up watching movies until a little after four. Unless you figure they all did it together as a Scout project, Marlene has a solid alibi."

Evan let a frustrated breath hiss out through his teeth as he looked around the yard. There wasn't much to see; it was just an excuse to look away from Beckett so he didn't have to say anything before he was ready. After a moment, he collected himself and looked back at the other man, who was standing there with his hands on his hips like Evan was the one who was someplace he shouldn't be.

"I suppose the Girl Scouts all know the Sheriff's dead and they're posting on Facebook as we speak," Evan said.

"No, slick, they don't and they aren't," Beckett answered. "I told them there'd been an accident, then called their parents and told them the same thing and asked them to come get their kids."

"I need to talk to the girls before they leave," Evan said shortly.

"I told them that, too," Beckett said. "I might be a cracker, but I've got twenty-four years in this game and I'm not feeble."

Evan propped his fists on his hips and sighed. "Where's Mrs. Hutchins?"

"Kitchen. The girls are all in back, in the den."

Evan looked past Beckett at the front door. "I'd appreciate it if you'd keep an eye on the girls and deal with the parents while I talk to her for a minute," he said. "Then I'll speak with the girls so the parents can get them out of here."

"I'll try to manage that," Beckett said, and turned to lead Evan into the house.

Evan followed Beckett into a small, square foyer. The hardwood floor was scuffed and dull, but it was clean. In the dim light from a small table lamp, Evan saw several photos on the walls, scenes from an evidently happy life.

A wedding picture, with a much younger and thinner Sheriff in a mullet and a cheap tux, and a small, pretty blonde woman smiling like she'd just been crowned. Several pictures that chronicled the life thus far of an equally pretty blonde girl; as a newborn, in a Brownie uniform with no front teeth, in a softball uniform with all of her teeth and a nice stance. In a graduation gown, looking relieved. Another wedding picture, this time with the daughter and a triumphant looking young man in a better tux.

To Evan's left was a living room that looked like it didn't get used much. To his right was a closed door. Straight ahead, at the end of the dark hall, Evan saw part of a well-lit room. All he could see of it was a fieldstone fireplace and the end of a couch with a blanket thrown over the back. He assumed that was the den.

"Which way is the kitchen?" Evan asked Beckett.

Beckett pointed at the living room. "Through there and on back," he answered. "I'm gonna go out front and have a smoke, wait on the parents."

"Good enough," Evan said, and he heard the front door open and close as he made his way through the formal living room, with the too matchy-matchy couches and chairs and the type of paintings you see at the Holiday Inn.

At the back of the room was an archway that led into a dark dining room elaborately over-furnished in well-kept 1970s oak. Evan wondered, a bit sadly, if the newlyweds had saved their pennies to purchase it, or if it had been a wedding present. On the opposite side of the room, a doorway opened into the bright kitchen. Evan smelled fresh coffee, and he wondered if Beckett had made it.

He stepped through the doorway into a kitchen that looked like it had been remodeled in the 90s or so. It was spotless and cheerful, though there were too many flowers and cookbooks and knick-knacks for Evan's comfort. At the back of the kitchen, in front of a sliding glass door, was a glass-top table for four. Sitting at it was an older version of Hutchins' bride.

Evan guessed she was in her early fifties or so, but even in a worn blue robe, with no makeup and her hair in a ponytail, she was still a pretty woman. Or would be, if her eyes didn't look so stunned and defeated. They were red, but dry, and she looked up at Evan without surprise.

"I made you some coffee," she said quietly. Her voice was more delicate than he'd expected.

"Thank you," he said, sad somehow that she'd thought she should be doing something for him. He had met her once before, when he'd been a guest for dinner the week he was hired, but he couldn't tell if she recognized him at the moment. "Mrs. Hutchins, do you remember me? I'm Evan Caldwell."

She nodded. "I remember you. Nathan—Chief Beckett—said you were on your way." She picked up a couple of balls of tissue as though she might throw them away, but she didn't get up.

"I'm very sorry for your loss," Evan said.

She swallowed hard and nodded.

"Is there someone I can call for you, someone you'd like to come be with you?"

"No," she answered, shaking her head. "Not right—not yet."

"Okay."

She opened her mouth to say something else, then closed it and looked out the window for a second. Then she turned back to Evan. "Let me get you a cup of coffee," she said, starting to rise.

Evan held up a hand. "Please," he said gently. "Let me get it."

She lowered herself again, looking at him hesitantly. Maybe it was that Southern compulsion to be the hostess, or maybe she just wanted something to do. "The cups are in the cupboard next to the fridge," she said anyway.

Evan turned around. The coffee pot, an older Mr. Coffee, was on the counter next to the refrigerator. He went to it, pulled two Corning Ware mugs from the cabinet, and poured two cups of coffee. He didn't like American coffee, but he'd drink it anyway. Next to the coffee maker were a sugar dish and a pint of Half n' Half. She'd set out a folded paper towel with a teaspoon on it, and that made him sad, too.

"How do you take your coffee, ma'am?" he asked, looking over his shoulder.

She blinked a few times, like she'd forgotten. "Just one sugar," she said finally.

Evan added one spoonful of sugar to each of the coffees, put some cream in his, and carried them over to the table. He set the cups down, then pulled out the chair next to her and sat. She didn't bother looking at her cup, just watched him pull a small notebook and a pen from the inside pocket of his jacket.

A lot of cops preferred taking notes on tablets now. Evan didn't. He used small, spiralbound books of graph paper, and rollerball pens. Pilot P-700s, blue. He couldn't think clearly without one or the other, so he ordered each of them by the dozen from Amazon.

He opened the notebook, a fresh one, and uncapped his pen. He looked up at Mrs. Hutchins.

"Ma'am, when did you last see or speak to your husband?" he asked gently.

She blinked a few times, and Evan saw a thin line of clear fluid drip from her nose to her upper lip. She wiped it away with one of the used tissues. "He left here about midnight, maybe a little later than that," she said. "He watched a movie with us, then he went into his study for a little while, and came and said he needed to go out for a little bit, for work."

"What movie did you watch?" he asked her as he wrote.

"We watched three," she said, sounding confused.

"Which one did he watch with you?"

"Oh. *Interstellar*. Then we put *Joy* on and he went into the study." She looked out the window, seeing nothing. "I wanted the girls to see movies with strong women in them."

"You're a Girl Scout leader?" Evan asked her.

She looked back at him and nodded. "Yes, ever since Amanda joined the Brownies." She started blinking again, but a tear still escaped from each eye.

"That's your daughter?" Evan asked.

She nodded.

"Have you spoken to her yet, ma'am?"

She shook her head quickly, and wiped at her cheeks.

"You'll want to let her know before it hits the news," Evan said. "And I imagine that'll happen very soon."

She nodded again. "I will. As soon as we're through talking," she said. "I'll call Brian and ask him to tell her. I just can't."

"Do they live here?"

"No, they're in Pensacola," she answered. "Brian's in dental school there."

Evan nodded as he wrote that down, then he looked back up at Mrs. Hutchins. "Ma'am, did your husband say where he was going so late at night?"

"No," she answered quietly. "He just said he had to meet with someone who had some information for him. He said it might take a while."

"Did he do that often? Meet with people that late in the evening?"

"Sometimes. Not often, no," she said. "But it wasn't unusual enough for me to think anything of it. Randy was never really off duty. He was very committed to his job."

"I got that impression," Evan said gently.

"He's four years from retirement, you know. We've been talking about getting a fifth-wheel, doing some traveling," she said, her voice breaking.

Evan didn't have a suitable response, so he just watched her with what he hoped was a sympathetic expression.

"That's one of the reasons he hired you, you know," she said. "He thought you might be a good replacement for him."

This time it was Evan's turn to blink. He had no ambition at all to be the Sheriff of Gulf County, or any other county for that matter. That wasn't why he'd come here. "No, I didn't know that," he said quietly.

She nodded and looked down at the tissue she was slowly shredding.

"What did your husband have with him when he left? Did you notice?"

"What do you mean?"

"Did he have his weapon, his cell phone?"

"Oh, I'm sure he did," she said, staring past Evan like she could see her husband leave again, make note of what he'd taken with him. "He never went anywhere without his gun, or his cell phones. He had one for work and one for…well, for us. Not for work."

Evan nodded, then jotted down a few things, primarily to postpone for just a moment his next line of questioning.

"Mrs. Hutchins, I apologize for having to ask this, but I do," he said finally.

She looked over at him, and he saw the dread in her eyes. That could be for any number of reasons.

"Is there any chance that his meeting last night wasn't work-related?" He didn't have to explain his meaning, and he had to respect her for not looking or acting like she'd been slapped.

"You mean a woman," she said simply.

"I'm sorry, but that is what I'm asking."

She sighed, and it almost struck him as a sigh of relief. "No. I'm not going to pretend we have a perfect marriage or that Randy is—was—perfect, either. But he wasn't messing around."

"Are you sure?"

"When we were younger, just married a little while, we had some issues," she said. "We were kids, really. But not for years and years. That's not something I ever worried about."

"Thank you," Evan said. "What was the number for his personal phone?" She recited it for him, and he wrote it down. "Did you try calling him when he didn't come home?"

"No," she said, shaking her head, her eyes widening. "I wouldn't do that, not when I knew he was working."

"Were you worried?"

She swallowed and then lifted one shoulder, almost in apology. "I always worry a little, but it's always okay."

Her eyes filled then, and Evan pulled a clean tissue from a box on the table and handed it to her. She took it without looking at him, and he waited for her to dry her eyes. When she had, she looked up at him and sat a little bit taller and straighter.

"It's always been all right," she said quietly.

She seemed a bit fragile, but Evan saw grit there, too. Whether it was the kind of grit that could empower her to kill her husband, or have someone else do it, was an unknown. The general rule was that it was almost always the spouse, the significant other, or the ex. Unless the victim was a cop. Then it could be anybody.

"I'm sure it's very stressful to be married to a police officer," Evan said automatically. He felt a tightening in his stomach. He wondered if or when Hannah had stopped worrying about him. Then he suddenly had the thought that maybe she still did, and the idea made him feel almost panicky. He squashed the idea almost instantly. "You're a strong woman."

She nodded and looked down at her untouched coffee.

"Mrs. Hutchins, have there been any incidents lately that concerned you? A prowler, someone strange in the neighborhood, people who call and hang up, anything like that?"

She answered quickly. "No, nothing like that, not lately."

"When?"

"Oh, I don't know, every few years someone eggs the house or dumps our trash in the yard, or makes a nasty phone call," she answered. "It happens."

"Has your husband mentioned anything? Been disturbed about something?"

Mrs. Hutchins thought for a moment. "Not really. Budget cuts. Getting antsy about retiring. He was tired." She balled up her most recent tissue and put it aside with the others. "But nothing like what you're asking. Nothing worrying, you know."

She looked back at the window, which was framed by blue and yellow checkered curtains. Flashes of early morning sun winked off the river just beyond the trees in the back yard. He watched Mrs. Hutchins for a moment, until she spoke so quietly he almost didn't hear her.

"Four years," she said. "It seemed like a long time."

Evan had nothing to say to that.

Forty-five minutes later, the frightened but also excited Girl Scouts had been questioned and dispersed. All of them verified that Sheriff Hutchins had left after midnight and that his wife had been in the same room with them until they'd gone to bed around 4am. Evan wasn't especially surprised; she might have had something to do with her husband's murder, but Evan didn't think she was the type to do it herself.

A friend of Mrs. Hutchins had come to sit with her while she called her son-in-law, and Evan had gotten permission to take a look at her husband's study. When he opened the door to the small room next to the front door, he'd found pretty much what he'd expected: a slightly outdated, masculine study, furnished with an inexpensive desk, a worn leather office chair with brown duct tape on the headrest, and an older desktop computer.

The paneled walls were decorated with various family pictures, a few law enforcement related photo-ops and certificates, and a good many pictures of Hutchins and other men on an older sport-fishing boat. It looked like it might be a late 80s, early 90s model, about a 25-footer. Evan wasn't sure of the make, but it looked like it got good use.

Evan sat down in the desk chair, which was permanently indented in the seat and emitted a good number of squeaks and groans. Once he was sure it wasn't going to fall apart, Evan relaxed and surveyed the Sheriff's desk.

One of those two-picture picture frames, with a shot of his wife from maybe ten years ago, and one of his daughter in what looked like a prom dress. A beaten-up Florida Gators travel mug full of pens and pencils. A small stack of mail that turned out to be current bills. Nothing attention-grabbing, just a few utility bills and one credit card statement in Hutchins' name.

Evan looked it over. It looked like Hutchins mainly used the card for gas and eating out. No large expenditures, nothing that looked hinky, like a hotel room or a stop at Victoria's Secret. That exhausted the desktop's supply of information, and Evan moved on to the drawers. The shallow drawers turned up more pens and pencils, an assortment of rubber bands, paper clips and business cards, and a broken pocket knife. The one deep drawer contained several hanging file folders.

A quick look showed that they were a fairly well-organized collection of paid bills, car titles, past income tax returns and various insurance policies. That folder caught Evan's interest, but only for a moment. The life insurance was a modest policy, not nearly enough to be considered motive. There was also auto insurance on Hutchins' truck and an '02 Caravan that was parked out in the carport. Whatever else the Hutchinses did, they didn't seem to blow money. A file full of neatly folded bank statements from that year and the prior one might shed more light on their financial picture. Evan pulled it and set it on the desk before turning on the computer.

There was no password requested, and Evan took a look around Hutchins' computer files. There wasn't a whole lot there that he found interesting. Mainly more family and fishing pictures, as well as a few Sheriff's Office gatherings. A pass through the Sheriff's browser history turned up several days' history with no gaps that would indicate that anything had been trashed. The history showed that Hutchins had checked his personal email almost daily, that he piddled around Facebook now and then, and that he liked to check the weather, the fishing forecasts, and the news. No porn, no chat rooms, no quickie divorce sites. Hutchins' email wasn't any more interesting, consisting mainly of ads, various newsletters, and a few law enforcement groups.

Evan was frustrated by the fact that no smoking gun presented itself, although he hadn't really counted on one. He shut off the computer, grabbed the folder full of bank statements, and walked out to the den, where Mrs. Hutchins sat on a plaid loveseat, blankly watching her friend carry a small trash bag around, tossing in candy wrappers and empty soda cans.

"Mrs. Hutchins?" Evan asked quietly from the doorway. It took her a moment to look up, then another moment for some expression of recognition. Her friend stopped picking up the trash for a moment, then went back to it, as though to show she wasn't paying too much attention to anything she shouldn't pay attention to.

Evan held up the file folder. "I'd like to take these bank statements back to the office to have a closer look at them. I'll make sure they're returned to you in a day or so."

Evan watched her work that out in her head for a moment, her eyes squinting just a bit. "You think my husband was taking money from someone?" she asked, a hint of anger in her voice.

"No, ma'am, that's not my reasoning," Evan answered gently. "I'd just like to make sure I've covered as many bases as possible, that I have a full picture of the last few months."

Mrs. Hutchins swallowed and her shoulders relaxed after a moment. "I guess," she said noncommittally.

"Thank you," Evan said. "I'll leave you alone now, unless you have any questions or you need anything from me."

"No," she answered, and went back to watching her friend, who had moved on to wiping off the coffee table.

"I'll let myself out then," Evan said. "If I can do anything for you, please call. I left my card on the kitchen table."

She didn't answer. Evan walked down the dim hall and stepped outside. A cruiser sat on the street in front of the house. A young deputy Evan knew only by sight was sitting in the driver's seat. The cruiser was just a precaution, and perhaps a small sign of support.

Evan started toward his Pilot, then cut diagonally across the front yard and walked over to the short dock. He saw that the creek was a decent-sized one. Several other docks floated behind several other yards.

The cuddy Evan had seen in the pictures wasn't there, but since it appeared to be used mainly for inshore fishing, it made sense to keep it at a marina in Port St. Joe. There was a small aluminum bass boat tied up. It looked like it got a lot of use, too. It was definitely better suited to the creeks and rivers. Evan wondered if Hutchins had fished the Dead Lakes much, and the thought made him feel a little morbid.

He lit a cigarette on his way back to his car, sucking gratefully on his first smoke since he'd gotten there. Then he tossed the file folder onto his front seat, and waved to the deputy as he pulled out of the driveway and headed back to town.

His cell rang a couple of minutes later. He glanced at the screen and saw that it was his friend and former boss at the Brevard County Sheriff's Office, Wyatt Hamilton. Wyatt had moved to Apalachicola, just down the road, a decade ago, to become the Franklin County Sheriff. He had recently resigned that position because he was in love with one of his investigators. Evan picked up the phone and connected the call.

"Hey, Wyatt," he said.

"Hey," Wyatt replied. "What the hell's going on over there?"

"It's a situation to be sure."

"Are you running the investigation?"

"Yeah," Evan answered. "A month on the job and now I'm working my boss's murder."

"What do you know?"

"Not much." Evan slowed for a coon that was apparently getting home late from a party. "One shot to the back of the head. No weapon, not even the Sheriff's service weapon. No idea of a motive yet. But he was a cop, so…"

"What the hell was he doing out in the Dead Lakes in the middle of the night?"

"I don't know that, either."

"Hinky," Wyatt said simply.

"Hinky," Evan agreed. "How well did you know Hutchins?"

Wyatt sighed. Evan could hear gulls in the background, and he wished he was wherever Wyatt was. Closer to the water at the least.

"I didn't really know him that well," Wyatt answered. "We had contact here and there, on cases that crossed the county lines, but we weren't friends."

"What did you think of him?"

"Seemed like a nice enough guy," Wyatt answered. "He's been re-elected about a hundred times."

"Yeah," Evan said distractedly. He lit another cigarette and took a long drag.

"This is some kinda crap for an outsider to have thrown on him," Wyatt said.

Wyatt had been an outsider in Franklin County, too, but Wyatt was much more likable than he was, Evan thought. They'd loved him almost instantly over there. And his former boss wasn't murdered.

"Yeah," Evan said again.

"Let me know if there's something I can do," Wyatt said. "Even if you just need to run over here and have a few beers."

"I will," Evan said. He would.

Wyatt waited a few beats before speaking again. "How's Hannah?"

Evan let a lungful of smoke out slowly. "The same." He spoke again before Wyatt could ask questions he didn't want to answer. "How are things with you?"

"Good. Maggie and I are getting married."

"I figured. I think that's great, man."

"Thanks." He paused for a moment, and when he spoke again, his voice was quieter. "We want you to come, but…I don't want it to be painful."

"It won't be," Evan said. "It's fine. Really. I wouldn't miss it."

He could hear Wyatt thinking, but when his friend spoke again, he changed the subject. "Okay, well, I've got to talk to some reporter about the state of the seafood industry or some crap. Unless they stand me up. You're much bigger news."

Evan winced at the thought of having to deal with the press. "Unfortunately. Listen, thanks for calling, Wyatt. I'll be in touch, okay?"

"All right. Keep me posted, yeah?"

"Yeah."

Evan disconnected the call and stared out at the narrow road, hemmed in on both sides by the meticulously uniform pines.

He was glad his friend had called, but that momentary reminder of his former life left Evan feeling acutely isolated. Wyatt was thirty miles or so down Hwy 98, but he, and everything else Evan used to call normal, could have been on the other side of the world.

He also felt a heaviness in his chest when he thought about how Wyatt had given up his twenty-plus year career for his lady, Maggie. Evan hadn't even used any of his vacation time for Hannah. A four day weekend to cruise over to the Bahamas was all he could spare. When he'd left Brevard County Sheriffs, he'd still had twenty-three days of unused vacation. He'd taken the money.

SIX

THE GULF COUNTY SHERIFF'S OFFICE
was located on FL 71 or Cecil G. Costen, Sr. Blvd, just
east of the small downtown section of Port St. Joe.

People generally referred to Port St. Joe as quaint, but
there was nothing quaint about the Sheriff's Office. It
was sandwiched between and behind the public library
and the courthouse, and both of those buildings were
significantly larger, though they all shared the same tan
stucco blandness that plagued many Florida govern-
ment buildings.

Evan pulled into an open parking space in the small
lot designated as belonging to the SO, and headed inside.
The sky had started to cloud up just a bit, but the air was
still hot and thick. The atmosphere inside the office wasn't
much different. A fog of grief and confusion seemed to
hover just under the fluorescent lights, and the place
was quieter, the people more subdued than usual. Janie

Pruitt, the young female deputy who manned the front desk, just blinked at him as he nodded in passing, and Evan could see that her eyes were rimmed in red.

A couple of other deputies either nodded or lifted a hand as he made his way down the east hall to the Sheriff's office, his shoes soundless on the utilitarian brown carpet. The office of his former supervisor was at the end of the hall, a few doors beyond his own, smaller quarters.

Vi Hartigan's desk was in the outer portion of the two-room office, and Vi herself was seated in her usual station. Vi was somewhere in her sixties, Evan guessed, with short reddish hair that had the substance of down, and a pair of rhinestone glasses that were always either perched at the end of her beaklike nose or hanging from a matching chain.

Vi looked up as Evan walked through the open door. Her eyes were not red, though they looked weary.

"Lt. Caldwell," she said in that deep, scratchy voice that always seemed to drop downward in tone, like a frown. "You've arrived."

"Yes," he said, though he didn't see any need to confirm her statement of the obvious. He stopped just in front of her desk, which was neat, but adorned with several framed photos of dogs, a single-cup electric teapot, and a tissue box covered in various shells.

"Did you get my voice mail?" she asked him, her blue eyes gazing at him over her bifocals.

"Yes," he answered. "Who is it that wants to see me?"

"James Quillen," she answered.

"Who is James Quillen?" he asked. "And who am I supposed to report to on this? I'm afraid I'm unsure about the procedure at this point."

"James Quillen is the head of the County Commissioners," Vi answered gravely. "And he can probably answer that question for you better than I."

"Okay," Evan answered. "When will he be here?"

"He's here now, in Sheriff Hutchins' office," she said. Her voice went dry and hoarse as she said their boss's name.

"Vi, I'm very sorry about Sheriff Hutchins," Evan said quietly.

"As are we all," she answered, sitting up taller, as though a straight spine would ease her obvious pain. "The Sheriff hired you because he admired your reputation, Lieutenant. Please see to it that you repay him by bringing him justice."

"I'll do my best," he said.

"Is your best very good?"

"Yes," he answered quietly. "So it seems."

She nodded curtly, the chain of her glasses rattling against large green dreamcatcher earrings. "Then I expect you to do it."

Evan nodded back at her, then stood there, unsure of his next move. "What's this guy like?"

"Lt. Caldwell," she sighed, like a patient kindergarten teacher. "I am merely the assistant to the Sheriff and his liaison with his staff and constituents. It is not my purview to tell you that James Quillen is a pointless sycophant. You will need to divine that on your own. Now, he's waiting for you, so please go speak with him."

She spun around in her chair, turning her back to him, and busied herself with running her fingers through a drawer of green file folders. Evan considered himself dismissed and walked over to the oak door with the black label designating it as belonging to Sheriff Randall Hutchins. He tapped on it twice, and opened the door.

The man behind Sheriff Hutchins's desk was subtly startling in appearance. It took Evan a moment or two to reconcile what he was seeing. Quillen didn't exactly look small, but he somehow made the desk and chair look bigger than they had appeared when Hutch had sat there.

He looked to be in his late fifties, with dark hair and a salt and pepper beard that was so finely trimmed that it looked painted on. He wore a decent but not too expensive gray suit. The man's eyes were so green that they had to be colored contact lenses. He smiled with warmth so sincere that it would have been impolite not to smile back, despite Vi's warning and his own uneasiness.

Quillen stood, with well-practiced dignity, and extended a hand, his smile expanding just enough to no longer be believable. "Lieutenant Caldwell," he said, his voice resonating in a way that suggested he used it often to direct the affairs of lesser mortals. "I'm Commissioner

Quillen, James Quillen, that is. So nice to finally meet you. I wish it were under, uh, better circumstances."

"So do I," Evan said, shaking the man's hand.

"Have a seat, if you would," Quillen said, extending his other hand toward the chair on Evan's side of the desk. "Please."

Evan sat, placing the file folder on his knee. Quillen remained standing for a moment. Evan had just started wondering if that was a power play, when the man finally sat back down. His face pinched in a show of ponderous thought as he slowly perused the office and its various accoutrements. Then he looked back at Evan, his eyes expressing sympathy tinged with deep, personal pain. "I imagine this has been a very busy and difficult morning for you, Lieutenant Caldwell. How are you holding up?"

"It has been busy," Evan said. "I'm guessing it will continue to be busy for several days."

Quillen smiled again, acknowledging Evan's polite point. "I won't keep you long, Lieutenant."

Looking at the councilman's teeth, Evan guessed he could buy a small sedan for less than Quillen had paid for his smile. The man was definitely invested in his political career.

"First of all, Evan, do you have everything you need for this investigation?"

"I think we have everything covered," Evan said. "So far, at least."

"I want you to know that you have the full backing and support of the County Commissioners. If there is anything we can do to help you resolve this case, anything at all…" Quillen peered across the desk at Evan, ratcheting up the sincerity in his stare.

Evan wasn't sure what Quillen expected him to need from politicians. "I'll let you know."

"I see you drive a…well what is that exactly? A Chevy?"

"My personal vehicle?" Evan asked. "I drive a Pilot."

"Ah, a Pilot."

Evan felt his forehead wrinkling. "That's right."

"Well, how about we, um, assign you a fleet vehicle, something more official? Like I said, we want you to have everything you need."

"Mr. Quillen, I appreciate that, but I really don't feel like this is the best time to discuss my vehicle assignment," Evan said politely.

"No, no, I understand. You have a lot on your plate today, but like I said, we want to make sure we support you in every way possible."

"I guess about the only thing I need right now is some clarification about chain of command," Evan said. "Although, a call over to the M.E to convey the urgency of the situation would be welcome."

"Grundy! Ha! That ol' codger. He's more of a mascot than anything else. We keep him around for sentimental reasons, mostly." Quillen's cell phone vibrated on the glass-top desk, but he ignored it. "It's those college kids that do most of the real work. They have all the new science, they're motivated, and they cost us about a quarter of what it would take to replace Grundy. But don't you worry about that. If there's any issue with the M.E.'s office, you let me know and I'll make sure you get what you need. You have my word on that."

"Okay," Evan nodded, "I'll keep that in mind."

"As to chain of command, well, that's the reason I asked to see you."

Evan wanted to say, *maybe you should have opened with that*. He refrained from vocalizing it, but worried his face conveyed the thought. If so, Quillen showed no sign of recognition.

Quillen continued. "For the time being, you will report directly to me, and the rest of the commissioners, of course. But I'll be your, uh, primary point of contact."

"Okay," Evan said, waiting for the rest of whatever it was Quillen had been working up to.

Quillen folded his hands on the desktop. Evan noticed a silver wedding band on his left hand and what looked like a fraternity ring on the other. After a deep breath and a pained sigh, Quillen finally got to it. "I need you to do something for me, Evan. Can I call you Evan?"

Evan nodded. His fingers desperately wanted to tap, and he needed a cigarette now more than he had all morning.

"We're aware of the circumstances of your coming here to Gulf County. We know all about your stellar career over in Brevard. We also know that you have no, uh, history with anyone in this town. You carry no grudges, owe no favors, etcetera. You don't have an agenda, so to speak."

"Mr. Quillen," Evan said quietly, standing. "I have an investigation that needs attending. With all due respect, I really need to get back to work." He resisted the urge to tap the file folder against his thigh.

Quillen smiled, relieved, as if Evan had just said *yes* to whatever he had in mind. "Very well, straight to the point then. I respect a man that understands the value of time."

He opened the lap drawer of the desk and removed a small wooden box, then walked around the desk so that he stood over Evan. He wasn't quite tall enough to be imposing, but he was trying.

"We have a county-wide election November of next year. That means it's going to be almost fifteen months before the good people of Gulf County can elect a replacement for Hutch. But we're going to need someone to sit behind this desk between now and then. We feel that you're the best man for the job."

The man seemed not to notice Evan's mouth opening, or the fact that Evan probably didn't look too excited.

"Accordingly, we've appointed you interim Sheriff of Gulf County, effective today."

Quillen opened the box and extended it to Evan. Inside, red velvet cradled a gold badge stamped *Gulf County Sheriff*. Thankfully, Evan knew it wasn't Hutchins'.

This was the second time that morning that someone had said something about him being Sheriff. It took Evan a moment to respond, so profound was his surprise, and his revulsion at the idea.

Finally, Evan asked, "You want me to fill in for Hutchins?" though the intent had been clear enough.

Quillen nodded, tilting the box in a manner suggesting that Evan should take it.

"How long do I have to give you an answer?" Evan asked.

Quillen cocked his head. "An answer? About taking over as interim sheriff?"

"Yes."

Quillen chuckled softly, "Son, no answer's required when a question hasn't been asked. This is what we've decided. Unless you're planning on resigning in the next little while, this is what we need you to do." He wasn't smiling anymore. "You don't have to run for the next term, but we do need you to step up to the plate for the time being."

"I see," Evan said, more as a verbal speed bump than anything else.

"Good," Quillen said, placing the box in Evan's hand. "I would love to stay and chat, but in this current crisis, I just don't have the time. Vi has been in this office just about as long as Florida's been a state. She can answer any questions you might have about the job. You also have the full confidence and support of the County Commissioners."

Evan thought about suggesting Quillen appoint Vi as interim sheriff, but Quillen didn't strike him as someone who appreciated sarcasm. As the commissioner stepped out the door, he called back to Evan, "I left my card on the desk. If you need anything at all, you call me."

Evan sighed as the door shut behind Quillen. There seemed to be more air in the room now that he'd left, but there still wasn't enough of it. He loosened his tie just a bit, then leaned back in Sheriff Hutchins' well-worn leather chair. He jerked himself upright as the chair threatened to dump him onto the floor. The Sheriff had outweighed Evan by at least sixty pounds, most of it applied to his width.

He ran a hand through his hair at he stared at Hutchins' desk. Letter trays containing files and papers that he knew nothing about and wasn't sure he should know anything about. Drawers he hesitated to open, even to look for a pen; filled as they were with things that belonged to someone he was not.

Yesterday, Hutchins' had been wiping at the coffee he'd spilled on his shirt while he'd asked Evan to run down a witness in an armed robbery over in White City. The coffee cup was still sitting on the desk, with the Gators logo on the outside and about an inch of too-light, very cold coffee in the bottom. Now Evan was sitting in an office he didn't know, having been given a position he didn't want or understand.

There were two sharp raps on the closed door. "This is Vi," came Vi's anchorman voice on the other side before he could answer.

"Come in," Evan said.

Vi opened the door, then sighed at him as she propped a hand on her hip. Her short, reddish hair was fine as down, and her bifocals were perched at the last stop on her beak. Evan thought she looked like a toddler buzzard, wearing the glasses on a rhinestone chain that had belonged to the elderly woman her parents had just consumed.

"What can I do for you?" she asked.

Evan started to answer automatically, then held up his hands as he realized he had no idea. "I don't even know precisely what it is you do," he said.

"I am your administrative assistant," she answered sternly, as though he'd just taken some other kid's milk money.

"I realize that," Evan said. "I just don't know what that entails."

"Everything you don't have time to do and I don't need a badge for," she answered. "I can pull the document listing my duties, but please be aware that we no longer have typewriters or Dictaphones and I no longer fetch coffee."

Evan worked at not sighing. "We'll figure it out." He could almost feel her getting ready with a retort, so he amended his statement quickly. "*I'll* figure it out."

He was surprised to see Vi's gaze soften just a hair, though he doubted she actually had an expression in her repertoire that could be considered soft.

"Lieutenant. I was very fond of the sheriff, as you know. We worked together for many years," Vi said, still managing to sound like she was reprimanding him. "It will take me a moment to get used to you sitting in this office. In his chair. You've been put in a very awkward position, for you. But I suspect, because of your resume and reputation, that you're most likely the best person for the job."

"Thank you, Vi."

"Very well," she said, and shut the door behind her.

Evan started making a mental list of his next steps. Foremost was a cigarette, and he stood up and rounded the desk to head outside, but was stopped short by an obnoxious buzzing behind him.

As he turned around, it was followed by Vi's voice through the desk phone's intercom. "Lieutenant--Mr. Caldwell, Sergeant Goff is holding for you on line three." Vi's voice droned through the speaker again, sounding oddly distant and tinny. He could also hear her through the door, and found that distracting. "Pick up the receiver and push the blinking button."

Evan walked over to the desk and took the call. On the other end, Goff said, "If you're done hobnobbing, Tosh just dropped off Hutch's truck in the impound lot. Paula asked me to go over it with you."

"Sure, Goff, I'll be right there."

Evan was eager for any information gleaned from the truck, but he was exceptionally grateful for the excuse to go outside.

·●✳●·

Tosh Bradley had just finished unhooking Hutch's truck, and was busy securing the hooks and cables to his tow truck when Evan entered the back lot. The sun was right overhead, and Evan felt his hair melting before he'd made it halfway across the lot. He pulled out his cigarettes and lit one of the them on the way.

Goff stood to one side, studying a black smudge on the truck's door handle.

"Goff?" Evan said as he approached.

"Hey," Goff replied, turning. "Paula finished collecting what she needed. She's headed back to the lab. She said she'd call you soon as she had anything to say."

"She get anything good?" Evan asked, squinting through white-hot light at the fingerprint dust on the driver's door.

"Don't suppose so. Said she got hair samples off about seventeen different people, that being by eyeball, not microscope. Might be more once she has a closer look. Same with fingerprints. Lots of samples, but none that's gonna amount to much. Hutch had folks in and out of that truck all day long."

"Hmm…" Evan said. "And we don't actually have any evidence from the scene to say for sure the killer was ever in the truck." He reached for his sunglasses, but he'd left them in his suit blazer in the office. "If the shooter is a local, and I would guess that he is, he could have had legitimate reason to be in the truck, so finding his prints there wouldn't mean much anyway."

"Yep. Paula doesn't have much hope for the stuff she got off the truck, but it's a stone and she's gonna turn it," Goff said. "On the upside, we did find the slug. It's a semi-jacketed .45 hollow point. Mushroomed out pretty good up front, but the back end's in good shape. It's got some clear striations, should be able to match it to a gun if one happens to turn up."

"Well, at least that's something," Evan said. "You think he might have been killed with his service weapon?"

"Nah, Hutch carried a nine." Goff took his SO cap off and wiped his forehead with the back of his hand.

"What about any items in the truck?"

"Nothing. Just his personal belongings that he's always got in there." Goff pulled a small notebook out of his shirt pocket, and Evan felt a sudden, though thin, kinship. "One of those insulated coolers with two warm Dr. Peppers, tackle box, a blue tarp and a brick from the truck bed, a few CDs. Hank Williams mostly."

"Did you find his weapon?"

"Nope," Goff said. "Didn't find his wallet or cell, either. Guessing the killer took 'em."

Evan folded his arms and squinted at the truck. Smudges of fingerprint powder covered the door handle, steering wheel, dash, console, turn signal lever, and several other surfaces. The scenarios ran through his head as he visualized the crime scene, what it would have looked like at midnight or two a.m. Who had the sheriff met out there? Or had he just run across someone? But why would he be out there otherwise? And why would he kneel like that?

"Whatcha thinking?" Goff asked.

"I don't know, yet. Not enough information I guess." Evan thought a bit longer about the morning, about the events after he left the crime scene. So far, the case was a collage of incongruities, the pieces still too ill defined to be properly fitted together. But one particular enigma kept pinging around in his head: the fact that Beckett clearly disliked Hutchins. And he seemed to be close enough to the widow.

"Let me ask you, Goff," he said. "Does it strike you as odd that Beckett made a point of suggesting the killer wasn't a woman?"

"That was a pretty big hole," Goff said. "We probably would have come to that conclusion on our own anyway. That was definitely a bigger gun than most gals carry."

"Most," Evan answered without commitment.

"The wife's got a Desert Eagle 50 cal. But that ain't usual."

"Hutchins' wife?" Evan asked, surprised.

"No, mine."

"Your wife has a Desert Eagle?" Evan asked. He'd met Goff's wife once when she'd brought Goff some lunch. She was even skinnier than Goff, if that was possible.

"She does," Goff said, nodding. "Looks damn silly holding the thing, but ain't no one gonna tell her that."

Evan looked at the deputy for a long moment, trying to ascertain whether he was serious. Finally, he asked, "Your wife have any reason to dislike Sheriff Hutchins?"

Goff looked up at him, and Evan realized it was the first time he'd seen the man smile. "She's got an alibi," he said, with a twinkle in his eye.

Evan took a last drag from his cigarette and ground it carefully under his toe. "You have any luck pinging the sheriff's phone?"

"Not a bit," Goff answered. "It's either off or out of business." Goff crossed his arms over his bony chest, then nervously uncrossed them and propped his hands on his gun belt. "So, you want me to call you Sheriff, Sheriff Caldwell, or just leave it at Caldwell?"

Evan grimaced and let out a sigh. "Am I the last one to find out?"

"Naw. I only know 'cause I walked in there when Quillen was tellin' Vi. It's just me and her."

Evan pulled out another cigarette and lit it before he squinted back at Goff. "It's not going to go over too well, I don't think."

"No, not right away it isn't," Goff answered. "Maybe not ever. But it's not 'cause they don't like you, it's just they don't know you. And you're from Cocoa Beach and all."

"Miami, originally," Evan said around a mouthful of smoke.

"Well, I wouldn't spread that around, I was you," Goff said.

SEVEN

EVAN HAD SPENT THE REST of the day poring over Hutchins' bank statements and waiting for Paula Trigg to call him from the lab. He'd also sent a team out to Dead Lakes to check the bank and water nearest the crime scene. He hadn't hoped for much, so he was pretty satisfied when that was what he got.

The bank statements were largely uninteresting. There were a few transactions here and there that weren't very clear, and he'd highlighted those and given them to Goff to run by the widow in the morning.

When Trigg finally did call, it was to say that, as Goff had told him, there were plenty of fingerprints all over the truck. She'd run half of them by the end of the day and the ones for which she found a match all had legitimate reasons to be there.

As Evan headed just out of town on Hwy 98, he looked to his right, out at the bay, and wished he was on it. He needed to think, and water helped him do that. But the early evening was becoming overcast, there was a decent chop on the water, and he had other obligations.

Sunset Bay was considered one of the best facilities in the state, and it was certainly designed to look the part. Evan coasted down the curving driveway, minding the speedbumps that seemed like they were placed every three yards. On either side of him were Sabal palms lit with solar spotlights, carefully planned flowerbeds, and black wrought iron benches that he'd never seen anyone use.

In the center of the expansive lawn was a small pond with a fountain in the middle, and more benches placed thoughtfully on its banks. Those did get used now and then, mainly by him.

He put his cigarette out as he parked, and stretched for a moment once he got out of the car. There were several small, one-story buildings on either side of the main building. They were set up as clusters of apartments for patients who were healthy enough for an assisted living situation. Evan walked through the double doors of the main building.

He waved at the receptionist as he crossed a large lobby that was decorated to look like a decent hotel in some more tropical locale, some place people would go for a more recreational reason.

Halfway down the hall of the East Wing, he raised a hand in greeting to the two nurses at the nursing station.

They smiled and waved in reply, but they knew him well enough to know he'd stop if he saw a need for conversation. He seldom did.

Evan let out a slow, even breath as he pushed open the door to Room 209. The room was intentionally cozy and cheerful, with a pale green loveseat under the window, and matching chair close to the bed. Framed seascapes adorned the pale peach walls.

The light in the room had a slightly orange cast to it, from the slices of sunset coming through the blinds, and the small lamp on the bedside table. The room was still and quiet, except for the gentle hiss of the ventilator. Nothing moved but the numbers on the monitors and the leaves of the palm outside the window.

Evan walked over to the bed and placed a hand on the rail. As he did every day, he checked for changes that rarely materialized.

Hannah's dark brown hair had been washed and dried. They kept it in the short bob she'd worn for years, and the ends curled just under her ears. Her long lashes rested on her cheeks, and her full lips were closed and motionless. She still had some chapping and bruising from the intubation tube they'd removed last month. She now had a smaller breathing tube running through a tracheotomy, which Dr. Simons said was less damaging to her mouth and throat.

Evan sighed and walked around the bed to sit in the upholstered chair next to her bedside table. Next to him on the IV pole hung the bags of saline and liquid nutrients that were ever-present. So, too, the urine drainage bag that was attached to the side of Hannah's bed.

Once he'd sat down, Evan realized that there had been a change since yesterday. Hannah's nails, which were normally bare and buffed, had been painted a sheer pink. It was barely discernible next to the pale skin of her slender fingers. Hannah had always spent a lot of time outdoors, and it still seemed odd to Evan sometimes, to see her so fair.

He resisted the urge to run a finger along the back of her hand, and leaned back in the chair.

"So, my boss has been murdered," he said conversationally. "Which sucks the most for him and his widow, but it sucks for me, too. The County's stuck me with his job for the time being."

He stared at the side of Hannah's head. The shaved spot over her ear had long since grown in, the holes from where they'd drained the excess fluid from her brain were just a memory. But he remembered them clearly. Sometimes when he looked they were still there.

It was still difficult to believe that both of their lives had been changed so completely by something as simple as a misstep, an unexpected bob of the boat, a slip as she jumped to the dock to secure the stern line. Her head had hit the side of the dock in just such a way as to turn what should have been an ER visit into a never-ending stay, first in the ICU in Cape Canaveral, then in the brain injury ward at Florida Hospital in Orlando.

And now they were here. He had sold their house and put a down payment on his boat with what was left after paying for this place. He'd left the Brevard County Sheriff's Office and was now being shoved into a position he didn't want, at a department where nobody knew him. Because she'd fallen off of a boat. Not his boat, but her lover's. A stranger to him, but not to her.

At the time, he was too angry and too wounded to give Shayne credit for staying at the ER even after Evan had shown up. Once the fury and the fire had mellowed to a deep ache, he'd grudgingly come to respect the man for it, but barely.

When he felt a sharp pinch of fresh anger in his chest, Evan looked away from the bed and up at the monitor that displayed readings of her heart rate, respiration, brain activity. It seldom changed, and he seldom expected it to anymore. He sighed and leaned back in the chair.

"Anyway, so now I'm supposed to be the interim sheriff, investigating what appears to be the execution of the former sheriff, and pretending not to see that nobody in the department thinks I'm the man for the job, including me."

Evan caught a movement in his peripheral vision and turned to look at the window. Through the blinds, he could see that the breeze had picked up; the little palm outside was getting excited about the possibility of rain.

He turned back to look at his silent, beautiful wife of five short years.

"Your cat has undertaken the task of peeing in my shoes for me," he said pleasantly. "I'm still a little upset with you for dragging him home and then sticking *me* with him two weeks later. I guess he's still upset about it, too. Either that or just hates me because he knows I loathe cats. We're thinking about going to counseling."

Half an hour and several lesser news stories later, he stood. He stared down at her face, so still for so long that it had taken on the presence of a sculpture. "I need to go. I'll see you tomorrow."

He stood there for another moment, looking at the little blue causeways that ran just underneath the skin of her hands, at tall of the old IV sites on her wrists, at the earrings he'd bought her for their third anniversary.

"I'll see you tomorrow," he said again, quietly. He leaned over the bed rail and kissed his wife on the forehead, then walked out the door.

He stopped at the nurse's station and nodded at the blandly pretty blond who was one of Hannah's nurses. Cara or Carrie or something, but he didn't want to look at the badge on her chest to be sure.

"How are you tonight, Mr. Caldwell?" she asked as she stood and picked up a chart.

"Fair," he said honestly. "And you?"

"I'm doing all right," she answered, grabbing a pen before she walked around the curved counter. "Hoping for some rain."

He nodded, meaning nothing. "Was it you that painted Hannah's nails?"

"Yep, that was me," she said.

"Thank you," he said. "Although I have to wonder why. Do you think she notices?" He hadn't meant it in a combative way, and he hoped, belatedly, that that wasn't how it sounded.

"Maybe," she said. "Do you think she notices that you never miss a day?"

"I don't know," he answered.

"There you go," she said as she headed down the hall. "Anyway, I didn't do it just for her."

Evan looked after her for a moment, then turned and walked back the way he'd come. He lit a cigarette as soon as he was the required twenty-five feet from the doors, exhaled his first drag into air that had become damp and heavy. Faint thunder rumbled from somewhere to the east. He wished it Godspeed.

He'd been completely blindsided by Hannah's affair. He'd had no idea she was unhappy. The only complaint he could remember her having, and it was frequent, was that he never talked to her about his work, about his day. He'd always tried to keep his work life and personal life separate, and he didn't want to talk to her about the darker side of his existence.

But now he did so, every single day.

The skies let loose just as Evan stowed his dress shoes in a cubby on the sun deck. All rain sounded like hail on a boat. It was one of the many reasons he'd chosen to live on one. He opened the door into the salon, leaving it open wide for the fresh air and noise, and headed for his stateroom in his sock feet.

He was relieved to find that there were no fresh urine comments in his hanging locker, and after he hung up his blazer and pants and tossed his shirt, underwear and socks in the washer, he changed into his favorite blue pajama pants and headed back up to the galley.

As soon as he stepped onto the galley steps, he spotted Plutes on top of the fridge, sitting tall, tail switching slowly, as though he were a juror waiting for a prisoner to take the stand in his own defense. Just below the Black Death, on the sole in front of the fridge, was the small philodendron that used to sit where the cat was sitting now. It lay limbs akimbo in a pile of potting soil, like a hit and run victim in a pool of their own blood.

Evan glared at the cat. "Why are you such an ass?" he asked. Plutes narrowed his eyes, and the tip of his tail ticked upward just slightly. Evan grabbed a small spray bottle of water from the counter and gave Plutes a quick misting. The cat's skin visibly crawled, like a small tsunami was passing just underneath his fur, and he flatted his ears, jumped down, and ran up the galley steps past Evan.

Evan grumbled to himself as he swept up and repotted the plant, and tucked it into a corner on the counter. Then he methodically prepared his routine evening drink, a warm mixture of cashew milk, coconut oil, honey, and turmeric. He poured it into one of the four white mugs he owned, and carried it out onto the deck.

The rain had slowed from a downpour to something more gentle, and Evan inhaled deeply of salt water, turmeric, and marine polish. The lights, and the noise, from the Dockside Grill were muted and dulled by the sheets of rain, and Evan felt like he and the boat were tucked into an air bubble.

He wished they could stay for just a while.

EIGHT

WHEN EVAN WOKE UP the next morning, he was relieved to find that nothing in his locker had been peed in, though one pair of dress shoes was out on deck and the other was in the trash. He dressed in his usual uniform, though today's suit was navy rather than black.

Evan's cell rang as he was putting sugar in his *café con leche*. The display showed it was Vi's line.

"Hi, Vi," he answered.

Not to be relieved of her identification duties, Vi intoned, "This is Vi," anyway.

"Okeedoke," Evan replied.

"Young Mr. Coyle just called," she said.

"Who?" As Evan crossed the salon, he glared at Plutes, who didn't care.

"The intern with the medical examiner's office," Vi said, clearly disappointed.

"Oh, the skinny kid, right," Evan answered as he stepped out onto the sun deck. It wasn't particularly hot yet, but the humidity was enough to dilute his coffee.

"He advised us that your autopsy results are ready," Vi said.

Evan looked down the dock, where The Muffin Girl was dropping newspapers at each occupied slip. "Okay, I'll head over there in just a few minutes," Evan said. "Anything else?"

"That's all you need until you get to the office," Vi said.

"Thank you, Vi," he replied, and clicked off.

He drank his coffee while he watched The Muffin Girl making her way toward his slip. He called her that because he didn't know her name, but she delivered complimentary newspapers every day, and on Sundays she also brought two muffins to each boat. This was the first time he'd actually been out on deck when she'd come by.

She was a tiny little thing, maybe five feet tall at most, and probably ninety pounds if she was wearing a heavy backpack. With her dyed black hair cut in a pixie, her ripped jeans, and her various piercings, Evan thought she looked like the love child of Thumbelina and Sid Vicious.

She didn't seem to see him leaning against the rail, but she didn't startle when he said, "Hey," either.

"Hey," she said back. Her voice was stronger than he expected it to be. Now that she was just a few feet away, he realized that she couldn't be more than sixteen or so.

"Go ahead and toss it," he said, holding out his free hand. She tossed the paper to him and he caught it. "Thank you."

She looked off to the side of him, then said, "Oh, hey, so he *is* your cat."

Evan thought her smile was much more delicate and pretty than the rest of her appearance led him to expect. He turned his head and saw Plutes inside, perched on the wooden shelf below the window.

"Him?" he asked unnecessarily. "We're roommates."

The Muffin Girl nodded. "Yeah, he walks around a lot," she said. "Up and down the docks and whatnot."

"Really." Evan was surprised to hear that. Although he always left a window open so Plutes could jump down to the sun deck and do his business, he'd never seen the cat actually get off the boat.

"Yeah. Like, he wanders around, you know?" She squinted up at him through the morning sun. "Like he's looking for somebody."

Evan felt something small lurch in his chest. He ignored it by taking a sip of his coffee. "Well," he said after a moment. "She's not here."

The girl looked at him like she was going to ask.

"What's your name?" he asked to head her off.

"Sarah," she answered.

"Your parents own the marina?"

She blew a bubble with her chewing gum. "No, I just work here."

Evan considered her for a moment. "What are you, sixteen?"

She shifted the canvas tote of newspapers from one hand to the other. "Seventeen."

"You seem to work here days and nights," he said.

"I know you're a cop or whatever," she said. "I got my GED and my mom could care less. It's legal for me to be here."

"Okay," he said simply, giving her a reassuring shrug of one shoulder.

"I deliver the papers and the muffins and stuff, clean up around the place, and help out in the office, you know?"

Evan nodded. "Sounds like a cool gig," he said.

"Yeah, I get paid minimum wage, but they let me stay on this little sailboat somebody dumped here and I can eat at the grill for free." She swiped her black athletic shoe on the dock. "I've been here almost a year," she said, and Evan heard a hint of pride in her voice.

"I would have liked that arrangement when I was your age," he said. He took another sip of his coffee and let her squint at him a bit.

"So, you're the new sheriff," she said.

"How did you know that?" he asked.

She jiggled the canvas tote in reply.

"Right."

"So, did you catch the guy that did it yet?"

"No, not yet," he answered, and drained his mug. "Which is why I need to get to work. But it was nice meeting you, Sarah. Thanks for the papers. And the muffins."

"Sure," she said, popping another bubble. "I'll see you around."

Evan nodded, and watched her turn and head back up the dock. Then he went inside to feed the nemesis.

The Gulf County M.E.'s office was in a one-story, tan stucco building with a rock garden and one palm tree out front. It looked like the average Florida dentist's office until Evan saw the small, tasteful sign.

A middle-aged African-American woman served as the office's receptionist, and she offered Evan a cup of coffee before leading him back to the autopsy room. He declined politely.

She opened a stainless-steel door at the end of a short hallway, and told him to have a nice day as he went through.

The autopsy room was small but pristine, and an ocean of white and stainless steel. There were four examination tables in the room, but only two were occupied. One had black toes sticking out from under the sheet, and the other had white toes, and the skinny kid in attendance, so he figured that was his destination. The kid looked up as Evan made his way over there.

"Oh, hey!" Danny Coyle said. His smile was huge, his teeth blindingly perfect.

"Where's Dr. Grundy?" Evan asked, trying not to sound like the kid was a nobody.

"Yeah, he had to run," the kid said.

Evan took a second. "Did he perform the autopsy on Sheriff Hutchins?"

"He had a gander at it."

"What?"

"I'm kidding, sorry," the kid said, then poked his glasses back up onto his nose before continuing in his rapid-fire manner of speaking. "Sure, he conducted the autopsy and I assisted. But, you know, conveying the results to law enforcement is part of my training."

"Okay," Evan said. "I get that, but this is the murder of a sheriff, and I'm the investigating officer for that murder. It's kind of customary for the M.E. to want to handle that conveyance himself, don't you think?"

"Sure, sure," Danny said. "But you know, he's, uh… he's a bit on the alcoholic end of the spectrum, you know what I mean? Only I'd appreciate you not mentioning that I said that, because I'm having a blast here. You know?"

Evan wished with all his might for the law against smoking in public buildings to be spontaneously repealed. When it didn't happen, he just cleared his throat. "Okay. Understood. A problem for another day. Just do me a favor, okay? Try to slow your speech to the speed of sound, so I don't miss anything important."

"Yeah, sure, no prob," the kid said, slightly slower than the average auctioneer.

Evan shook his head slightly, but he couldn't help liking the kid. "You might want to think about cutting back on the Monsters or the Red Bulls or whatever you're living on."

"Oh, no, no. I don't touch the stuff," Danny said with a big grin. "I'm a juicer, right?"

Evan squinted at the boy. "Heroin?" he asked.

"Aw, no, no! That's funny," Danny said, then looked serious. "Cucumbers, kale and so forth, you know?"

"Ah, juicing," Evan said.

"Right? You yank the fiber out of those fruits and veggies and it's like shooting those natural sugars and antioxidants right into your bloodstream, you know? I've got more energy than most squirrels."

Evan thought the kid was also built like one, but he refrained from suggesting he might want to throw a pork chop into his juicer, from time to time.

"Okay, so what have we got?" Evan said, pulling his notebook and pen from his breast pocket.

"What you've got is a grey-black discoloration from the soot at the entry wound, a faint abrasion ring, muzzle imprint, circumferential skull fractures radiating outward from the wound. The bullet passed through the cranial cavity, cleared out his sinuses, and exited just under the left nostril, causing significant tissue damage to the septum and upper lip. What you haven't got is any GSR or bruising on either hand. The entry wound is dead-center on the midline, at the top back of the head. So, he didn't do this himself. You've got all the tell-tale signs of a single contact shot to the back of the head. Cause of death: massive brain damage due to gun shot, manner of death: homicide."

"We didn't find the gun, so I was already thinking someone else might have been there," Evan said. "Anything about the weapon used?"

"The entry and exit wounds are consistent with the .45 bullet that was recovered at the scene. The doc found a copper fragment inside the sinus cavity from the bullet's jacket. If there is any doubt, your ballistics guy can match the fragment to the rest of the bullet, so that's kind of a slam dunk."

"No other injuries? Defensive wounds? Indications that he was bound or that he struggled?"

"Doc didn't find anything." Danny said, leafing through the autopsy report. He pulled out the third page, adjusted his glasses and said, "Well, there's a bandage on his neck, where he had a mole removed, but that's been there a few days."

"Yes, it has," Evan said. "Did Grundy run toxicology? Any drugs or alcohol in his system?"

"Plenty of alcohol in Grundy's system," Danny said, with a furtive glance at Evan, trying to determine whether he caught the joke, and whether he appreciated it.

Evan gave no indication of either.

"But the sheriff was clean," Danny added quickly. "Elevated adrenaline levels, but that is to be expected. I went ahead and packaged up a sample to send to the state crime lab. They might pick up something the doc missed, but none of the regular suspects showed up on our tests."

"Time of death?" Evan asked.

"Between 1:00a.m. and three."

Evan surveyed the small autopsy suite. Everything necessary for a proper post-mortem was present, except a competent M.E. To Danny he said, "If Dr. Grundy does happen to make an appearance today, tell him… You know what, never mind. Just email a copy of that report to the SO." He closed his notebook and slipped the pen into its holder.

"Actually," Danny said quickly, "I can't email it. Doc hasn't set up that clearance on my computer. And… well, I had a couple other things I wanted to point out."

"Other things?" Evan asked.

"Yeah, so, there were a couple of other…things. Stuff I found kind of interesting that didn't seem to pop much for Dr. Grundy, you know?"

Evan stopped midway to putting his notebook back in his pocket. "What kind of things?"

"Okay, so, the first one may not be super exciting or anything, I just found it curious," the kid said. "But the Sheriff's pants, the knees."

"What about them?"

"You want me to get them for you, or just tell you?"

"Just tell me," Evan said. The kid was sharper than Evan had originally given him credit for; he figured he might explain it well enough.

"Right, so it wasn't particularly damp or dewy at two-thirty - which is the doc's best guess for time of death, btw. Anyway, around four-thirty, five o'clock it was dewy, sure, but not so much when the Sheriff was killed."

"Okay."

"So, the knees of his pants were pretty dirty. A little more in the way of grass stains and dirt than I would expect to see, given the lay of the land there where we found him."

"Okay," Evan said again, only to let the kid take a breath.

"So, to my way of thinking, right, in order for him to have so much staining on the knees of his khakis, he either had to be kneeling somewhere else for a while, someplace wetter and grassier, but that doesn't make much sense, right, because if you got a guy on his knees, you go ahead and shoot him, correct? You don't say okay, that's enough kneeling over here, now I need you to kneel over there."

"Sounds sensible," Evan said. Evan was starting to think he was really going to like this kid within one or two more conversations.

"I know, right? So, the only thing that makes sense to me is that he was kneeling longer than the time it took for him to get down there and somebody to pull the trigger. Like quite a while, which sort of plays right into this other thing I was looking at."

"Which is what?"

The kid took a deep breath, which pretty much caved in his chest, before he continued. "Okay, so blood splatter, right? Not exactly my specialty or anything, clearly, but I am a big fan."

Evan didn't bother hiding a small smile. "So there's interesting blood splatter?"

"So true! Because his hands," the kid said. He lifted both of the Sheriff's hands. "Come around here, so you can see his hands from the other side."

Evan walked over to stand behind the kid. Danny was holding Hutchins' hands out horizontally, thumbs side up. There were several small brown stains, more like dots, on the outside edges of the thumbs, and a few on the first two fingers of each hand, on the inside edges.

"Blood?" Evan asked unnecessarily.

"Right, but in a place that doesn't immediately make sense, okay?" The kid pulled the hands away from each other until they were about eight inches apart. "We might see this if he was holding his hands like this, right, but I can't think of any reason for somebody to do that, unless they're telling somebody about a fish they caught or getting ready to do The Robot, right?"

Evan smiled. "Agreed."

"But, if his hands were like this," Danny said, placing them palm to palm, "Then it starts to look right to me. Given the trajectory of the blood and other matter from the exit wound. Because it's going to start out, just for a second, in a narrow pattern and then *whoosh*, immediately go wide, right?"

"Right. So, what are you saying? You think he was bound? Is there any evidence he was handcuffed or tied?"

"No, none," the kid said. He put the Sheriff's hands back down at his sides, then propped a hand of his own on one hip. He shoved his hipster glasses back up with the thumb of his other hand before he spoke. "No, I think maybe he was praying. Which, you know, makes me sad."

Evan stared at the kid a moment, then looked down at his former boss. The thought made him a little sad, too.

NINE

THE FIRST THING EVAN noticed as he pulled in to the SO parking lot was the impromptu memorial wall that had sprung up just to the left of the Sheriff's Office main entrance doors. Flowers, pinwheels, teddy bears, and all manner of other stuff festooned the little nook where on other days there were usually just a couple of UPS packages or a few cigarette butts.

As Evan approached, he saw several miniature Florida Gator's helmets among the bouquets and hand drawn cards. Someone had written "Hutch" across the back of a Port St. Joe High School football jersey and pinned it to the wall. Evan stood and scrutinized every memento and card, looking for something that might not belong, but there was nothing that jumped out at him.

Upon entering the office, he noticed another unusual thing: every deputy on the force had shown up for work today, regardless of their official schedule or the fact that it was a Saturday. There also seemed to be about a dozen reserve deputies and Citizen Patrol volunteers in evidence. There were several deputies in the conference room midway down the hall, and everyone else pretty much crammed themselves into any available space in the hallway itself.

As Evan made his way toward the conference room, he passed the stretch of wall on which several framed photos memorialized the SO officers who had died in the line of duty. He wondered, sadly, how long it would be before Hutch's picture moved from the wall behind his desk to the wall of death.

As Evan "Excuse-me'd" his way through the people milling in the hallway, the half-dozen conversations in progress began to shut down. The mood was subdued and solemn, but the conversations were anxious and animated. They were there to console each other and to hold the community together in the most practical of ways, by finding the sheriff's killer.

Evan stopped in the doorway to the conference room, and picked out Goff's face among the fifteen or so that looked back at him. Evan wasn't prepared to address the entire staff, so he just passed a few nods around the room, then tipped his chin at Goff.

"Goff, can you come to the, uh, office, please?" Evan was uncomfortable calling it *his* office anyway, but he felt as though torches and spears would come out if he did so in the midst of this crowd.

Goff nodded and scissored his way through the bodies in the room, then followed Evan down the hall. After a few paces, a low murmuring started up behind them. Evan led Goff to the office he had used since arriving in Port St. Joe. He nodded or said a word of greeting to several deputies, which they all returned, but their manner was different. It reminded him of how they had greeted him the first few days he had been employed there, as if they had never met him and needed to take his measure.

He carried the autopsy report in a file folder which he tapped against his thigh as he walked. He and Goff didn't speak until they were in Evan's old office, which still contained all of his things. Goff seemed surprised to find himself there, rather than in the big office beyond Vi's desk. Evan pulled a vinyl chair over to face his desk, and waved at Goff to sit in it, then he walked around his desk and sat down himself. He folded his hands over the autopsy report and huffed out a breath before asking, "Goff, did you know the sheriff to be a praying man?"

Goff was clearly surprised by the question, and his Adam's apple worked itself up and down a few times before he answered. "He'd make Sunday mornings, like everybody else, sometimes say the opening prayer at the football game, back when that was allowed. No idea if he did any praying in his free time."

"You wouldn't expect him to be the type to drive out into the swamps at two in the morning to get closer to God, would you?"

"What'd God be doing in the swamp?" Goff asked, dismissively.

Evan nodded, granting Goff the point. Then he pushed the autopsy report across the desk. "Grundy's findings. Have a look if you like, but there's nothing there we didn't already know," Evan said, "Paula hasn't come up with anything useful in the way of fingerprints or hair from inside the truck. Were you able to get anything good from the widow? From Marlene?"

Trigg had reported that the remainder of the prints showed nothing irregular. She had compiled a list of the matches for Evan but he didn't expect much to come of it, other than a lot of overtime.

"Not much, no," Goff said. "We went over those bank statements you gave me. All thirty-six months. Nothing much stuck out as unusual. Regular deposits in, regular withdraws out. Nothing unexplained. I asked her about other accounts, safety deposit boxes, all that. Got nothing."

"And you discussed his routine with her?"

"Yep. She knew where he was just about every minute of any given day. If he wasn't working, he was home with her, and if he wasn't there, he was coaching football or fishing. And if he was doing any of those things, she usually knew where."

"Okay, and nothing stood out to her as unusual in the last few days?"

Goff shook his head. "Naw. And I don't think she was keeping anything back, either."

Goff pulled the autopsy file closer and opened it up, began reading the summary report on top.

Evan nodded and watched the man read for a moment. "I'd like to get a rundown of his whereabouts this week. What was he working on? Where did he go? Who did he talk to? Do you think Marlene would be willing to sit with you again so you can put together a sketch of his last few days?"

"She might be willing, but she won't need to," Goff said, pulling a spiral note pad from his breast pocket. "I got it from her on our first visit. Last five days, all whereabouts and activities accounted for. Right up until he left in the middle of the night and didn't come back."

Evan accepted the note pad, eyebrows raised. "Nice work, Goff. I thought you said you didn't get anything good from her."

"Well, we didn't sit there watchin' TV together," Goff said mildly. "I got a lot of notes, but I don't think there's any one of 'em that's gonna lead us straight to the killer. If it's in his movements the last week or so, I don't think it's gonna jump out and kiss us, you know what I mean?"

Evan nodded, placed Goff's notebook beside the open autopsy file, and considered the differing merits of the two reports. "Look, Goff. I'm going to need your help.

This was an uphill case before Quillen shoved this pro-motion on me. There's an awful lot of ground to cover. I need everyone working together and doing their part, even if it's not the exciting stuff. And I don't know if they'll do that just because I asked."

Goff didn't argue the point, but acknowledged it with a nod. "But every one of them wants this guy caught or dead. Preferably both. That's why they'll do it," he said. "You make that the thrust of it an' they'll follow."

Evan nodded. He pulled a legal pad from a drawer and placed it on the desk, intending to list avenues of investigation, then match those efforts with the avail-able deputies. As he put pen to paper, his phone rang.

"Caldwell," he answered.

"This is Vi," Vi intoned. "The files you are going to request are arranged on the sheriff's desk. Would you like to review them there, or shall I bring them to you?"

"The files?" Evan asked, raising his eyebrows at Goff.

Vi sighed impatiently, evidently disappointed in Evan's slowness, and the resulting need to explain things which should have been discernable to the average twelve-year-old. "The files of those recently released, frequent offenders, agitators, political opponents, current inves-tigations, threats, grudges, and general malcontents."

Evan felt the corner of his lip lifting of its own accord. Perhaps Goff was right about the level of cooperation he could expect. To Vi, he said, "If you already have them set up in there, go ahead and leave them. I'll be over there in a few minutes."

"Very well," Vi said. "Is there anything else you need?"

"If you could, please let everyone know that I will be addressing the office at…" Evan consulted his watch. It was 11:14. "…at 11:30. Explaining where we are with the investigation and handing out assignments."

"11:30," she said.

"Yes. Also, other than going over the files you collected for me, I 'm going to keep working from here for the time being. I'm not going to stall the investigation just to move my stuff into a bigger office."

"That sounds reasonable," Vi said and Evan thought he detected a note of approval in her voice. "Will that be all?" she asked.

"Yes, Vi. Thank you."

Across the desk, Goff was leaning back in his chair, a sly grin lifting the corners of his mustache. "See, you're learning. Get that old gal on your side and you'll own the place in no time."

"I don't actually want to own it," Evan said. He slid the legal pad across the desk, then pulled another fresh one from his desk drawer. There were probably a dozen more in there just like it. He got anxious when they ran low. He pulled a Pilot Precise V-7 pen from his blazer pocket. There were a few dozen of them in his desk, too.

"Can you go through your notes and list everyone Hutch talked to during his last two days?" he asked Goff. "I'm going to want someone to interview each of them."

"Got it."

On his own pad, Evan started writing down column headings. *Dive Team, Financial Statements, Home Phone Records, Office Phone Records, Home Computer, Office Computer, Cell Records*. He hesitated for a moment then added Widow to the list. He looked up at Goff who was poring over his note pad as if he'd never seen it before.

"They just have the one child?" Evan asked.

"Who?"

"Hutch and Marlene?" Evan said.

"Yeah, Amanda," Goff answered while writing. "She's grown and gone, married some guy in Panama City or Pensacola or one of them places."

"Did you ask her about any hard feelings in the family? Any enemies not connected to his work?"

"Nope. And I didn't ask her about affairs, neither. Figured I'd leave the really crappy questions for you, seeing as how you're the new sheriff and all."

Evan looked at him over the top of his legal pad for a long moment, but Goff didn't look up. Eventually, Evan said, "Well, I appreciate that." When that got no response, he asked, "Was there talk or suspicion of an affair?"

"Nope, none that I've ever heard," Goff said. "Kinda hard to be running around on your old lady when she knows where you are every minute of the day."

"What about her?" Evan asked. "Did Hutch know where she was every moment of the day?"

This time, Goff did look up. His eyes narrowed. "I don't think he felt like he needed to know. Marlene's a good woman…and folks around here know better than to be stepping out with the sheriff's wife."

"What if the sheriff was out of the way?"

Goff leaned back in the chair, producing a dry creak. Evan didn't know whether the sound came from the chair or Goff himself. "I guess it wouldn't hurt to add that to your list there. But I can tell you, ain't nobody gonna believe Marlene had anything to do with this."

Evan nodded and looked down at his notes. He wouldn't write it on the pad just yet, but he wasn't dismissing the idea either. There was something unnerving about the way this case was coming together. It had a vibe, a hidden energy, like a current moving beneath a deceptively calm surface, that Evan perceived but could not yet quantify. He couldn't even guess yet where this case would go, but whatever path it took, Evan doubted there would be anything routine about it. He sensed the final resolution would be somehow very personal.

When he raised his head again, Goff was studying him. Evan placed his legal pad on the desk and slid it across to Goff. "Do you feel comfortable making the assignments?" he asked. "You know our team better than I do. I think you'd be good at matching skills to tasks."

"Sure," Goff said. "I can do that."

"Pair me up with one of the senior deputies and give us three or four of the more interesting names on that list. We'll do a couple interviews and by the end of the day some of this other info should be filtering back in."

Goff nodded as he perused the list. After a moment, he raised his eyebrows and said, "Dive team? Dead Lakes is 'bout as black as three-week old coffee…and not the good kind, neither."

Evan wondered what kind of coffee Goff considered 'the good kind' but decided it might be better if he didn't know. Instead, he asked, "You don't think they'll find anything down there?"

"Oh, they're like to find just about anything," he said, shaking his head. "No telling what folks get up to out there. More than likely they'll find evidence of cases we don't even know we have, yet. But as far as Hutch's gun, or his cell phone…I wouldn't put money on it."

"You think we've got guys willing to give it a try?" Evan asked.

"We don't have an official dive team, but you'd have a hard time finding a deputy here who doesn't dive."

"You dive, Goff?"

"Not in this century, but I could if called upon."

"I'd rather have you working elsewhere," Evan said. "Do we have dive equipment?"

"Yeah, we've got the underwater metal detectors and some dive gear," Goff said as he went back to reading Evan's list of investigative inquiries. After a moment, his eyebrows knotted and he said, "You got 'Cell Phone' on here. I told you I tried to get the phone company to ping his cell. Got nothing."

"Right," Evan said. "It's probably in the swamp, along with his gun and the murder weapon, if the killer had any sense. But the cell company should be able to tell us which towers it was pinging before they lost it. They should also be able to tell us what time it went dead, presumably shortly after Hutch was killed."

"Makes sense, I guess," Goff nodded. "And I'm figuring once we pull call records from his home and office, you're gonna want someone to talk to everyone he talked to?"

Evan nodded. "Someone to talk to them, yes, as well as a list of all the names, regardless of the reason for the call, even if it was just a telemarketer."

"I think we should go ahead and round up any tele-marketers we come across. Lock 'em up for general mal-feasance."

Evan tried not to smile as Goff scratched and scrib-bled on Evan's pad for a few minutes, then cleared his throat, nodded to himself, and said, "Yep, I think that oughta just about do it. You want to look over this before we present it to the troops?"

"No, as long as you've got someone covering each of those, I think we'll be all right," Evan said. He looked at his watch again, then said, "Let's go see what they think."

TEN

ONCE AGAIN, ALL CONVERSATION ceased when Evan stepped out of his office. All eyes turned to him. The faces of the deputies and volunteers no longer showed a scattered blend of sorrow, shock, anger, or detached confusion. Their expressions had hardened to smoldering determination. These men and women intended to pour all their combined energy into running Hutches' killer into the dirt. The only thing Evan could not tell was whether they saw him as part of that pursuit, or as an impediment.

Evan made his way into the conference room, Goff just behind him, and found some open space at the long, oval table. Through the wall of windows at the far end of the room, he could see the palm trees getting excited about some kind of upcoming weather. He wished he was out there.

"Everyone," he addressed the room, "As I'm sure you've already heard, the commissioners have appointed me to run this office until a new sheriff can be elected. I know some of you disagree with that decision. I understand that, but I don't much care. I didn't have any more say in it than you did, and we have much more important things to do, so I don't expect us to waste any time bickering about it." He paused, then asked, "Are there any questions or comments on that matter?"

The crossed arms and set jaws of his deputies suggested that the issue was not settled, but none of them chose to pursue it just then. A few pairs of eyes just dropped to the carpet when his gaze passed them.

"Very well," Evan continued, "Let's focus our attention on the matter at hand. Here's what we know at this point. The sheriff was killed early Friday morning, between the hours of midnight and two-thirty a.m. The cause of death was a single gunshot to the back of the head. He was kneeling at the time he was shot."

This produced low, agitated murmuring in the crowd. Evan let them have their moment before he continued. "The murder weapon is a .45 caliber semi-automatic handgun. We don't know make or model yet, but ballistics has the slug, so they should be able to give us that information soon. We have not recovered a possible murder weapon. The Sheriff's duty weapon and cell phone are also missing."

"I just spoke with the M. E's office, and have reviewed the initial crime scene forensics. Whoever shot Sheriff Hutchins didn't leave us much to work with. We have very little in the way of physical evidence. At this point, we have several dozen interviews that need to be conducted. I want to reconstruct every hour of Hutch's week prior to his death. I want to know everyone he met with or talked to on the phone, and I want us to talk to each of them."

There were a few quick nods and raised eyebrows around the room. Evan sensed he'd earned some credibility for actually knowing how to do his job.

"Vi will be setting up an hour-by-hour calendar on the wall here," he continued. "Goff's working on pairing officers up with each interview. As you conduct your interviews, add your information to the appropriate place on the calendar, in addition to the regular reports you file. This will allow all of us to see the progress and look for leads or avenues of investigation."

Evan heard someone toward the back of the crowd whisper, "Avenues of investigation," giving the phrase an uppity sneer. A couple people chuckled dismissively, but the majority of the deputies either ignored the jibe, or turn annoyed faces in the direction of the comment. Evan knew their disapproval had more to do with their respect for Hutch than their defense of himself, but he was grateful for it all the same.

He continued without reference to the comment. "Goff has a list of duty assignments for each of you. These consist primarily of these interviews with people who had contact with Sheriff Hutchins over the last 72 hours. Most of these people aren't suspects in any way, we're just building the history. Make your reports thorough. If you believe the subject you're interviewing might need a closer look, note it accordingly in the file and pass it back to Sgt. Goff for follow-up.

"Those of you not assigned to interviews, and the community volunteers, will be heading out to Dead Lakes to do a wider sweep, looking for either the murder weapon, the sheriff's duty weapon, his cell phone, or any other evidence that may be connected to this killing." Evan looked around at the few volunteers who had managed to find a spot in the conference room. "Sgt. Goff will brief you volunteers in more detail later, but please, if you find something, call out, text, dial the phone...but *do not* pick up anything you think might be evidence. We all appreciate your willingness to help, but we need to be very, very careful about the handling of evidence. When we catch the person responsible for Sheriff Hutchins' death, we will not be watching his lawyer get him off for a mistake we've made."

Evan caught a few nods of agreement in his peripheral vision.

"If any of that's there, it's in the water," someone said from the back of the room.

Evan turned to look at a man in faded jeans and an Apalachicola Seafood Festival T-shirt from 2010. "Most likely," Evan said as he nodded. "We'll be sending divers into the lake."

A couple of deputies whistled through their teeth.

Goff cleared his throat, silencing the dissent. "I made the assignments," he said. "Come find me out back of the station if you got a problem with it." No one expressed any interest in taking him up on that offer. Goff was a little guy, Evan thought, but he came across big.

"Look, people," Evan said, "this is going to be a difficult few days, but we all want the same thing. Everyone in this room is here to solve this killing, to find out who killed Hutch and bring that killer to justice." Evan looked around the room, making eye contact with everyone he could. "The dedication and loyalty on display here would have made Hutch proud of all of you. It would have made him proud to be your boss. Let's use that loyalty and determination to motivate us to work together to get this job done. Can we do that?"

Heads nodded and several deputies made mmm-hmm noises. A big bull of a man named Holland had been leaning against a file cabinet. He now stood up straight and asked, "What about the part where you tell us to act professional and not take matters into our own hands?"

"Do you need that part of the speech? I'm sure you've heard it enough on TV." Evan said. He returned Holland's challenging stare., but noted that one corner of the man's mouth had kipped slightly upwards.

"Nah," Holland said. "Saw that just last week I think."

Evan turned to the rest of the crowd and said, "If you did need that reminder, you just heard it from Holland. I don't doubt your professionalism or your dedication." What he didn't say was that if they needed that reminder, it wouldn't have done any good coming from him, anyway. He closed with, "Goff has your assignments."

Goff had paired Evan with one of the other three sergeants in the department, a man named Peters. The man hadn't given any indication, one way or the other, how he felt about Evan. He was around forty, with hard planes to his face and a blond crew cut that would have made any drill sergeant happy. He had been on the job almost twenty years and had the respect of his fellow deputies.

As they walked to an unmarked Crown Vic assigned to the Criminal Investigation Unit, Evan noticed a tattoo peeking out from below the sleeve of Peters' uniform shirt. The tattoo was faded to a faint blue. It looked like the Marine insignia, but Evan couldn't tell for sure.

Peters had the keys to the Vic. Evan walked to the passenger side and waited for Peters to unlock it. There were woods on two sides of the property, and Evan watched the smaller branches waving in the damp wind that had advanced on Port St. Joe in the last hour or so. A look at the sky told him rain was coming eventually.

He'd appreciate the drop in temperature, but wondered if the rain would come through the window he always left open for the idiot cat to get out to his litter box.

"Who we looking at today?" Peters asked, as Evan got into the car.

Evan began to flip through the six files Goff had handed him, these from the stack Vi had compiled. He recognized two of the names, but was unfamiliar with the cases. The last name he remembered well.

"We pulled Johnny Bowles, Eric Scruggs, a couple of Eubanks, a Morrow, and Ricky Nickell Jr."

"There's a bunch of winners for you," Peters said as he cranked up the AC. " If brain cells were dynamite, all of 'em together couldn't blow each other's noses."

"I don't know much about Bowles or Scruggs, but I helped Hutch serve a protection order against Nickell. Seemed like a real piece of work."

"Yeah that boy's got some issues, alright. We call him Ricky Take the Nickle," Peters said. "He can't keep his mouth shut to save his life."

"Take the nickel as in the fifth amendment?"

Peters grinned and shook his head, making a *sheeesh* noise through his teeth. "Nickell stood up in court, behind the defense table, mind you, while he's on trial for domestic violence. This joker stands up and shouts, 'Yeah, I slapped that woman. She don't know when to shut her damn pie hole!'" Peters let out a high-pitched laugh, then said, "Man, I can't tell you—I was assigned court duty at that time, working as the bailiff—can't tell you how hard it was not to crack up right there on the spot. Nickell spent his time in county for the DV, plus an extra three days for contempt of court."

"Huh," Evan mused. "Hutch told me, when we served the protection order, that Nickell has so many protection orders against him that if I see him with any female, it's PC for an order violation."

"That might be overstating it, but not by much," Peters said. He had sobered significantly at the mention of Hutch's name. "Nickell is up in White City. Marrow is, too, but the rest are here in town. You wanna take a run at Scruggs first?"

"Sounds good," Evan said, pulling out of the station onto Highway 71, "What can you tell me about him?"

"The short version? Eric's a small-time hood. He's got a big mouth but not much to back it up. He's usually got a little meth or weed on him, so we can bust him on that if we need to, but he's not worth the trouble. That's my guess, anyway. He doesn't have the stones for something like this."

"No?" Evan asked. "Why is he on our radar?"

"Oh, 'bout five years back, before the high school expelled him, he was on the football team. Hutch was, well, I guess you'd call him the 'co-coach.' He wasn't gonna be anybody's *assistant* anything, but he had too much on his plate to be the fulltime coach, so he was there when he could be and let the real coach run the show the rest of the time. You get me?"

"Sure," Evan said, "sounds like Hutchins."

"Well, Hutch busted Eric and a couple other boys for smoking weed after a practice. He tried to handle it off-book, you know, scare the boys straight but not jam them up too much. It worked on the other boys, but Eric took offense. Since then he has made threats on line and in person."

"But you don't think he would have made good on those threats," Evan said. "Does he have any violent crimes or weapons charges on his record?"

"Nah, like I said, he's got a big mouth, that's about it," Peters said. He tapped the files on his palm and smiled. "Now, his dad is a different story. William 'Willy' Scruggs has the reputation, and the rap sheet to back it up. If this was twenty years ago, I'd say he was our man, for sure. But he's not getting around too quick these days."

"He's the one that was big into liquor store and gas station robberies?" Evan asked.

"And meth running and auto theft and any other vice that was dangerous enough to pay big and pump adrenalin"

"I didn't see him in the files Vi pulled. Is he somebody we need to be talking to?"

"Well, we're probably going to be talking to him. Eric lives with him. But he's not a player anymore. He and Hutch knocked heads a few times back in the early nineties, when Hutch was just a deputy and Scruggs was a mullet-wearing Trans-Am driving bad ass. But Scruggs got old early. Meth'll do that to you. He hasn't had any run-ins with us for over a decade."

Peters pulled the cruiser in to the driveway of a squatty little white duplex with a wheelchair ramp on one side and a Little Tykes play kitchen on the other.

"Scruggs is gonna be on the right, with the wheel-chair ramp," Peters said. "For Willy, not Eric."

He and Peters exited the vehicle and knocked on Scruggs's door. After several seconds with no response, Peters pounded the door again, calling, "Sheriff's depart-ment. Open the door!"

They heard movement inside, and a not-unusual noise that Evan recognized as grumbling. Peters looked at him and shook his head. The noises inside grew louder. When the door opened, they were met by the older Scruggs, Willy.

"If you're here for the kid, you ain't up on local gossip," he said by way of greeting. He was in his mid-fifties, but his grey skin and faded-out eyes made him look closer to seventy. A clear tube ran oxygen into his nostrils from a tank on wheels that stood beside him. His torso seemed somehow disproportionate, as if he had been stuffed by an unskilled taxidermist.

"We just want to have a word with Eric," Evan said. "May we speak to him?"

Willy Scruggs chuckled. It sounded like a kid blowing bubbles in chocolate pudding with a straw. He looked at Evan and said, "This must be that new hotshot they got from Fort Lauderdale or wherever."

"Cocoa Beach," Peters corrected.

Scruggs coughed and waved a hand dismissively, as if either place amounted to the same level of inconsequence. "I guess they don't teach 'em to listen too good over that way, huh?" The man turned, wobbling as he did so, and shuffled deeper into the apartment. The wheels of the portable oxygen tank squeaked beside him. "He ain't here and I don't figure he did whatever it is you're after him for. I ain't shooing you away, but I can't stand longer'n a few minutes at a time, so if you want me to say more, you're gonna have to come in and sit."

Evan and Peters followed him into a small living room furnished with an overstuffed easy chair, a couch, and a console-style tube television. Willy pulled his oxygen over to the chair before collapsing into it, then waved a hand in the general direction of the couch. The cushion on the left side had been squashed almost flat, while the armrest on the right was covered in a light dusting of sand. Evan surmised that someone, probably Eric, made a habit of sitting sideways on the couch, while propping his shoes on the opposite armrest. This would be the position that would allow optimum viewing of the television. He chose the flattened left cushion because it put him closer to Willy and kept him out of the dirt.

"Don't ever get old, boys," Willy said. "it's a real kick in the crotch." He only had fifteen years or so on Evan, but those had obviously been hard years.

"I can't say the alternative has much to recommend it," Evan said.

Willy raised his eyebrows, as if considering Evan's point, then scowled and shook his head, "Like you'd know. What're you trying to pin on Eric?"

"You been watching the news, Willy?" Peters asked.

"What would I wanna do that for?" Willy scoffed. "Ain't never nothin' new on the news no more."

"Mr. Scruggs—" Evan started.

"Crap, Peters!" Willy said, "You hear that? He called me 'Mister,' like he thinks I'm gonna think he respects me or something." He let out a short burst of laughter that devolved into a coughing spell. Evan thought he sounded like an outboard motor that had been filled with paint.

When he quieted, Peters said, "Willy, someone went and shot Hutch. Killed him. Early yesterday morning."

Willy Scruggs's dim eyes hardened, seeming to come just a bit more alive. He sat up in the chair, dropping the pretense of dismissive contempt.

Peters continued, "Now, I don't believe Eric had anything to do with the killing, but we're talking to everybody that might have had something against Hutch. We need to talk to Eric just so we can cross him off the list. Do you know where he is?"

"Somebody killed Hutch?" Willy asked.

Evan nodded, and waited.

"What do you know," Willy muttered, settling back into the chair again. "Now, why would somebody go and do a thing like that?" He took a framed photo from his side table and stared at it in his lap. "Eric didn't do that, I know that for a fact. If I thought he had done it, I'd have taken care of it already." Evan didn't know if the warble in Willy's voice was due to his frail state, or if the man was about to start crying.

"Is that a picture of your son, Mr. Scruggs?" Evan asked.

Willy made a *pfft* sound, flapping his loose upper lip. "What the hell would I want a picture of him for? If I ever want to see his lazy ass I just look to where you're sitting and there he is." He turned the frame around so Evan could see the photo of a glowing twenty-some-thing blond holding a bundled blanket with a tiny pink face peeking out. "This is my girl and her baby, my grand-daughter."

"They're lovely," Evan said. "What are their names?"

"Jordan's my little girl, and her little girl's Avery. Only thing right I did in my life…"

"Willy, we're not here to talk about your daughter," Peters said, annoyed. He was still standing. "We're here to see Eric."

Willy curled his upper lip again, dismissing Peters. "Eric ain't here. Probl'y won't be back for a while from

DAWN LEE MCKENNA & AXEL BLACKWELL

what I hear. He's been in ICU up to Panama City since last weekend. Got into some fentanyl, thinking it was Oxy, I guess. Point is, anything that happened around here, Eric didn't do it."

"That'll be easy enough to verify," Peters said.

"Verify this, Peters," Willy said, making a show of slowly raising his middle finger.

"Cute, Willy," Peters said with a sneer. "I think we're done here."

"You were done as soon as you came through the door," Willy shot back. "I told you he didn't do nothing."

"You know what, Peters?" Evan said, "Why don't you head out to the car? I'll be right out."

Peters turned and stared at Evan, surprise and irritation evident on his face. After a beat, he pursed his lips, nodded, then said, "Well, I guess you are the boss, aren't you?"

Evan smiled politely.

Peters scoffed, then turned on his heel and walked out the way he'd come in.

Willy Scruggs laughed his yogurt-gargling laugh, pushing his head back into the headrest. "I guess you told him, didn't you?" he said. "I went to school with that guy, if you can believe it. He's always been an ass."

"Be that as it may, Mr. Scruggs," Evan said as he stood, "He and I both appreciate your cooperation and the information about your son. I hope he has a speedy recovery."

"Yeah, I guess I hope so, too," Willy said.

Evan saw the man was gripping his daughter's photo so tightly that his knuckles had turned white. He said, "Willy, I noticed you started talking to us about your daughter when we told you that Sheriff Hutchins had been killed…"

Willy nodded his head, pressing his lips together. His eyes had taken on a reddish tinge around their rims, "The way I figure it, I only got her 'cause of Hutch. Her an' Avery. Ol' Hutch busted me up pretty good. I spent twelve years in the state pen 'cause of him. And that's what saved my life. All the boys I ran with back then, they died while I was away. Car wrecks, OD's, just bad business and such. I'd'a died, too if he hadn't locked me up."

"Sometimes that's what it takes," Evan said. "Sometimes we have to lose too much before we change."

The older man looked over at Evan, his eyes narrowing, as though he was reappraising him.

"Hell, if he'd got to me sooner, maybe I wouldn't be all tore up," he said finally. "I'm dying of kidney failure and about three other things besides. Avery's my first grand-baby. Jordan says she's gonna have three more. I probably won't be around to see them, but whatever time I do get, it's 'cause of Hutch. I owe him, you know. I'm not in touch with too many guys anymore, but if I hear anything I guess I'll pass it along."

Scruggs looked back down at the picture in his lap and Evan suddenly felt intrusive.

"She really is a beautiful girl," Evan said. "Thank you for inviting us in, Mr. Scruggs."

Willy nodded, then turned his eyes to the photo. Evan saw himself to the door.

ELEVEN

PETERS WAS LEANING AGAINST the cruiser, typing on his phone, when Evan crossed the small yard. Peters looked up as Evan said, "You think you and I can work together, or should I team up with someone else?"

"Maybe I was out of line, Caldwell, but you don't know this place and you don't know these people," Peters said. He didn't sound like he thought he was out of line.

"Maybe," Evan said, "But this is what I do know: you get someone like that talking, you let them talk."

"Let'em talk, huh?" A grin spread across Peters' face. "You'll love Ricky then." He opened the driver's side door as Evan opened his.

"Listen, Peters," Evan said evenly. "If you're trying to make me feel like an outsider, you're late to the party. But let me explain something. I don't want to be sheriff. I intend to get out of it any way I can, but I take the investigation of Hutchins' death very seriously." Peters glanced over at him as he cranked up the car. "I wouldn't undermine you or make you look weak in front of a civilian, and if you try it again with me, I'll cut you off at the knees, do you understand? It'll get in our way."

Peters turned the air on full blast, then looked back over at Evan. "I guess I can work with that," he said.

The interviews with David and Nathan Eubanks were mercifully short. Neither brother had any interest in visiting with law enforcement and were quick to provide an alibi. They had been at the Thirsty Goat until last call the night Hutch had been killed. David had paid his tab by credit card and was able to show as much on his on-line bank statement. Nathan had paid cash, but said plenty of folks, and the bar's camera system, could alibi him.

By the time they showed up at Johnny Bowles's apartment, word of the interviews had gotten out. Johnny greeted them at the door with Clapton's *I Shot the Sheriff* blaring out of his sound system. At first, Johnny thought it was funny, but Peter's quickly convinced him otherwise. After a brief interview, Evan concluded that Bowles was an idiot, but not likely a murderer.

The atmosphere thickened as they drove inland toward White City and away from the fresh gulf air. The paper mill had closed over seventeen years ago, long before Evan first visited Port St. Joe, but mile after mile of paper-mill trees still lined either side of the highway. The pines had been planted in rows as precise as lines of type on a page. As far as scenery went, it could be better. Evan found the symmetry and monotony somewhat unsettling. He kept his eyes on the road.

At first, they drove in silence. Then Peters called Gulf Coast Regional Medical Center in Panama City and confirmed Willy Scruggs's story. Eric had, indeed, been admitted to the ER for a fentanyl overdose and had only been released that morning. Peters reported this to Evan, which reopened lines of communication between them. By the time they reached White City, the tension had settled back to ambient levels and the two were exchanging general small talk.

It was a little after three in the afternoon when they arrived at the Nickell residence. Ricky Nickell's trailer sat in a dirt patch behind a screen of pines and cypress trees. Four F150s and a GMC pickup truck loitered at one end of the lot, one up on blocks, one slumped on flat tires like a middle-aged woman after an all-night drunk.

Large black oil patches stained the ground beneath each of them. A girl with oil-black hair, wearing high-heeled western boots, tie-dyed yoga pants and a pink sports bra, wandered around the trucks, picking butterflies out of the air, except there were no butterflies.

"Well look here. It's Kinzy," Peters said. "She's a favorite party favor on the local tweaker scene. Help yourself out here, Caldwell, don't try the 'let 'em talk' approach on her."

"Yeah, I think I could have figured that out on my own," Evan said.

He waited until Kinzy was on the far side of a truck before opening his door. He could hear her either muttering or singing to herself, but couldn't catch any individual words. By the time Evan and Peters reached Nickell's trailer, she had them identified as an audience. Her voice grew louder as she made a bee-line towards them.

Evan pounded on the door, calling, "Mr. Nickell, Gulf County Sheriff. Please come to the door."

"...the door Ricky the door come to the door it's the police of chief to the door mister nickel in a pickle pickled beets beat beaten pickles..." Kinzy's voice vacillated between strident scolding and sing-song playfulness.

She reached the foot of the steps where Evan now stood. "Helloooo, officer," she cooed. "What can I do for you?" The girl's pupils had dilated to the point that her irises were barely visible, their color indiscernible. Evan also noticed a smattering of small round welts on her bare mid-section. "Ma'am," Evan said, "we need to talk to Ricky." In his peripheral vision, he saw Peters shaking his head and grinning.

"Yeah, they didn't want to open copper, you know the Branch Davidian tile?" Kinzy asked. "Well they educated us to unite with abounding slip sloppy sequins sequence sequester them up there, right, real decisive like? But the bees keep coming out!"

"Ma'am..." Evan tried again.

"Did you explain the neat hum notice?" She demanded, hands on hips. Then she turned to Peters and snapped, "Why the hell is there isn't less legs in there?" She stopped speaking abruptly, holding one bent arm out to her side like a mannequin, and looked around as if confused.

Peters ignored her and said to Evan, "That white Ford is the truck he currently drives. Means he's in there. You just have to keep knocking."

"That's right!" Kinzy scolded, violently shaking one finger at Evan, "You just knock and knock and knock but don't knock it until you tried it cause you just don't know do you? But I do. It's in there. It's cause of the hot steady acoustics in a quick minute. You got it. It's his Ford built Ford tough tough luck, lady," She burst out laughing.

Evan had met dozens like her, but he never stopped wanting to take a shower when he met another meth head. It was like they enveloped anyone nearby in a thick, oozing coat of despair. He knocked on the door again. "Ricky Nickell, open the door. Gulf County Sheriff."

A weary, beleaguered voice came through a screened window, "Dang, Kinzey, give it a freaking break already!" Evan noticed several BB sized holes in the screen.

Kinzey stopped laughing and commenced another string of words that only tangentially connected to each other.

Evan talked over her, "Mr. Nickell, I need you to open this door, sir."

"I'm coming!" came the answer, followed by, "*Kinzy!* Shut up!"

"You shut up you nippy praise minute!" she shot back. "Quick frogs oil soil! You crank! Thanks tank rank stank…"

"Go back over by the trucks or the bees will get you, Kinzy!" Ricky yelled. This was followed by a loud snap. The window screen twitched and Kinzy yelped. Her string of words accelerated, now at a much higher pitch as she scurried away from the trailer. A new red welt appeared in the middle of her lower back.

Evan felt a mild bump of adrenaline and color rising in his cheeks. He grabbed the door knob and pulled. It swung open a couple inches before catching on the security chain. Peters began to protest, probably about needing a warrant, but he didn't get that far. Evan wrapped both hands around the edge of the door and wrenched it open, ripping out the chain. The cheap aluminum door bent and flew open, banging against the side of the trailer.

Evan was through the opening. A stick figure dressed in boxer shorts was standing in the middle of the room holding a Daisy air rifle. "I said I'm…" he started, then his eyes popped wide when he got a look at Evan. "Hey you can't…it's not a real…"

Evan was on him before he could finish. He snatched the air rifle with his left hand, bringing it up horizontal, then grabbed it with both hands and drove it into

Ricky's chest. Ricky lost his grip on the rifle, stumbled backward three large steps, and crashed into the wall, putting a crack in the beige paneling. The whole trailer rocked. Ricky plopped onto his butt, staring wide-eyed up at Evan.

Evan tossed the Daisy away. It clattered into the kitchen, breaking something glass. Both of his fists had balled of their own accord, but he took a deep, measured breath and slowly uncurled them. After another breath, he said, "You find that entertaining, Mr. Nickell? Shooting that girl with a pellet gun?"

"Ain't a pellet gun, just BBs," he said in a petulant tone. "Besides, you can't just bust down my door…"

"You were assaulting that girl. With a weapon. While two law enforcement officers were banging on your door," Evan said, calming himself. "Probably one of the dumbest things I've seen all week, and that's really saying something. And now you're under arrest for it."

"But, but it's just Kinzey…"

"And since I had to enter the premises to stop the assault, I also have cause to arrest you for marijuana possession, judging from the smell."

"I don't *possess* any weed, man. We smoked it all," Ricky said, closing his eyes and rolling his head slowly from side to side. "What're you harassing me for, man? I got like this monster hangover, man, an' Kinzey won't shut up and now my door is all busted."

"We're here to talk to you about Sheriff Hutchins," Peters said.

"What? He got another straining order for me? I told that self-righteous old man that he ever bring me another one of those I'd cram it down his throat 'til he choked." He lowered his head into his palms. "I need some Kool-Aid, man."

"When was the last time you saw the sheriff, Mr. Nickell?" Evan asked.

"I don't know…when he came an' told me I couldn't see Julie no more, I guess," Ricky said. "Pervert wants 'em all for himself."

"So, you were pretty upset with the sheriff?" Peters asked.

"Sure I am! He's an ass…Wait a minute, why you asking me where he's at? Huh?"

"Can you tell us where you were Thursday night, and who you were with?" Evan asked.

"What? No! I don't gotta answer any of your questions! You can't even come in here without a warrant," Ricky said, looking up from his palms. "I know my rights!"

"What are they?" Evan asked.

"What are what?" Ricky said.

"Your rights. You said you know them. What are they?"

"I, um…I have the right…I have…" Ricky's face flushed. He glared at Evan, then at Peters. "I don't gotta tell you my rights!" He finally blurted.

Peters chuckled and shook his head, arms crossed on his chest.

Evan said, "That's okay, Peters will give you a refresher. Mr. Nickell, you're under arrest for assault with—"

"But that was just Kinzey!" Ricky nearly screamed. "She wouldn't stay away and my head is slamming." He looked around, bleary eyes wide. "I want to press charges, officer! I want to charge her with assault 'cause she was assaulting me with her ever-yapping mouth."

"Mr. Nickell, focus," Evan tried.

"No, no, get this man," Ricky said, becoming animated. "You need to arrest *her*, not me. It was self-defense, man. I couldn't listen no more or I'd have killed myself, woulda just shot myself in the head. It was her or me, man. It was the only way to get her to shut up!"

"I think he's still half blitzed," Peters said.

"You're half blitzed, pig!" Ricky shouted.

"Go ahead and cuff him up," Evan said. "We'll let him stew a bit. The weapon and the weed will get us a warrant. We can search this place and use anything else we find to motivate some cooperation out of Mr. Nickell, here."

"I ain't got no weapons, man. No firearms at all, 'cause of my DV's," Ricky protested. "Not allowed to *possess* a gun. That's why I have the Daisey."

"On your feet, Ricky," Peters said.

"Wait, no, man. You can't arrest me. It was self-defense. I told you…"

Peters expertly stood Ricky up, spun him around and snapped the cuffs on him as he Mirandized him.

His protests continued as Peters dragged him out the door. "Man, I ain't got nothing on, man! I ain't got no pants. My pubicals'll be hanging out all over the place, man! You can't take me in like this!"

"Nobody cares about your pubicles, Ricky. Now shut up and sit still or I'll go get the Daisy," Peters said as he slammed the car door.

Evan joined Peters by the cruiser, and looked at his watch. "Have we actually got time for this?"

"Not to do it right," Peters said. "If you really want to book him and toss this place we'll have to head back to Port Saint Joe. You didn't leave but one or two deputies in town, so you and I'll be stuck with all the paperwork. It'll be dark before we'd have a chance to get back to our next interview."

Evan wished they had driven separate cars, but that had not been an option. The fleet was a bit light to start with, and with the extra manpower today, every vehicle was in use. He looked to the trailer, then over to Kinzey, and finally to Ricky Nickell.

He said, "Here's what we're going to do. Toss him in the tank and book him on simple assault. We'll seal this place, but not waste time on a warrant just yet. If he's still all wound up in the morning, we can use the threat of a warrant to squeeze a bit of cooperation out of him."

"If I just do the biographical input today but hold off on writing up the report until the morning, we should be able to get back out here in under an hour," Peters said.

"Let's give that a try," Evan said, then nodded to Kinzey, "What are we going to do about her?" She had taken up scolding the fender of the white truck.

"She likely won't be coherent 'till next week," Peters said. "I've got a cousin, Sheryll, here in town. She knows Kinzey. I'll give Sheryll a call, see if she can come pick her up, run her home."

"Ask your cousin if she can drive her down to Sacred Heart Hospital. Get her checked out, and have them document the welts." Evan said.

Peters nodded. He had already dialed and was holding the phone to his ear.

Evan watched Kinzey while Peters conversed with his cousin. The girl had apparently given up on convincing the fender of anything. She got down on all fours, matted hair draping her face, weeping and explaining the inner workings of her mind to insects that probably didn't exist and certainly didn't care.

Evan grabbed the cold bottle of Fiji water he'd stopped for on the way, and walked over to the girl. "Kinzey," he said quietly. She looked up at him, some mixture of fear and anger on her face. Evan held out the water, condensation cooling his palm and dripping from his fingers. After a moment, she took it, then sat down in the dirt. When Evan turned back to the car, she was clutching it to her birdlike chest. For the hundredth time in his career, Evan was grateful he didn't have a daughter.

Peters waved him over, although he was halfway there already. "Sheryll's on her way, should be here in about two minutes. You want to take off?"

"Let's wait," Evan said. "Just for her safety."

"Not sure there's much left to save," Peters said.

"You ever get the feeling you've missed something?" Evan asked.

"Like what?"

"Like some worldwide paradigm-shift where it makes sense for a girl to do that to herself?"

Peters studied Evan for a moment, then said, "Let's just see if we can figure out who killed Hutch, huh? Then we can focus on trying to save her for the eighteenth time."

Evan nodded, still watching Kinzey. A few minutes later, Peters' cousin arrived and escorted the girl away. Ricky Nickell had fallen asleep in the back of the cruiser. Evan and Peters drove the seven miles back along Highway 71 primarily in silence.

TWELVE

RICKY NICKELL DID NOT want to be booked for assault, or anything else, for that matter. His protests, general lack of cooperation and an episode of fainting caused the process to take much longer than it should have. It was well past five by the time Peters managed to get Ricky tucked in. Evan used the time to type up a search warrant application for Nickell's trailer and emailed it to the judge, but had not yet heard back. He could have called and asked for a rush on it, but decided to hold off. The judge would see it first thing in the morning. He didn't need to rush to tick off the local judges by keeping them in their offices late.

Many of the deputies were returning to the station after pursuing their assigned tasks. They were recording their findings on the white board Vi had placed in Evan's office. He decided to conference with his people now and put off the second trip to White City. Once the warrant came through, he would do the search and the Morrow interview in the same trip.

It had been a long, full day, and tomorrow promised to be just as demanding. The dive team would begin their search around 10:00 a.m. Goff expected to receive a full report from the cell phone company in the morning. Evan was encouraged by the vigor with which the deputies had tackled their assignments. The whiteboard calendar was almost completely filled in, and a thick stack of reports waited for him on his desk.

Two items in particular caught his attention. First, Paula Trigg had left a folder containing eight photos of the tire tracks Goff had pointed out. Evan realized all eight were actually the same shot but processed using different filters. It was clear Paula had spent several hours digitally manipulating the image to maximize its clarity. At the back of the folder, she had included a hand-drawn sketch of the tire track and a note. The sketch highlighted an odd feature that was evident in some versions of the photo; the edges of both tire tracks had a dull sawtooth pattern, but the right tire track also displayed a repeating void along its outside edge.

Paula's note explained her deduction about the significance of this pattern: *The ragged appearance of the tires' edges suggests these were off-road tires with a coarse, open tread, probably from a 'mudder' or 'swamper' type tire. The void along the outer edge of the right tire indicates one of the lugs is missing from that tire. I calculat-*

ed the tire's diameter at approximately 120 inches, based on the distance from one void to the next. These will look somewhat out of place as they are fairly large. Especially considering the wheel-base and track calculations, which indicate we are looking for a smaller truck.

The second item that caught Evan's interest was a note from Vi. She had taken a call from Sally Bivens, a local real estate agent. Sally claimed she had seen Sheriff Hutchins' boat at a dock in Mexico Beach, a tiny coastal town a few miles west of Port Saint Joe. Vi had included in her note that Sally tended to be a bit flighty, and a bit of an attention hog, so to take the tip with a grain of salt.

The note was one of many dubious tips that had come in over the course of the day, but this one interested Evan because, until he read it, Hutch's boat had been the last thing on his mind. He had known that the sheriff owned a boat, and that he spent many hours a week fishing from it. Evan had seen his boss on the bay more than once.

But now that he stopped to think about it, he hadn't seen Hutch's boat in any of its usual places since the sheriff had been shot. He looked at Vi's note for several minutes, trying to recall the last time he had actually seen the boat. It bothered him that he hadn't included it on his list of investigative inquiries.

He placed the note on top of all the other files. When he returned to work the following day, his first priority would be to contact Marlene Hutchins and ask her where she believed the boat to be. Then he would call the realtor. For now, he needed to get away from all of it.

· ● ✳ ● ·

The Dockside Grill always did a good business, between boaters who found it convenient and locals who liked the feeling of having a boat without actually getting one. Evan liked the place. The food was good, the staff, mostly college kids, was friendly and efficient, and if he couldn't cook for himself at least he could be within sight of his home while someone else did the cooking.

Tonight, Evan sat out on the covered side patio, along with half a dozen other diners. He leaned back against his chair as he sipped from his bottled water, looked out at the boats and the sunset, and awaited his grouper Po-Boy.

Although Evan rarely went out at night, or at all, he sometimes found himself wanting the company of strangers. Not that he talked to anyone, other than the bartender or server; he seldom did, unless spoken to first. It wasn't so much that he wanted to be *with* people. It just made him feel less alone to be *among* them. Sometimes, he just needed to be around people for whom violence didn't seem to be an everyday thing. He didn't need it very often, but he did tonight.

The little red-headed server who was majoring in marine biology headed his way. He couldn't remember her name, and he stole a quick glance at her name tag while she set down his food.

"Here you go, Mr. Caldwell," she said, placing a small bowl of cheese grits beside his plate.

"Thanks, Rene," he said.

"You want another bottle of water?"

"Actually, could you ask Benny to pour me a glass of cranberry juice?" Benny was an African-American kid with a short afro who tended bar and was getting ready to get his Masters in Elementary Education. He wanted to teach kindergarten, and Evan just liked that for some reason. When he did want to talk to somebody, he sat at the bar and listened while Benny told one story after another. It was soothing.

"Sure thing," Rene said, already zipping away. "Back in a sec."

Evan scraped half of the remoulade from his sandwich, unrolled his silverware, and started eating. The air was heavy and dank and he wished it would rain. He also wished the sound system was playing something other than 70's rock. Although he liked a varied selection of music, he had no affection for Queen.

Rene came back with his cranberry juice, and Evan asked her to deliver a five-dollar bill to Benny next time she went to the bar. He ate most of his sandwich alone, watching the water in the marina turn from a gray-green to just gray and then moonlit black in what seemed like just a few minutes.

Then he paid his check, leaving Rene ten dollars he didn't have a better use for, and headed back to his car.

·●✴●·

Few cars waited in Sunset Bay's front parking lot that evening. Evan was later than usual, and most other visitors had gone home. He finished his cigarette, thought of his hard-won victory over smoking, of the twelve years he'd proudly done without it, and how he'd started again the day they'd told him Hannah would never wake up. He'd lost two things that day.

On that cheerful note, he walked inside and down the almost silent hallway to her wing. Here and there, he heard muffled voices behind closed doors, but this wasn't a section of the facility where many patients talked, or where many people talked *to* them. He'd been told that Hannah was one of only three comatose "residents," but this wing was devoted to those who spent much of their time unconscious or in some kind of critical state.

He lifted a hand to the two nurses that were working the station, and a moment later he entered Hannah's room, letting the door *swoosh* shut behind him. Hannah's curtains, curtains she'd made for their breakfast nook, had been drawn shut against the night, and the room was almost cozy, bathed in the soft, amber light of her bedside lamp. He'd wondered once what the nurses would do if he'd just gone to sleep in the stuffed chair and stayed the night, but he never had. He hated to admit it, even to himself, but as much as he needed to be here, he was always relieved to leave.

He stopped at her nightstand for a moment, saw the latest card from Hannah's mother. She had mourned already, though she drove up once every couple of months from Melbourne Beach. She always left some trinket of Hannah's, some memento. But she never called or tried to see Evan, and she always came during the day so she wouldn't run into him.

Though he and Marjorie had never grown close, they'd been friendly before the accident. Marjorie wasn't slighting him or even blaming him; she just needed to not see him, or listen to him talk about Hannah. Evan understood that she'd needed to move past the loss of her only child, and he bore her no ill will for it.

Evan sat down in the chair, slid his feet partway out of his shoes to give them some respite.

"So, I met this girl today," he said, as though they were in the middle of a conversation. "She was strung out on meth and who knows what else. I couldn't help thinking that you would have immediately gathered her to your breast and tried to nurture her out of her misery." He sighed. "I didn't mean that as a snipe. I just knew you'd want to fix her."

Hannah had been an event planner by trade, and a very successful one. But she'd spent a lot of time working with a non-profit that mentored high-risk girls. Evan had been proud of her, but he couldn't remember at the moment if he'd ever actually told her that. There were a lot of things he'd just assumed she knew.

"Your cat is intact, by the way," he said.

Just then the door opened slowly, and the young nurse named Jessica stepped in hesitantly.

"Mr. Caldwell? May I come in?"

"Of course," he answered. She let the door close, and stepped farther into the room. "How are you tonight?" he asked politely.

She nodded and smiled as an answer, and put one hand on Hannah's bed rail. She used the other to smooth down the top of her sheet. Evan guessed her to be in her early twenties. He knew she'd only been a nurse for a couple of years. He watched her fiddle unnecessarily with Hannah's pillow, waited for her to say or ask whatever she'd come to say or ask.

He was trying not to expect something bad concerning Hannah when she finally spoke. "Have you caught the person who shot Sheriff Hutchins yet?" She was looking at Hannah when she asked.

"No, not yet," Evan answered, taken aback. "But I really can't talk about that, Jessica." He said it politely.

She nodded for a moment, then took a deep breath and let it out. She finally looked at him. "I wanted to talk to you about something I really can't talk about, either," she said quietly. "I feel like I should, though. But, then I think I'd be hurting someone rather than helping anybody."

Evan picked at his thumbnail for a moment while he tried to look accepting and kind.

"Jessica, I'm guessing this isn't about Hannah," he said gently.

"No."

"Whatever it is you have on your mind, it's up to you whether or not you talk to me about it," he said. She just nodded. "Is it about this case?"

She let out another breath, this one slower. "Yes. I don't want to hurt anyone, but I never felt right about nobody ever looking into it."

"I understand you being hesitant," Evan said. "Clearly, your intentions are good."

She nodded again. "I think it's the right thing, but maybe not the best thing." He waited. "Before I came here, my first year out of nursing school, I worked in the ER at Sacred Heart."

"Okay."

"Well, one night my second or third month there, Sheriff Hutchins brought his wife in with a dislocated shoulder. They said that they'd been coming home from going out to eat, and his wife opened her door and started to fall out. They said he'd grabbed her forearm to try to keep her from falling out, and he'd accidentally hurt her."

It took Evan a moment to speak. "Was she intoxicated?"

"No," Jessica answered, shaking her head. "She said the door was just really heavy, and she'd lost her balance when it swung open. Something like that."

"But it bothers you," Evan said.

She sighed. "I was new here. I'm from New Smyrna Beach originally, but I came up here for nursing school, at West Florida. I didn't know the sheriff or anything." She looked down for a moment, rubbing her finger along the bed rail. When she looked back up, she seemed resigned. "I said something about it to the other nurse that was with me, when we were going back to the nurse's station later, and she said it wasn't the first time. She seemed like she wanted to just forget it, and I dropped it. But I always felt wrong about dropping it."

Evan tried to ignore a sinking, slightly nauseating sensation in his stomach. "What about the doctor? Did he question it?"

"He asked them questions, but he didn't seem to think there was any reason not to believe them, or to doubt their explanation."

Evan was lost in thought for a moment, running various "if then, do" loops around in his brain.

"I really wasn't sure what to do when I heard about the sheriff," she said after a minute or so. "I mean, if he was abusing her and she did something about it, he probably had it coming, frankly," she said, standing up straighter, ready to defend her position. "But it still seems right to say something."

"It was the right thing to do," he reassured her. "Try not to second-guess it too much."

"I just don't want to do her any harm," she said.

"I don't want to hurt her, either, Jessica." Evan slipped his feet back into his shoes, though he wasn't ready to leave yet. It didn't feel right to be conducting official business in his Nautica socks. "Even if her husband hurt her, that doesn't necessarily mean she had something to do with his death. But I have to look into it."

"Okay."

They looked at each other for a moment. "I appreciate you talking to me," he added.

Jessica nodded. "That's one of the reasons I came to work here. I can handle accidents and illnesses and death, but I just couldn't take all the violence and the drugs and the children and everything else that comes into the ER every night."

Evan thought about his meal at the Dockside Grill, about his need to be in a "normal" world. "I get that," he said.

"Yeah, I suppose you probably do," she said. She looked like she was going to leave, but she stopped. "You know that I violated the patient confidentiality laws, right? I could get into serious trouble, lose my license."

"You won't," Evan answered. "Nobody will know."

"Okay. Thank you." She looked at Hannah. "She looks good."

"She does," he said, and they both were lying.

He watched Jessica leave, then leaned forward and put his elbows on his knees. This was a piece of news he wished didn't exist. Him bringing to light any suspicions against Hutchins' character wasn't going to win him any support in the SO, or anywhere else for that matter.

If Hutchins did beat his wife, and that was still an "if", Marlene might have killed him or she might not have. Even if the thing was true, it still might not have anything to do with his murder. On the other hand, the possibility that someone else might have killed him for the abuse presented itself, and that was a whole different mess.

Evans sat back and sighed, looked at Hannah. He caught himself thinking that at least he never raised a hand to his wife. In fact, he couldn't remember raising his voice more than a time or two, even when they fought. But that was probably due to inattention rather than restraint.

If Hutchins did abuse his wife, Evan wanted to get all worked up with righteous indignation, but then he wondered if neglecting his wife was really any better than hitting her.

Then he wished he had a cigarette.

THIRTEEN

EVAN SPENT MOST OF THE next morning getting a warrant to check Marlene Hutchins' medical records at the hospital, without earning the wrath of Judge Winters for calling him on a Sunday morning. This he had to accomplish by getting Vi to tell him who would be the friendliest judge to harass, without letting Vi know what the warrant was for. All in all, it was an exhausting and stressful proposition, but by early in the afternoon, he had the warrant in his email. He printed it off immediately, grateful that Vi wasn't in the office breathing down his neck, and hit the road.

The upside of it being Sunday, when Evan would much rather be out on the water, was that people who might otherwise be doing themselves injury seemed to be staying safe; the ER was downright quiet.

After talking to the doctor in charge of the ER that day, who continued the chain of weekend interruptus by calling the director of the ER at home. The director felt the need to pass on his pain by calling the hospital administrator, who appreciated being dragged away from a family barbecue, and cheerfully gave the okay for the warrant to be honored. In the interim, Evan enjoyed drinking several cups of horrific coffee while he read two magazines for diabetes patients.

Once Evan had the records in hand, he shed himself of the hospital atmosphere and went back to his boat, where he found Plutes sitting on the sun deck, surrounded by crumbs. He'd gnawed through the plastic wrap on one blueberry muffin, and apparently napped on the other. The newspaper was unmolested.

Evan threw the cat into a crab pot and dumped him over the side. After enjoying that satisfying fantasy, Evan made himself a real cup of coffee and sat down in the galley dinette to look over the records that he'd fought for so valiantly.

Marlene Hutchins had been to the Sacred Heart ER three times in the seven years that Sacred Heart had been in existence. In October of 2011, she'd been treated for a sprained wrist that she said she got by tripping over the dog and trying to break her fall. In May of 2014, she'd gone to the ER with a broken nose from slipping in the shower. The last visit was in January 2015; the dislocated shoulder.

Her husband had brought her in all three times, and none of the doctors had seemed inclined to check for, or at least note, any other signs of injury, or any suspicions of abuse.

Evan was a cop, and he'd only been to the ER once in the last seven years. That was when Hannah had been taken to the hospital in Cape Canaveral. There was every possibility that Marlene was an accident-prone woman, but Evan's gut told him that wasn't the case.

He went up to the sun deck for a cigarette and a think. The abuse rang true, but the idea that Marlene had something to do with her husband's death felt wrong. Evan had misjudged people more than a few times, but he was more often on point. However, the premise that Hutch had been killed for the abuse couldn't be ruled out at all.

He snuffed out his cigarette and called the dispatch office that was shared by the SO, Port St. Joe PD and Wewa PD. Within five minutes, he'd learned that Chief of Police Beckett had signed off at midnight on the night Hutch was murdered. Apparently, that was his normal sign-off time, even on his days off. So, he didn't have the easy alibi of being out on a call at the time of the murder. That didn't necessarily mean anything, but Evan wanted it to.

Beckett was actually on duty that afternoon. Apparently, he worked two Sundays a month so that each of his officers had a Sunday off at least once every other month. Evan tried not to like that much.

DAWN LEE MCKENNA & AXEL BLACKWELL

He spent the twenty-minute drive out to Wewa listening to his lungs scream for air that had been filtered by salt water. The further he got from the coast, the more claustrophobic he felt, despite the fact that he had no trouble with small spaces.

Evan caught up with Beckett outside of a white, one-story building with an unimpressive sign stating it served the best pizza in Wewa. Evan made a mental note to not run out here some Friday night to check it out.

Evidently, the alarm had gone off in the closed building, and two-thirds of the police department had turned out to see what was amiss. One sixth of the department was leaning against his Monte Carlo, drinking a bottle of orange soda. He watched and waited, a slight smile on his face, as Evan got out of his Pilot and walked over.

"Looking for me?" Beckett asked.

"I am," Evan said.

"So I heard," Beckett said with a wink. "How can I help you?"

"I was wondering where you were between midnight Thursday and three Friday morning."

"I heard that, too," Beckett said.

"So you've had time to rack your brain, then."

"It was pretty quick," Beckett said, adjusting his sunglasses. "I was sleeping. At home. Alone."

"No dates with your local fan club?"

"No, but I'm no Sonny Crockett," Beckett said. Evan appreciated the 904th reference to *Miami Vice* since he'd moved there. "I'm not as young as I used to be. All of my dalliances end before the eleven o' clock news. And I always sleep alone."

"That's not especially helpful, as alibis go."

"Why would I need one?"

"Because you care about Marlene Hutchins," Evan answered.

"So does her mother," Beckett answered, and he'd lost any hint of a playful mood.

"You think Mom would put a bullet in Hutchins' head for beating her daughter?"

Evan could swear he felt a cold draft oozing from Beckett's body to his own. The other man's eyes narrowed behind his green lenses, and he'd gone very still.

"Did you know anything about Hutchins being abusive?" Evan asked after a pregnant silence.

It took Beckett a moment to answer. First he took off his glasses, folded them, and hung them in his pocket. "About two years after he and Marlene got married, I went over there to pick him up for some sport fishing. Marlene had a bruise on either side of her jaw. He was still in the shower, but I got it out of her that they'd had a fight the day before, and he'd grabbed her jaw and hauled her around the living room by it."

"Okay."

"So I dragged his naked ass out of the shower, hauled him out to the back yard and beat the crap out of him,"

Beckett said without pride or apology. "Told him if I ever heard of him layin' a hand on her again, I'd kill him."

"So did you?"

"Marlene and I didn't have any contact after that, except to see each other around town. Hutch and I didn't speak outside of law enforcement business. I never heard a word about any more abuse."

"Is that a fact?" Evan asked.

"How do you know he was hurting her?" Beckett asked. "Did Marlene tell you that?"

"No. The possibility was presented to me." Evan pulled out his cigarettes and lit one. "But if you're telling me there was at least one incident, I'm going to assume the allegations are true."

Beckett looked off to the side, staring at the quiet street.

"I'm going to ask you point blank," Evan said after a moment. "Did you know Marlene Hutchins was being abused?"

Beckett's jaw tightened, the vein on the side of his neck popping. He finally turned back to Evan. "No. But if I had, he'd have been dead long before you got here, Hollywood. And they'd *still* be looking for his body."

Evan didn't want to believe him, but he had a feeling the man was telling the truth. It was evident that he was thrown by the idea that Marlene Hutchins was the victim of continued abuse. One thing he did believe was that if Beckett had killed Hutch, he probably wouldn't have just left him there. This area had to be loaded with dynamite places to hide a body.

"Okay," Evan said simply. "Talk to you later." He started back to his car. "By the way, Hollywood's in Broward County," he said over his shoulder.

"I don't care where the hell it is," Beckett said without inflection.

Evan believed that, too.

FOURTEEN

EVAN SPENT MOST of Monday going over every notation in the autopsy report and in Trigg's evidence file, and following up on a bunch of useless leads while he waited for the search warrant for the Nickell estate. Oddly, it took longer for that than it had the warrant for Marlene's medical records. Evan supposed the judge might be getting back at him for Sunday.

The sky had taken on a faint orange tint by the time Evan and Goff finished the search of Nickell's trailer and the grounds around it. They came up with several bits of drug paraphernalia, but not much else. The pipes and syringes would get Ricky some time in County, but probably not enough to leverage him into giving up information on a murder, if he even had such information.

They did find several hundred spent bullet casings from a variety of weapons scattered throughout the dirt lot. They collected all the .45 shells they could find, about two-dozen. Analysis through the ballistics lab might be able to tell them if these had been fired by the same model of weapon that killed Hutch. It was another long shot, and neither Evan nor Goff expected it to pan out.

As they packed the evidence bags into the cruiser's trunk, Goff asked, "You still wanna talk to Tomorrow?"

Evan looked at him, opened his mouth, but didn't know what to say. After a beat, he said, "I'm sorry, Goff. I don't know what that means."

"That interview you and Peters didn't do last time you were up this way, kid named Tommy Morrow, A.K.A. Tomorrow."

Evan looked at the peach-tinted sky, consulted his watch, then said, "Yeah, I guess we'd better."

Tomorrow was just around the bend of a dusty gravel road. His lot bore a strong similarity to the Nickell place. The primary difference was two trailers occupied this lot instead of just one. Several pickups lined one side of the driveway. Most appeared inoperable.

Evan spotted a pair of legs sticking out from under one of the trucks, next to a tool box and an air compressor. As they parked their cruiser, the man attached to the legs wriggled out from under the truck and stood to watch them. He was thin, but muscular, rather than anorexic as Nickell had appeared, and dressed in thick canvas overalls and matching work gloves. Evan wanted to pass out just thinking about being that covered up.

"That's our boy," Goff said.

On the drive over, Goff had given Evan the rundown. Tomorrow had been trying to hock stolen power tools at a pawn shop in Panama City. The store owner called the police when he noticed Tomorrow's ID was a fake. The kid split, and made it back into Gulf County, but did so a little too quickly. Deputy Crenshaw got him on radar doing close to ninety miles an hour. After stopping the vehicle, Crenshaw heard the BOLO from Bay County, recognized Morrow as the suspect and made the arrest. On top of the reckless driving, false ID, and possession of stolen property charges, Morrow also got dinged for several ounces of weed in the glove box.

It was a good bust for Crenshaw, but nothing out of the ordinary. And not in any way connected to Hutchins. What put Tommy Morrow on their radar was what had happened after. He had pleaded guilty to seven misdemeanor charges and one felony charge for the drugs and was sentenced to eighteen months in county lockup.

For some reason known only to himself, Hutchins had attended Morrow's first parole hearing. He'd testified in his favor, and apparently pulled strings behind the scenes. Tommy Morrow had been released from county jail after serving only four of the original eighteen months.

It was odd behavior for Hutchins, but no one thought much of it at the time. However, Tommy had been released less than two weeks before Sherriff Hutchins had been killed. Now, his special treatment seemed to merit a closer look.

Tommy approached them as they exited their cruiser. He seemed nervous and perhaps a bit confused.

"Um, can I help you with something?" he asked.

"Tommy Morrow?" Evan asked.

"Yes, sir," Tommy replied. He wore oily leather work gloves, which he started to remove, as if about to shake Evan's hand, but then he stopped and shoved his hands in his back pockets instead.

"I'm Evan Caldwell from the Gulf County Sheriff's Office, and I think you know Sergeant Goff…"

"Um, yeah, sure," Tommy said, then smiled nervously. "My probation officer was just out yesterday. He said I was in compliance. I ain't done nothing since then to mess it up."

"Tommy, we just need to ask you a couple of questions about your relationship with Sheriff Hutchins," Evan said. "This isn't directly related to your probation, so relax, all right?"

"Oh," Tommy said. "Okay."

He didn't look like it was okay. He shifted from one foot to the other, and gnawed on a lip that couldn't bear any more gnawing. He was scared, for sure, but there was something there, almost a sweetness, that made Evan not want to scare him any more than he could help.

"Hutch got you a hell of a deal," Goff said. "You might not be the crispiest cracker in the box, but I know you're not stupid enough to go and mess that up, right?"

"Oh, you got that right," Tommy said with a chuckle. "Man, he was real good to me."

"Yeah, Tommy," Evan said. "You heard someone killed him, right?"

Tommy's eyes darted back and forth between the two, "Well, um, yeah. We all heard it. It's all anybody's talking about, man," he said. "Y'all don't think I did that, do you?"

"Well, Tommy, that's what we're here to talk to you about," Evan said. "It doesn't make much sense that Hutchins would go and do you a good turn only to have you kill him for it…"

"No, no that don't make too much sense at all," Tommy said, shaking his head. Evan wondered what the man's IQ was. He didn't seem challenged, just a little behind the curve.

"We were just wondering why Hutch went to all the trouble to help you out like that in the first place," Goff said.

"And then two weeks later, somebody shoots him," Evan added. "We have this really odd behavior by Hutchins, involving you, two weeks before he was killed. So, you see why we had to come out here and talk to you, right?"

Tommy shifted his feet again and shrugged. With his hands stuffed in his back pockets, the gesture accentuated his shoulders. "Well, I guess so, but I don't know what one thing's got to do with the other."

"How about you start by explaining to us exactly why Hutch went to all the trouble to get you out of trouble," Goff said.

Tommy shrugged again, as if this was obvious. "I known Hutch all my life, just about. I went to all those football camps he put on, played on his team all through high school. I just figured he liked me or something. You know, he thought I'd do okay with a second chance and all. And also 'cause of my brother."

"Your brother?" Evan asked.

"He's a Gator," Tommy said, beaming. He looked as proud as a new daddy.

Goff looked at Evan and said, "Tommy's brother is Gavin Morrow, University of Florida's third string wide receiver you'll never hear of again. Caught one pass, sprained an ankle, and rode the bench for the rest of the season."

"You know what, Goff," Tommy said, "I don't need to listen to you running down my brother. This is my property. Maybe y'all have the right to come on here to ask me questions or whatever, but I don't have to listen to—"

"Whoa," Evan said, stepping between Tommy and Goff. "Let's stay on track here, all right? You're telling us this was just some sort of favor?"

"Well, yeah, I guess you could call it that," Tommy said, "More for Gavin than me, though. He was real proud of Gavin playing for the Gators." This last part he said emphatically to Goff over Evan's shoulder. "Hutch told me he was gonna try to spring me early 'cause Gavin might lose his scholarship if he couldn't play next year. He knew we were all real proud to have one of our brothers going to the university. And he's got pretty darn good grades. For us, anyway. So, he told me he figured that would motivate me to stay straight, you know. 'Cause if Gavin loses that scholarship, the only way he can stay there is if we send him money."

"You're saying Hutch got you out of jail early so you could pay for your brother to stay in school?" Evan asked.

Tommy nodded. "Yeah, me and my other brother," he said gesturing with his left hand toward one of the trailers. Suddenly, against his will, Evan thought of Larry, Daryl and Daryl from that Bob Newhart show.

"What is it, exactly, that you do to afford U of F?" Evan asked.

"My brother and me are mechanics. We both work at Dan's Tire Shop in town, and we also do side jobs here at the place," he said, waving an arm in the direction of the lined-up trucks.

Evan looked down at his notebook, then asked, "These tools you stole, who'd you steal them from?"

"The who?" Tommy asked.

"You pled guilty to stealing power tools and trying to pawn them," Evan prompted.

"Oh, them," Tommy said, again seeming relieved. "No, I didn't actually steal those tools. I pled guilty to *possession* of stolen tools. Somebody else actually stole them. I got 'em in payment."

"For what?" Evan asked.

Tommy looked like he was sorry about that last part, but he recovered with a big smile, and swept his arm in the direction of the dead trucks. "For services."

Evan nodded, consulting his note pad. "And by 'services,' you are referring to providing marijuana to this individual in exchange for stolen tools, correct?"

"Um, well, yeah, but that all got taken care of already," Tommy said, fidgeting. "I thought you said you were out here about what happened to Hutch. I want to cooperate with helping you and all, but I'm not saying nothin' to get myself back in trouble, man. Especially now that Hutch ain't around to help me out."

"I'm just trying to get the facts straight, make sure we're all on the same page," Evan said. He was silent for a moment, studying Tommy. He frowned then said, "You were looking at some serious jail time, at the State Pen. Pretty heavy stuff for a guy your age, yeah?"

Tommy looked down at his feet as he kicked at the dirt, "I guess."

"Then Hutch comes along and helps get you out on early parole. How did that make you feel, Tommy?"

"How'd it…man, I was sure grateful. I was. Hutch did a really good thing for me. For my brother, too."

"You feel like you owe him?" Evan asked.

"Well, sure I do. He didn't have any reason to help me out like that…except my brother, you know. I can't believe he's gone."

"Listen Tommy," Evan said, moving in a bit closer. "Some of the guys you know from your dope dealing days, some of the guys you met when you were locked up, they didn't like Hutchins too much. Some of those guys might be real happy he's dead, right?"

"Well, sure, I guess. But, they shouldn't."

"One of them might even have a guess as to who did it," Evan said, "and they're not likely to share that guess with me."

Tommy's shoulders slumped. "You want me to ask around? See if anyone knows who did it?"

"You don't have to go asking around, Tommy, just keep your ears open. Let me know what people are saying. You can do that, right?"

Tommy's face pinched as he looked at the dirt. "But I ain't supposed to hang out with them kinda people anymore."

"No, you don't want to jeopardize your parole, Tommy, just keep your ears open, okay?"

Evan thought he was going to object to being a snitch. But when Tommy finally looked up, he realized the kid was struggling to control his emotions.

"Yeah," he finally said, nodding, "I guess I can do that. It should never have happened, not like that." He looked away, watched a skinny little dog with half an ear gone as it galloped off after something only it could hear. "If I hear anything, I promise I'll tell you."

"Thank you, Tommy."

Evan gave Tommy his card, then followed Goff back to the cruiser. When they pulled out, Tommy was where they'd left him, standing beneath a purpling sky. Him, the broken-down truck, and the chewed-on dog.

Evan hadn't been this depressed since yesterday.

FIFTEEN

IT WAS TUESDAY MORNING, three full days into the investigation, and despite the diligent efforts of his team, Evan didn't feel any closer to finding the killer than he had felt when he was staring down at Hutchins' body.

The sheriff had connections and contacts with such a diverse variety of people that it was difficult to see every angle or to identify all of the possible variables. His job put him in touch with all levels of the state's political machine, and put him in very close proximity to its worst criminal offenders. As an elected official, his campaigning and community involvement put him in touch with everyone in between.

Evan and his team had carefully recorded every lead, every tip, every hunch, but Evan couldn't help but feel that important pieces were slipping through the cracks.

He hadn't had enough time to follow up on the tip about the sheriff's boat, which bothered him. A stack of files and reports waited for him on his desk that he hadn't had a chance to review. At least half a dozen interviews had not yet been conducted due to the individuals not being readily found. On top of the murder investigation, Quillen had scheduled a press conference to introduce Evan as the interim sheriff. Apparently, it was his idea of being helpful.

Before he could address any of those concerns, however, Evan had to check in with the dive team out at Dead Lakes. Four of the deputies had been taking turns with the metal detector under the still, black water surrounding the crime scene. They had each intimated that it was a fool's errand, and that idea had been reinforced by the ten hours of unproductive searching the day before. Evan hoped his presence at the scene might bolster morale. He also wanted to see the progress first hand to determine if it was indeed a useless endeavor.

He checked his watch as he headed toward Wewa. It was just past 9a.m. He figured it wasn't too early to call Marlene Hutchins.

"What can I help you with, Lieutenant?" She asked after he introduced himself. She sounded tired but not sleepy.

"Ma'am, I apologize for calling this early. I have a few details I need to discuss with you. I'll be in the area this afternoon. Would it be all right if I came by?"

"I'll be here all day," she said, her voice flat and disinterested. Evan wondered if she had been drinking, or perhaps been given something to dull her pain.

"I'll come by around two o'clock, if that works for you," he said. "It should only take a couple minutes."

"That'll be fine," she said.

Evan was about to thank her, but she had already hung up. He had been to dinner once at the Hutchins's house, when he first came to Port Saint Joe. Marlene had been warm and kind, solicitous of his needs and indulgent of her husband's blustery manner.

Evan had also noticed a bit of steel just below her soft surface, not the steel of strength, but more of sharpness, like a barbed hook hidden beneath the soft feathers of a well-tied lure. Her voice now conveyed none of those qualities. It was, instead, empty and detached, like a derelict raft that had come unmoored.

His own thoughts were adrift now as well. Marlene was alive but somehow empty. Hannah was also alive but empty, though more profoundly empty than the sheriff's widow. Hannah wasn't going to wake up, ever. The doctors had told him this months ago, but the enormity of those words could not be absorbed, not all at once. Instead, they wormed their way into his consciousness at odd intervals, sometimes like a hollow opening up in the center of his chest, sometimes like a fever, sometimes like a stomach full of ice. Mostly, however, he felt numb. Mostly, he felt exactly how Marlene had sounded just now.

Evan cleared his throat and gave his head a little shake. He passed the sign that said the Dead Lakes were just ahead. He'd be there in a few minutes. He put the thoughts of Hannah back in their box, and stuffed the box into its closet, though he didn't expect it to stay there. The flurry of activity at the dive site would help, for a little while.

A deputy lifted the barricade out of Evan's way as he pulled into the recreation area. Evan recognized him, but couldn't recall his name until he saw his badge.

The area had remained closed to the public since the shooting to protect any evidence that had not yet been discovered. Evan hoped to allow it to be reopened within the next day or two, depending on what turned up between now and then.

A Sheriff's Office boat seemed to hover silently over the water. Around it, the lake's black mirror surface was dotted with what looked like bright orange softballs, maybe two-dozen of them set at irregular intervals. As Evan approached, he saw that each ball had a number stenciled on its side. He realized these were marker buoys indicating the location of items found by the divers.

The actual items had been arranged on a tarp under a white canopy near the lake's edge. A yellow plastic triangle stood beside each item displaying a number that corresponded to the number on the marking buoy in the lake where that item had been found. All the finds were approximately the same color – black or brownish rust. On first sight, Evan knew nothing found so far had anything to do with Hutchins's murder. Everything on the tarp had been in the lake several months, at least.

A second canopy had been set up to facilitate the dive team and other Sheriff Department personnel. It covered a picnic table, and a large cooler. There was also a coffee urn and microwave that could be powered by a gasoline generator, but none of these were running as Evan approached. He saw Paula Trigg and a couple deputies huddled around an array of laptop computers and file folders on the table.

After exchanging greetings, Evan asked for an update on the status of the search. This was met with bemused grins and murmurs. Paula nodded toward the other canopy and suggested he take a look, then followed him over.

If the items hadn't been caked in rust and black mud, Evan might have thought he was at a yard sale. The haul included expected pieces, like two fishing rods and an electric outboard motor, and several less likely finds – a large monkey wrench, a Weed Eater, an old manual typewriter, a cast iron tea kettle, most of a trombone, seven mangled golf clubs, a transistor radio, and other less identifiable bric-a-brac.

"Took us a while yesterday to calibrate the detector," Paula told him, hands stuffed into her jeans pockets. "We spent the first couple hours pinging off beer cans and fishing reels."

"Did you dive yesterday?" Evan asked. He hadn't remembered seeing her name on the dive team roster.

"No, stayed topside to help manage the equipment and catalog the finds," she said. "So far, they haven't found anything relevant. Problem is, they can't tell what they've found 'till they bring it to the surface. That's why we brought all this junk up. It's too murky on the bottom to see anything. Except for the typewriter. They brought that up because it's cool."

"What's that?" Evan asked, pointing to an odd lump labeled "14."

"Heck if I know," Paula said. "It's not a gun and it's not a cell phone, and it was down there long before last Friday, so I guess it doesn't really matter what it is, huh?"

Evan looked at her for a long moment, noticing her tweaked left ear. That, and her diminutive stature, gave her an almost elfish appearance that belied the woman's formidable competence. "That was excellent work on the tire tracks," he said eventually. "I never would have guessed you'd be able to get that much detail."

"Thank you," she said simply, looking out across the lake.

Evan couldn't read her expression. "You think this is a waste of time?" he asked.

"Of course, it is," she said and shrugged. The movement caused a circle of scar tissue on her neck to fold in delicate wrinkles. She was a pretty woman. He wondered if the scars bothered her. "Unless we find something," she continued. "Just about everything you do in a murder investigation is a waste of time, if you want to see it that way. When you're looking for your lost car keys, everywhere you look except the place they are is a waste of time, right?"

A *ploik* sound in the lake caught Evan's attention. He looked that way and saw ripples radiating in perfect rings from a new orange marker that had just popped to the surface. A moment later, a diver appeared beside it, holding up what looked like bicycle handle bars.

Evan's waning enthusiasm expressed itself through a slow sinking sensation just below his diaphragm.

"The gun is out there," Paula assured him, "I'd bet my sneakers on it. Probably the phones and Hutch's gun, too. If that's all that was out there, I'd say we had a fair chance at finding them. But with all this clutter…" She waved a hand at the mess spread across the tarp, then shook her head. She moved on without finishing the thought. "The lake system is extensive. The killer could have ditched the gun in the water here, or a mile from here." She hesitated, then turned to Evan. "I guess you got to do this, but I don't think you can put any hope in it."

Evan nodded and studied her for a moment, then shook his head. "Thanks, Paula," he said. He pulled his pack of Camels from his blazer pocket, shook one out, and lit it.

"You got another one of those?" she asked.

He tapped one out for her and offered her a flame from his lighter.

She filled her lungs, then slowly exhaled through her nose. "It's hard being the new kid in this town. I was born and raised not too far from here, and I've been back going on five years now, but most of them still think of me as the big city cop," she said. "Course, I'm not a man, so maybe they don't see me as much of a threat."

"Well, that'd be a mistake, I figure," Evan said. He drew a long pull on his cigarette, feeling the smoke warm his throat and fill his lungs.

She gave him a grin. After another puff, she said, "You might have figured this out already, but if you've got anyone to worry about in this town it's Quillen. Kind of a crappy thing for him to do, sticking you in the middle of this mess. You can expect that sort of thing from him. He wants everyone focused on you so he won't get any of the pressure or blowback from this case… and so he can get up to whatever it is he gets up to over there in the councilman's office without too many people watching."

"What exactly does he get up to?" Evan asked.

"Tell me when you find out," she said, taking a final drag and flicking the butt. "You're the detective."

He was trying to formulate a response when his cell phone rang. It was a Port St. Joe number, but Evan didn't recognize it.

"Thanks for the smoke, Caldwell," Paula Trigg said. "Got to get back to it. I'll call if we get anything."

He nodded to her as he answered the phone. A raspy, crackling voice greeted him.

"Is this Evan Caldwell?" the man asked.

"Yes sir," Evan said, "who am I speaking with?"

There was a phlegmy cough and Evan knew the answer before the man said it. "This is Scruggs. Willy Scruggs. You and that fool Peters were out at my place couple days back asking about my kid, Eric."

"Yes sir," Evan said. "How's Eric doing?"

"Well, he ain't dead, if that's what you're asking," Willy answered, sounding irritated. "I didn't call about him."

Evan waited a moment, but when Willy said no more he asked, "What did you call about?"

Willy hesitated a beat, then said, "Look, I might know something you want to know, okay? I still know a couple of guys, you know, and I hear talk sometimes."

"I see," Evan said. "What have you heard, Willy?"

Evan heard that horrible cough again. This time the old man had the courtesy to hold the phone away from his mouth. Out on the lake, another marker popped to the surface. Evan watched for the diver to emerge.

When the coughing ceased, Evan heard irritated muttering, but Willy was not talking to him. In the water, the diver surfaced. Evan felt a sudden jolt of adrenalin when he saw the pistol in the diver's hand. The diver's eyes popped, as well, when he saw what he held. But the excitement died just as fast. The gun was as rust caked as the old typewriter. It might be *a* murder weapon, but it wasn't *the* murder weapon. And whatever case it had been part of had either already been solved or filed away years ago. Evan felt his disappointment dragging him closer to something like depression. And depression was not something he could deal with right now.

He could hear Willy's labored breathing on the other end of the line, but the man still had not replied. Evan prompted, "Mr. Scruggs, is there something you want to tell me?"

"No, I don't *want* to tell you a damned thing. I'm not a snitch, and I'm not real fond of cops in general or you in particular."

Evan waited, expecting the cough again, but it didn't come.

After a moment, Willy continued, "Look, I'm only calling because I owe Hutch, alright? Because Hutch looked out for Jordan, but now he's gone. He ain't here to watch out for her."

Evan thought he knew where this was going. "Is she in some kind of immediate trouble, or do you just want me to keep an eye on her? On your daughter and Avery?"

"Avery's father is a piece of walking dog—" he broke off in a coughing fit, then was quiet for a long time.

Evan had begun to walk, going nowhere in particular. The natural beauty, offset by the natural weirdness, of the place drew him in. He walked along the water's edge, moving into a stand of pines and cypress.

When Willy came back, his voice was more of a harsh whisper. Evan's phone crackled and chirped as the signal strength faded in and out. Willy said, "Listen, she's had some trouble with him. The baby daddy. It's all in Hutch's files." He choked back another cough. "Damn it. Listen, I can't be there for her anymore, Hutch can't either. You're not my first choice but you're all I got left I guess."

Flattery was not his strong suit, Evan surmised.

Willy continued, "I need you to look after those two, just the job you're sworn to do anyway, all right? You give me your word on that and I can let you in on what I heard."

Evan looked out at the lake. The boat and marker buoys floated on the water far from where he had expected to see them. He noticed the white canopies on the shore, also not where he thought they would be, and realized he ran the risk of getting himself lost if he wandered too far from the lake.

He wasn't sure how best to answer Scruggs. He had no way of knowing if the man's information was of any value at all. He had received several dozen tips so far and none had led him anywhere. He hadn't had to haggle for that information, and didn't believe he should have to trade for information that ought to be given freely.

Of course, *should* and *ought* were concepts that didn't often figure heavily in a murder investigation. If people behaved as they were supposed to, there wouldn't *be* any murder investigations.

Evan said, "Mr. Scruggs, if you had an understanding with Hutch, I believe I can honor that as well. If your daughter has trouble with her ex, she can come to me."

"I don't want her to have to *come to you!*" Scruggs yelled, or tried to yell. It set off another coughing spell, which he choked down to finish his thought. "I want you to *be there* for her. I want you to *make sure* folks *know* that my girl has got someone looking out for her."

Evan waited, making sure Scruggs was finished. Then he said, "I can do that, Mr. Scruggs. I can do that with significantly more focus once I've cleared Hutch's murder. If you know something about that, you need to tell me."

Scruggs made a sound that could have been a growl, or a grumble, or maybe he was just suppressing another cough, Evan couldn't tell. Then he said, "Fine, alright, here's the deal. There's a crew of guys looking to move some, uh, product up the coast. They've been scouting the area the last few months, just getting the lay of the land, mostly, right? And these guys have been getting local charter guys to take them out, show 'em the area."

Evan waited, walking a bit farther into the shade of the trees, while Scruggs choked back another coughing fit.

"This crew, folks call 'em the Tallahassee Ten. They didn't have nothin' to do with killing Hutch. In fact, the only reason I heard any of this is I know some guys that were hoping the Tens were gonna want to move their stuff through this area, were hoping to get in on a piece of it, right? But now they're all pissed 'cause once Hutch got shot the Tens decided it was way too hot to make any moves anywhere near here. A murdered sheriff is real bad for business. You with me so far?"

"Yeah, I hear you," Evan said. He was walking again, following a path along the water's edge. Something wriggled away from him just beneath the lake's dark surface, a frog or small snake, perhaps.

"Well, here's the inside info; the Tens had pulled out already, before Hutch got shot. They got spooked because they found out that their charter guy was working as a CI for Hutch. He was GPS'ing all their routes and stops, collecting names and itineraries, and passing all of it straight to the sheriff. And that guy works out of the marina right here in Port Saint Joe."

Evan hadn't heard a peep about this from Hutchins, but he knew the Sheriff kept some of his cards very close. He asked, "So, you think maybe the Tallahassee Ten killed the sheriff because he knew too much about them?"

"No! I just told you, the Tens didn't do it. They wouldn't have got nothing from killing the sheriff except more heat. These guys aren't idiots," Scruggs said. "It was the charter guy, must have been. He got squeezed in the middle – rock and a hard place sort of thing I reckon.

Hutch made some deal with that guy, and it went bad, and the kid shot him. Simple as that."

"Okay," Evan said, stepping over a fallen pine bough.

"You start working as a CI, you're putting your butt on the line, big time. The 'C' in CI stands for confidential. That means the sheriff's got to keep your identity secret. That's the deal. If I ever took a CI contract and the cop screwed up and leak my info to the Tens, I'd put a bullet in that dude's head faster than he could turn around. It's the way the game is played, man. You get me?"

"You're telling me you believe the shooter was a charter boat captain operating out of the Port St. Joe marina?"

"It's a kid they call MacMac. Probably thinking there's no way he could have done it, but go check it out. Get into Hutch's CI files. You'll see. He's your man."

MacMac was Mac McMillian, a cocky blond beach bum who lived on his boat and paid the monthly mooring fee by taking tourists fishing. Calling him a charter boat captain was a bit of a stretch. Thinking he had somehow got Sheriff Hutchins to kneel down and take a bullet in the head was a giant flying leap. On the other hand, Evan remembered seeing his number several times on Hutch's cell records, which was odd. MacMac did not seem like the type of guy Hutch was likely to socialize with, and Hutch had his own boat, had no need of a charter service.

Evan thanked Scruggs for the information and assured him the he'd keep a sharp eye on Jordan, then clicked off. Across the expanse of dark water, a diver surfaced. He held a short discourse with his partner in the boat, both shaking their heads, then the diver climbed aboard. A moment later, the boat slowly motored to shore. Evan felt his heart sinking.

An old pine had fallen and now lay sideways across the path, jutting out over the lake. A spinning lure and a tangle of monofilament line dangled from one branch. Evan sat down on the log, with his back against the trunk of a cypress, and tapped a cigarette out of his pack. As he lit it, he thought about what Paula had said about wasting time. Wasting time was all well and good until you ran out of the stuff. He wondered if that was what Hutch had been thinking in his last moments. His mind started trying to connect that idea with decisions he would soon need to make about Hannah, but thoughts like that were deeper and blacker than this lake, and too dark to consider just now.

He drew the smoke in, watching the cherry flare, then rolled his head back until it rested against the cypress. That's when he saw the .45 aimed directly at his face.

SIXTEEN

EVAN CHOKED, COUGHING UP the lung-full of smoke he had just inhaled. Three different thoughts stamped themselves into his mind at the same instant, but none of them made sense.

There was no need to duck for cover or draw his weapon, as his reflexes indicated he should. The gun was aimed at him, but there was no one to pull the trigger; nothing waited behind it but tree limbs and clear blue sky. The pistol was tangled in a clump of Spanish moss, snagged on a low-hanging pine bough about ten feet up in the air.

Evan stared at it for a long moment, bemused almost to the point of being mesmerized. He understood what he was looking at, but the ramifications were staggering. The killer had attempted to throw the murder weapon into the lake, but somehow managed to hook it on this overhang instead. Fishing lures festooned that branch, and those around it. The shooter had made the same mistake that countless anglers had made before him, casting a little too high.

But there would have been no splash. The killer should have realized the gun didn't go into the lake. *There's no way he would have gone to the trouble of walking the gun all the way out here just to leave it hanging in the tree,* Evan thought.

"But there *was* a splash…" he whispered to himself, because the shooter didn't just throw his gun, he would also have thrown Hutchins's gun, and his cell phone. Evan let his mind play through the scenario.

After shooting Hutch, the killer wanted to get rid of the weapon, but knew better than to toss it in the lake near the body. Evan looked across to where the dive team was enjoying their lunch break. He could hear them laughing and talking around the table, though he was too far to make out any words. At the rate they had been going, it would have taken weeks to search from their current location to this spot.

So, after the killer shot Hutch, he came all the way down here to throw the guns, phones, and anything else that might cause him trouble. Maybe enough of that stuff hit the water that the killer didn't realize the actual murder weapon had not gone into the lake. Or maybe he noticed, but couldn't find it in the dark. The killer was nervous, anxious to get out of the area, and who would have guessed that a gun tossed into a lake could end up caught in a tree? It was almost ridiculous enough for Evan to start laughing…almost.

Instead, he dialed Trigg, intending to ask her to bring the dive team across to his location to see what else the killer had tossed, and to collect the pistol from the tree. The call didn't go through. Evan was about to try again when he saw the 'no service' indicator in the upper corner of his phone. He frowned at it. Scruggs had called not twenty minutes ago, where had the signal dropped?

Evan didn't want to walk away from the weapon. An uncharacteristic superstition had gripped him, a surety that if he took his eyes off that improbably suspended weapon, it would disappear, or he would be unable to find it when he returned with the evidence tech. He didn't want to disrupt any evidentiary value by collecting the gun himself. And he didn't want to fall in the lake, which was the likely outcome if he attempted to climb up the tree to retrieve the gun.

He tried the cell again, and again it told him there was no service. Evan looked up at the pistol, a black Glock, .45 caliber. Sunlight winked and twinkled through the thick canopy. It flashed off lazy ripples in the black water.

Evan sighed, and felt a shiver go up his spine. He'd run into plenty of sharks in his time, had been caught in more than one rip current, been bitten by a barracuda, and stepped on a homicidal sea urchin down in St. Thomas. He understood the dangers of salt water, but loved it all the same.

He didn't understand fresh water, or the smelly crap people called fresh water. He didn't know the snakes that were reportedly everywhere, or which ones were venomous. He didn't trust the sticky, heavy, hairy crap at the bottom of inland waters. He was going in anyway, just a little.

He slipped out of his shoes and socks, hiked up his pant legs and waded out into the water, just far enough to be in full sunlight. A million years' worth of decomposition squished up between his toes, and he wondered where he'd get new feet.

He eyeballed the angle of his shadow, calculated the approximate position of the sun, then used the flat glass face of his cell phone to flash sunlight across the lake at Paula and the deputies gathered at her table.

He could see them starting to notice; one head turned, then another, but Evan wasn't sure if they would understand his intent. He was trying to remember if he knew enough Morse Code to try that. He could Google it on his phone if he had service. But, of course, if he had service he wouldn't need to. He was relieved beyond measure when his phone rang.

"What are you doing?" Paula asked when Evan answered.

"Um," Evan said, "Trying to communicate. With you."

"I see," she said. "Anything in particular, or are you just going for a merit badge?"

"My phone said no service. I tried to call a few times, but…you know, nothing."

"Yeah, there's only the one cell tower out here. It doesn't usually get much use, but with all the deputies and reporters, there's not enough band width for all the calls and texts and emails. You got a fifty-fifty chance of getting through. What did you call about, anyway? And what are you doing all the way over there?"

Evan nearly forgot what he had called about. What Paula told him about the cell tower was suddenly as important as the recovered murder weapon. A single cell tower for the whole area, a tower that rarely saw much traffic, could narrow a very long list of possible suspects down to maybe three or four, maybe one or two.

"Evan?" she prompted

"Oh, right," he said. "I found the gun."

Lunch was over. Within minutes of Evan's call, Paula Trigg and all four divers arrived at Evan's location. Less than half an hour after that, a diver located Hutchins's revolver. A total of four cell phones were recovered from that area over the following two hours, as well as a few unrelated artifacts of backwater Florida. Two of the phones were later found to belong to Hutchins, his work phone and his personal phone. The other two turned out to be burners.

It took several attempts to retrieve the tree-bound Glock, and one deputy did end up falling in the lake during the process, but they eventually managed to get it bagged without it going into the water first.

It was sneaking up on two o'clock, the minutes slipping by almost unnoticed, by the time all these pieces had been recovered, documented and packaged for transport. Evan felt the momentum of the case suddenly shifting in his favor.

He called Marlene. It took six tries before the call went through. He informed her that he wouldn't be able to make it to her house for their two o'clock meeting. He apologized and assured her that he would come by the following day. She thanked him for the call, sounding just as dazed and vacant as she had that morning, but Evan felt a good deal better than he had on his way out there.

He was beginning to doubt that the probable domestic abuse had anything to do with the case. If Beckett had been involved, Evan felt pretty sure he wouldn't have made such a clumsy mistake with the gun. And the depth of Marlene's distress argued against her willing participation in the murder. Evan felt that the visit with her was no longer the top priority in the investigation. He did need to know one thing, though, and he felt comfortable asking this over the phone.

"Marlene," he said, "when was the last time you saw Hutch's boat?"

She hesitated for a long moment. When she spoke, her voice carried more emotion than Evan had heard in it all day. "He took me out in it. Last Wednesday. Took the afternoon off work and…" she trailed off. Evan heard sniffling. Then she finished, "We stayed out until after dark. It was nice. Sunset on the water. We had a fish he caught. It was very nice."

"That was Wednesday?" Evan asked. "Six days ago?"

"Was it only six?" Marlene said, "I guess it was just six days ago."

"Ma'am," Evan asked, "do you know where his boat is now?"

"Why, I'm certain it's at the marina," she said. "That's the only place it ever is if he's not on it. Sometimes it's here at the house. But not now. It must be at the marina, isn't it?" She had slipped back into her detached voice.

Evan assured her it was nothing to concern herself with, told her he would visit her the next day, then clicked off. He scratched some notes on his pad, then called Goff…or tried to, anyway. After the third failed attempt, he decided to postpone the call and instead went to check on Paula's progress.

The divers had been eager to go under, once the first phone had been recovered, but now that they had found everything that Evan had hoped to find, their enthusiasm had waned. No one complained when he told them to pack it in. After a few quick instructions to the crew and a brief conference with Paula, Evan hopped in his car and headed down Highway 71, back to the office. Halfway there, he managed to get a signal and called Goff. He asked Goff to put out a BOLO on Sheriff Hutchins's boat, a 1989 twenty-three-foot Sea Ox, white, with a two-foot diameter Florida Gators decal on both sides of the bow. Then he asked Goff to pull up all the cell records they had received.

Paula had no trouble finding finger prints on Hutchins's phones, even after three days under water, but all the prints belonged to Hutchins. The burners, his revolver, and the Glock had all been wiped clean. All four sim cards were missing from the phones. The serial number on the Glock had not only been filed off, but a line of X's had been stamped into the bare metal where it had been. Paula explained that this would make it almost impossible to recover the numbers through any of the common forensics tricks.

This was a disappointment, but in light of the day's developments, not a major one. Paula packaged the Glock and prepped it to be transported to the ballistics lab in Tallahassee where it would be tested to confirm that it was, in fact, the murder weapon, and to attempt to match it with any other shootings in the data base.

Evan felt like celebrating. He might go home that night and smile at the cat.

SEVENTEEN

"SHERIFF CALDWELL? THIS IS Officer Cal Rochester over here at Panama City Police. I have that boat you're looking for."

Evan's eyes shot to his clock. It was just past four and the BOLO had been issued less than two hours ago. "That was fast," he said. "Listen, can you keep an eye on it until I arrive, should be under an hour. If you see anyone aboard, hang onto them until I get there."

There was a long pause on the other end of the line, followed by an *uhhhh…* sound, suggesting Rochester was confused. When he finally spoke, he said, "No, I mean *I* have the boat. I bought it from Hutch a couple weeks ago, just picked it up Thursday afternoon."

This time it was Evan who was thoroughly confused and unable to respond for a moment.

"Sheriff?" Rochester asked, "You there?"

DAWN LEE MCKENNA & AXEL BLACKWELL

"Yes," Evan said. In addition to the unexpected status of the boat, Evan still felt uneasy about being addressed as Sherriff. "So, you have the boat in your possession? You bought it from Hutchins?"

"Yes sir," Rochester affirmed. "I've been hounding him for years to sell me that boat. Been kind of a joke between us for a while. Then a couple weeks ago he says, 'Hey, Roach, you really want to buy that boat? It's yours, man.' He named the price and I paid it, simple as that. He wrote me a bill of sale, if you want to see it."

"Well, I guess I better have a look at that," Evan said, feeling almost as dazed as Marlene had sounded. "How much did he sell it for?"

"Eighty-five hundred. Probably could have got ten for it, but like I said, I got the buddy discount. I doubt he would have sold it to anybody else."

There had been no indication in Hutchins financial statements that he had received that much money anytime in recent months. Evan made a note to re-examine the financials, but had a hunch the money wouldn't turn up there. He asked, "Did you pay him in cash?"

Rochester hesitated. When he spoke, his voice carried a hint of caution. "As a matter of fact, it *was* cash…took it out of my boat fund. I've been saving up for years. You can check. Man, I didn't have anything to do with what happened out there, brother. No one in all the Panhandle would believe I had anything to do with that. Hutch was one of my best friends, man."

"Officer," Evan said, "I have no reason to believe you had anything to do with Hutchins' death. But I have a feeling that him selling the boat did have something to do with it. Do you follow? I am wondering why he sold that boat. You were surprised when he said he'd sell."

"Well, sure. Yeah, I was surprised. But I wasn't about to turn him down, either, not at that price."

"Did he say why he was selling it?" Evan asked.

"I asked him. Not sure whether he actually answered me or not, now that I think about it. He gave me the impression that he needed money for some family business. You know, personal stuff he didn't want to talk about," Rochester said. "I didn't pry."

Evan asked Rochester to fax him a copy of the sales receipt for the boat and Rochester said the fax would be there within the hour. Evan thanked him and ended the call.

He sat back in his chair, puzzling over the day's developments. Outside his window, a hint of yellow now tinted the blue haze as the afternoon crept toward evening. Evan flipped his legal pad to a blank sheet. He stared at it for a moment, then started writing.

Glock, shell casings found at Nickells. Match? Mac McMillian, CI? Tallahassee Ten? Cell tower. $8500. He circled the money two or three times.

He was about to add *Domestic* to his list, but again hesitated. The domestic angle was a hunch, and hunches didn't need to be written down; they tended to hang around as long as they remained relevant. He looked at his notes again. The $8500 looked like a metaphoric exclamation point. Missing money added a new dimension to the investigation. Hutchins had apparently arranged, or at least attended, a clandestine meeting with an unknown subject in a secluded area in the middle of the night. And $8500 was missing, or at least unaccounted for. It looked a lot like a blackmail, maybe over the abuse. But if the killer had got $8500 from Hutchins, why had he then killed the man?

He needed to know what happened to the money. Evan would ask Marlene when he saw her tomorrow if Hutchins had hidden cash anywhere around the house, but he was already pretty certain she didn't know anything about the money. He was also certain that the cash was an integral part of this case.

He grabbed the phone and punched the intercom button, ringing Vi's desk

"This is Vi," she answered, just in case.

Of course it is, Evan thought, but didn't say. "Yes, Vi," he said instead, "I need to look at the Sheriff's Confidential Informant files. Do you have those?"

"They are in the Sheriff's office, in the file marked Confidential Informants, in the A through F drawer. Would you like to get them yourself or shall I bring them to you?"

"No, don't trouble yourself, Vi, I can get them, thank you."

"You'll need the key. That file cabinet is locked."

"Okay," Evan said, "Do you have the key?"

"Evan, the confidential informants are confidential. Only the sheriff had access to those files. And only the sheriff had a key."

"I see," Evan said. "I guess we'll need to call a locksmith, then. I need those files."

"It's almost five, Evan. You'll have to pay afterhours rates if you call a locksmith now," Vi said in a tone that made Evan feel like standing in the corner. "Why don't you just use the sheriff's key?"

"Yes. That's an excellent idea," Evan said. "Let's do that. Where might I find the sheriff's key?"

"It's in the African Violet on his bookcase."

"Thank you," Evan said, again wanting to say, *of course it is*, and again refraining. A brief flash of ridiculous comedic irony struck him – he was suddenly certain that Vi had already figured out who had killed Hutchins, through her sheer, indomitable omniscience, and she was just waiting for him to figure it out. He assumed when he did finally piece it together and announce the name of the killer, Vi would tell him, *of course it is*.

"Is there anything else?" she asked.

Evan refocused his thoughts. "Um, yes, Vi. If Goff and Trigg are still in, would you ask them to come see me? I'll be in the sheriff's office."

"I suppose you should be," Vi said, then hung up.

"Let's step out back," Evan said when Paula Trigg and Ruben Goff appeared in his doorway. "I need a smoke."

The three assembled around a concrete picnic table in the courtyard behind the building. Most of the other day-shift deputies were gathering their things or had already left for the day. Somewhere nearby a barbeque grill had just been lit. Evan smelled burning lighter fluid on the late afternoon air. Soon it would be replaced by the fragrance of charcoal and sizzling beef. Evan hoped to be back on his boat before it got to that point.

"I'll make this quick," he said, laying the note pad on the table. "Hutch had $8500 cash in his hand Thursday afternoon. He sold his boat. The following night, he met with someone, and now that money seems to be missing."

"Blackmail," Trigg said.

Goff looked to the side and spit.

"Goff," Evan said, "You said you went over the financials with Marlene ? Did you get any indication from her, or from the numbers, that there might be that much extra money stashed anywhere?"

"Nah," Goff said. "She doesn't have that money. Not unless Hutch stuffed the mattress with it, but he wasn't that type."

Trigg was shaking her head. "There's no way in hell he'd sell that boat, not unless he was desperate." She looked at Goff for confirmation.

"Sooner sell his house I reckon," Goff nodded. "Somebody have him over a barrel, you think?"

"But why kill him?" Trigg asked. "If someone had blackmail material worth that much money, why kill the goose that laid the golden egg?"

"Hutch was more dangerous than any old goose," Goff said. "If I'd been responsible for Hutch losing his boat, I wouldn't want that guy around to come after me later. That's for damn sure."

"Problem is," Evan said, "if blackmail was the motive, the only way to trace that back to the killer is either find the money, which is a long shot, or figure out what the killer had to blackmail Hutchins. If we go that route, it means we're going to be trying to dig up dirt on him, and that isn't going to go over around here. Not at all."

The corner of Paula's mouth had turned up in a cynical grin and she was shaking her head again.

"Just yesterday you were going around asking folks if Hutch beat on his wife. That sure didn't win you any friends." Goff had crossed his arms and was frowning. "You keep pissing on his grave around here and you're liable to end up in one next to him."

Evan looked up at him sharply. "That got around pretty quickly."

"Why you think everybody's been giving you the dead eye all day?"

Evan shook his head. He didn't bother telling Goff that these were the looks he'd been getting for days.

Goff met his gaze. "You gotta chase this lead, no doubt, but you better tread lightly when you do."

"I hear you," Evan nodded. "It's something you two need to be aware of, that's all. I'll take the lead on that, but if you pick up on anything that feels like it fits a blackmail scenario, I need to know about it, right?"

Trigg and Goff nodded.

"We have a couple other things going," Evan said, gesturing to his note pad. "Paula, I need you to send those .45 shells we found out at the Nickell place up to Tallahassee, see if they match the weapon we recovered today."

"I already did that," she said. "They're rushing everything I send, high profile case and all. We should have results tomorrow."

Evan smiled. To Goff he said, "Tomorrow, you and I are going to do a couple more interviews. We'll be talking to Marlene again, then we'll check out a charter captain named Mac McMillian, see what he knows about the Tallahassee Ten."

Goff made his *pfft* sound through his mustache, "There's been a lot of folks wagging their chins about the Tallahassee Ten, lately, but I'd be surprised if they did this. Those boys ain't brilliant, but few dopers are dumb enough to kill a county sheriff."

"McMillian was a CI, working for Hutchins," Evan said. "I got a tip that he was running Tens around on his boat, scouting missions, I guess, then reporting back about everywhere they went. You guys hear anything about this?"

Trigg and Goff both replied in the negative.

"Yeah," Evan said, "me neither. Vi confirmed that McMillian was a CI, and that Hutchins had a file on him, but that file isn't where it was supposed to be. I just looked for it and came up empty-handed."

"You think it was McMillian that Hutch went out there to meet?" Trigg asked. "I mean, I agree with you, Goff, most drug smuggling organizations won't intentionally pick a fight with the police, but," she touched her damaged ear, "every once in a while, they do."

"Bottom line," Evan said, "we've got missing money and a missing file. The file is on a guy who was playing both sides, taking money from Hutchins for information. Taking money from the Tens for scouting smuggling routes. So, we're going to go talk to that guy and see if we can find out what was in that missing file, and why the file went missing."

"I guess that makes sense," Goff said.

Trigg was nodding her head.

Evan said to her, "Paula, when you come in tomorrow, I need you to go over the cell records again. I requested a list of all activity recorded on the tower that covers Dead Lakes between 10:00 p.m. and 4:00 a.m. on the night of the murder."

Paula was grinning again, a predatory twinkle in her eye. "I'm going to see both of Hutches phones show up there at the time he arrives. I'm going to see what time the phones go dead, when they go in the lake, and I'm going to see the killer's phone as well."

"Exactly," Evan said. "Also, you'll see at least one phone on those two locals who called it in. Check their number to eliminate them." Evan paused, then added, "This isn't a home run. We recovered those two burner phones. If the killer thought this out as well as he seems to have, he didn't bring his regular cell out there with him. But it is possible. Definitely worth looking at."

"Definitely," Paula said. "Worst case, we'll be able to lock down some of the timing."

EIGHTEEN

EVAN HADN'T REALIZED he was exhausted until he got home to the marina. Once he stepped onto the sun deck and slipped off his shoes, he suddenly felt the need for a shower, food, and sleep, all at once if possible. He knew some of it was due to the hours he'd been pulling and the stress he felt over doing this case right, but some of it was also just coming down off of the adrenalin of finding the gun. Adrenalin only took you so far.

He was relieved to find that Plutes had chosen to favor Evan with only minor insurgency during his absence. There seemed to be extra cat litter kicked out onto the sun deck, which Evan unwittingly trod on and had to dig out of his socks. He had to wonder how cats even managed to step in to a litter box; the stuff was like walking on somebody's broken molars.

Evan had some pasta and shrimp for dinner. Plutes had pureed gerbils or whatever it was that slid out of the expensive little can. Then Evan did the dishes, took a shower, made some of his golden milk with the turmeric, and carried it into the V-berth a few steps down and aft of the salon.

He'd taken the mattresses out of the berth, and replaced them with several plastic totes, each one carefully labeled. He switched on the light, set his cup down on the shelf next to it, and opened the next box in the rotation.

When he'd decided to sell his house in Cocoa Beach, he'd finally gone through all of Hannah's things and packed them up. Each tote full of her possessions had been carefully organized and labeled, and most of them had gone into the storage unit he'd rented in Port St. Joe once he'd actually moved.

The totes containing her paperwork, bills, checkbooks and other personal things from the last year had come onto the boat with him. There were five, and this one was the third in line.

The irony wasn't lost on him. He was a cop who investigated other people, evidently when he should have been spending more time with his wife. Now he was investigating her. Over the last several months, he had slowly made his way through the last year of his wife's conscious life, trying to see what he hadn't seen at the time.

The fact that his wife had fallen off of her boyfriend's boat had completely blindsided him. The fact that they'd been seeing each other for over six months had been more than he could take in right away. He'd had no idea that his wife was unhappy, other than her occasional, or probably frequent complaints that he separated *his* life from *their* life, as she put it. He certainly hadn't suspected that she was unhappy enough to have an affair.

At first, he'd wondered how she'd found the time, but he quickly realized that the sixty or so hours he worked every week happened at all hours of the day and night. She could have had a boyfriend and a second job without him noticing any absences.

Evan pinched the bridge of his nose, where a sharp ache threatened to become a major headache. Then he reached into the tote and pulled out a Victoria's Secret box that he knew had contained the yellow bathing suit she'd ordered online. He could only remember seeing it once; the time they'd taken the cheesy sunset gambling cruise on a whim.

Inside the box were all of the bank statements he'd found from the previous year. Hannah hadn't been as uptight about organization as Evan was, but she'd kept a pretty good handle on her finances.

He pulled out the envelope containing her Capital One statement from two months before her accident. Nothing jumped out at him on the first page. Several visits to Starbucks, the physical therapist she'd been seeing to help with her lower back, a few purchases at Home Depot, probably for the paint and other things she'd gotten to redo her home office. Lots of gas.

Halfway down the second of three pages, he saw a charge for some place called the Indian River Art Studio. A painting or some vase or another? But exactly one week later the same charge appeared. And the week after that. Forty-five dollars each time.

He folded the statement back up and put it down, grabbed the one for the following month. It hadn't even been opened. There he saw the same charges, exactly seven days apart. Lessons. She had to have been taking some kind of art lessons.

Evan sat down on the edge of the wooden platform, the statement resting in his lap. His wife had been taking art lessons several weeks in a row, and he hadn't even known. He hadn't even known she liked art.

The next morning, Evan left the Sheriff's Office and headed back out to Wewa to talk to Marlene Hutchins. He'd planned on bringing Goff with him, but Goff was out on a burglary call.

The air was so thick you could walk across it, and it wasn't even ten yet. Evan chose between smoking with the window open or doing without in the air conditioning, and the AC won. Even so, he felt like he needed another shower already by the time he pulled into the Hutchins' driveway.

Marlene Hutchins opened the door and invited him in, took him back to the kitchen and offered him coffee. This time he declined in favor of a glass of water. Marlene didn't seem at all nervous or anxious. She didn't seem much of anything, and Evan was pretty sure she was taking some kind of sedative.

"Mrs. Hutchins, is there anything I can do for you?" he asked once she'd sat down across the table from him.

She looked at him and took a moment to answer, not because she was a little out of it, but because she didn't seem to know what the answer was. Finally, she shrugged one shoulder. "You're already doing it."

Evan nodded. "Ma'am, it's come to light that your husband sold his boat a couple of weeks ago."

"Sold it?" She showed her first emotion of any depth, and it was surprise. If there was $8500 in this house, she didn't know a thing about it. "He wouldn't sell that boat," she insisted.

"But he did, ma'am. I have the bill of sale," Evan said kindly. "He sold it to a friend of his, Officer Cal Rochester over in Panama City. Do you know him?"

Her confusion was genuine. "Of course, I know him," she said. "They've been friends…well, a long time." She shook her head. "But he wouldn't sell that boat. I don't understand what you're saying."

"Were you having any financial troubles?" Evan asked. "Help for your daughter, a new transmission, anything come up lately that was going to be hard to pay for?"

She shook her head again, slowly. He could see her trying to work it out, and he felt for her. "No. We've always been pretty simple people. I mean, we drive used, we like to eat at home, we don't need much. We've always just put away what we could for retirement. The house is paid off, we paid it four years early."

"So you can't think of any reason why he'd sell a boat he didn't seem to want to sell? And not tell you?"

She blinked at him a few times, and he saw a hint of that sharpness he'd noticed when they'd first met. "Well, he wasn't having an affair, if that's what you're getting at. I told you that already."

"Yes, you did, and that's not what I meant, I'm sorry." Evan took a drink of his water, put the glass down carefully. It hydroplaned just a hair on the ring of condensation that had already appeared. "Mrs. Hutchins, can you think of anything that someone could have found to blackmail your husband for?"

"No, of course not," she said. "He didn't see other women, he didn't do drugs. He was strictly above-board at his work…I don't know why you would ask me that."

"What about allegations of abuse?" Evan asked quietly.

"Abuse?" She tried to look like she had no idea what he meant, but he saw a flicker of fear in her eyes before she locked it down. "Of who? No, that's just…"

"Of you, Mrs. Hutchins. Was your husband violent with you?"

"Don't be ridiculous," she said angrily. "He wasn't that way."

"You've been to the ER three times in the last few years, for injuries that could be explained a few different ways."

"They were explained the way they happened, Lieutenant," she snapped. "My husband was a good man. He tried very hard to be a good husband." She seemed to realize that 'tried' might not be the best word she could have used. "Do I look like the type of woman that would tolerate that kind of thing? I wasn't raised to allow myself to be treated that way."

"Mrs. Hutchins, I'm not trying to hurt you any further, or to hurt your husband," Evan said.

"Then you shouldn't say such things," she said, her eyes tearing. "He liked you. And he loved me."

"He spoke very kindly of you," Evan said.

"You shouldn't say such things."

She blinked away her tears. Evan watched as one fell to the Formica table and the sunlight made it look like a diamond.

·•✳•·

Half an hour later, Evan was paying of the biggest bottle of Smart Water that the convenience store had when Beckett showed up beside him.

"You looking for me again?" Beckett asked with a grin.

"Not this time," Evan said as he swiped his card.

"Hey there, Nathan," the old man behind the counter said. "How's it going today?"

"Pretty fair, Boyd. How's things with you?"

"Can't complain. Got the air fixed, finally," the man said.

"I can see that," Beckett said. "Anderson and them give you a fair price?"

"They did." The old man handed Evan his receipt. "Thank you, come again. Sure thing, Chief. Took good care of us. I was a day away from havin' a heart attack in here."

Evan started for the door, and heard Beckett coming behind him.

"You take care now," Beckett said.

"You do the same."

Evan twisted the cap off of his water and took a long drink as he walked back to his car, Beckett's footsteps right behind him. Evan reached into the car and grabbed his cigarettes, and Beckett waited while he lit one.

"So what brings you to town?" he asked finally.

Evan exhaled away from the Chief before answering. "I had an appointment with Marlene Hutchins."

Beckett nodded and looked away, over at the soccer mom filling her gas tank. "How's she faring?"

"As well as you'd think," Evan said.

Beckett turned back to him. "Heard you might have found your murder weapon."

"Might have," Evan said.

"Well, that oughta clear me good and well."

"How's that?"

"If I'd done it, you wouldn't have found the weapon," Beckett said. "You sure as hell wouldn't have found it up some tree. I'm a lot of things, but I'm not a screw-up."

"If it makes you feel any better, I already figured that," Evan said.

"Well, gee. I sure appreciate that, Captain Miami," Beckett said without rancor.

"Have you ever even been to South Florida, Beckett?"

"As a matter of fact, I have been to the bright lights and big city a time or two, Caldwell. '92, when Hurricane Andrew stopped by. Took five thousand gallons of Culligan water down to Homestead. Where were you in '92, Caldwell?"

Evan didn't have to think much. Everybody in the US knew where they were when Kennedy was shot. Everyone in South Florida knew where they were when Andrew hit.

"In a foster home in Miami Gardens," he said casually. He opened his door, leaned in to turn on the ignition, and cranked up the AC.

"Foster kid, huh?" Beckett almost sounded like he was impressed. "That must have sucked."

Evan took one last drag, then dropped and toed out his cigarette. "Sometimes," he said, in a dismissive tone. He climbed into the Pilot. "I'll see you around," he said.

"I'm sure it's our destiny," Beckett said.

NINETEEN

HIS MEETING WITH Beckett had left Evan conflicted. On the one hand, he felt certain that the small-
town chief of police had not been involved in Hutchins
murder, which was good. He also felt certain that Beckett
had not been aware that Hutchins had a tendency to
settle domestic disputes with his fists. Which was also
good. What was not so good was that Evan was coming
to believe, very strongly, that Beckett *would* have murdered Hutchins if he had known. He'd have done it long
ago, in fact. And he'd have left no evidence behind.

Evan wasn't sure what to make of his new certainties. But that would have to wait for another day. Beckett
was a wildcard, but he was a wildcard that hadn't been
dealt this hand.

As conflicted as he was about the chief, he was certain
about the dead sheriff, and his widow. Her denials were
meant to convince him, but they were also meant to con-

vince herself that she hadn't been the kind of woman to take years of abuse. Someone should tell her that staying in an abusive marriage wasn't as simple as strong or weak, loved or not loved.

It also occurred to him that maybe she couldn't actually accept that Hutchins had hurt her because that opened the possibility that someone had killed him in order to stop the abuse, the very possibility Evan was attempting to investigate. But if that had been the motive for the murder, then Marlene would feel that his death had been her fault.

Evan's teeth had started to hurt. He realized that he had been clenching his jaw muscles so hard that they now bulged. His hands, too, ached from clutching the steering wheel. The convoluted rationalizations and justifications – the lies and alibis people created to protect themselves from their fears, fears which seldom had any basis in reality – always led to darker holes than the ones they were conjured to avoid.

Abuse victims often protect their abuser because they've been conditioned to believe that, even though the abuse is bad, it is not wrong. It is not wrong because it is their own fault. And because they deserve the abuse, the abuser is actually the victim, being forced by the bad behavior of their spouse to lash out physically. And because the abuse is the victim's fault, any consequences that abuse brings is also the victim's fault. At least, that's what plenty of social workers and psychologists had explained to him in emergency rooms and living rooms all over South Florida.

Evan felt a chill despite the afternoon's intense sunshine. The thick humidity that had congealed under his shirt felt as if it were turning to frost against his skin. Evan feared he was very close to slipping through his own safety net of self-deception. He had been telling himself plenty of lies, one set before Hannah's accident, a different set since. Lies about who he had been and who he now was, about Hannah, and about their relationship.

The biggest lie was about time – it can wait, we'll sort it out when life slows down a bit. But life doesn't slow down, ever. Life is a chunk of iron hurtling through space at ten times the speed of sound, accelerating as it encounters a gravitational pull and accelerating still more until it hits the atmosphere and burns away to nothing. Or slams into the skin of the planet, erupting in a torrent of dust that clouds the atmosphere and kills off all the damned dinosaurs.

It was too humid and Evan was too tired to fall down a rabbit hole of doubt and self-recrimination.

So instead of thinking about that, he called Goff and asked him to help interview MacMac.

·●✳●·

"Nearly missed him," Goff said, nodding in the direction of the docks. He had arrived at the marina just moments before Evan, but looked as if he had been leaning against that rail all day. Down on the dock, Mac

McMillan locked the cabin of his boat and shouldered a pack. His physique and hair suggested he was off to audition for a fragrance commercial. Goff spit over the rail and muttered, "I've got dentures older than this kid."

Evan grinned and lit a cigarette. "He's coming to us, which I appreciate. It's too damn hot to go out there and get him."

MacMac didn't notice them waiting for him until he was most of the way up the gang plank that led to the Dockside Grill, the office and the parking lot. When he did see them, his cheeks colored and he set his jaw. "Wow, you guys just don't get it, do you?" he asked before Evan could introduce himself. "'Confidential' means nobody else is supposed to know about it."

"Know about what?" Evan asked.

MacMac looked at him, then turned to Goff. "Is this your new boss? I'm guessing that's it, since you're in a uniform and he's in a suit."

"If you think he's the boss, what're you asking me for?" Goff replied, but with only mild interest.

"Mac McMillan," Evan said, "I'm Interim Sheriff Evan Caldwell. This is Sergeant Goff. We need to ask you a couple of questions about your involvement with Sheriff Hutchins and the Tallahassee Ten."

MacMac threw his head back and uttered a short burst of mock laughter. "My involvement?" he asked. "My involvement was I tried to do the right thing, but apparently Sheriff Hutchins couldn't keep a secret to save his life…" He stammered, then said, "Sorry, I didn't mean it like that…but, you know what I meant. He was sloppy and it got him killed and it's probably gonna get me killed too if you keep coming around in uniform, in broad daylight, asking me questions where anybody can see!"

"Would you rather come down to the Sheriff's Office with us?" Goff asked. He had drawn his handcuffs without making a sound, neither Evan nor Mac had noticed, but he made a show of clinking them together now.

"No, I don't want to go to the station. Are you nuts?" He raised his right hand, palm out, and solemnly vowed, "I swear, I will never again do the right thing."

"I'm not sure I understand, Mr. McMillian," Evan said. "It sounds like you believe that something you said to Sheriff Hutchins resulted in his death. Do I have that right?"

MacMac was silent for a moment. He glanced between Evan and Goff, then looked back to Evan. "Can we please not be standing right here in the middle of everything?

"Sure," Evan said. "We'll walk you to your car."

The three of them walked through the passageway that ran between the marina office and the laundry and shower rooms, Evan in front, Goff in the rear, and McMillian in the middle. Evan waited until they'd gone down the steps and were in the parking lot.

"Where's your vehicle?"

McMillian raised his free arm and pointed. "The Ford over there," he said. He seemed pretty happy about making new friends and getting an escort to his truck. It wasn't lost on Evan that it was a Ford.

"So, do you have some reason to think The Ten had something to do with the Sheriff's murder?" Evan repeated. "Because, if that's the case, either you talk to us willingly or we'll have to charge you with obstruction, or possibly accessory after the fact."

"If it helps," Goff offered, "we can slap the cuffs on and let you ride in the fancy cop car." He craned his neck to look over one shoulder, then the other. "Case any bad guys are looking."

"You think this situation is funny?" MacMac snapped.

"It ain't the situation I'm laughing at," Goff said.

MacMac turned to Evan. "Either arrest me or shove off. I have places to be." He pushed past the two men, intending to sulk to his truck.

"Maybe it won't just be accessory we'll arrest you for," Evan said to his back. MacMac stopped and turned back around. "Hutchins was keeping secrets. You're keeping secrets. You're telling us it was one of those secrets that got him killed."

Evan let that hang in the air for a minute. "Your file is missing, Mr. McMillian, from Hutchins's office. You don't happen to know where that file is, do you? How it got out of a locked file cabinet in the sheriff's private office?"

MacMac took two large steps toward Evan, bringing their faces uncomfortably close. "What are you suggesting?"

"I'm suggesting you retreat from my face," Evan said, without a change in tone. When MacMac didn't immediately move, Evan lifted his cigarette to his lips. Its cherry flared an inch or two from Mac's eye. The younger man blinked a few times and took a step back.

"I'm suggesting," Evan continued, "that you give us a full and detailed account of everything you know or think you know about the sheriff and the Tallahassee Ten. Including everything that was in that file."

"No freaking way, man!" Mac said. "Are you crazy? Are you even listening? I talked to Hutch, man. I didn't have to do that, you know. I was just trying to be a good citizen, or whatever, and now he's dead. All I talked to him about was smuggling, or, you know, suspected smuggling. What the hell you think's gonna happen if I start talking to you about *murder*? Huh?" He threw his hands up and looked around as if hoping some bystander would see his obvious logic and come to his aid.

Goff was his only audience, and if the logic impressed him, he gave no sign.

"And I don't even know who the hell *you* are," Mac said. "At least I knew Hutch. How am I supposed to trust some fancy slick from Miami?"

Goff spit on the pavement, then stepped forward and jammed a long, bony finger into the trench between

MacMac's puffy pecs. "You drifted in with the tide not two seasons ago, and you'll be gone again before your boat grows barnacles, like as not. Don't go playing yourself off as a local."

Mac took another step back and again raised his arms in exasperation, this time looking to the heavens for support. When he had completed the display, he said, "I ain't talking. Arrest me if you're going to, but this conversation is over." He took two more backward steps, arms still out to his side, palms up. A grin seeped across his face as the distance between himself and Evan grew. "That's what I thought," he said, turning his back to them and walking to his truck. "You got nothing. Can't arrest me because you don't have a charge that would stick."

Goff raised an eyebrow at Evan. Evan gave him a slight shake of his head. He followed MacMac to his truck, but made no move to stop him. MacMac tossed his duffle onto the passenger seat of his Ford Ranger, then climbed in and slammed the door. Evan half expected a middle finger, but the cocky kid only glared at him through the window. Evan folded his arms across his chest and watched the truck back out and pull away.

It was then that he noticed the tires. The truck was primer red, lifted almost two feet over factory specs and riding on radials that were nearly bald and puffier than MacMac's muscles. But what really caught his attention was the missing lug on the right front tire.

"You know," Goff said, arms crossed, head cocked, "that might just be the truck we've been looking for."

·●✳●·

"Paula, It's Evan," he said, consulting his watch. Its hands seemed to be moving much too quickly. "You up for a bit of overtime?"

"That depends," she said, "Whatcha got?"

Evan pulled out of the marina parking lot, heading back toward the office. Goff followed in his cruiser. "I think we have a match on the truck that was parked beside Hutchins's on the night of the murder," Evan explained. "It's missing a lug on the right front. I collected an oil sample from the pavement in the parking lot. Do you think you'd be able to confirm a match with the sample collected at the scene?"

"I can take a look, run it through a few tests, but I doubt I can give you an absolute yes or no," she said. "Too many possible contaminates from every other vehicle that ever parked there."

"I don't need anything absolute yet," Evan said, "just need to know if I'm barking up the right tree."

"Yeah, I hear you. I'll take a look, let you know if it's at least close. Speaking of barking, though, if you want me to stay past six, I'll need to run home and pick up Ernie. He gets sulky if I'm late."

"Ernie?" Evan asked. "He's your dog?"

DAWN LEE MCKENNA & AXEL BLACKWELL

"Well, he ain't my boyfriend," Trigg said. "Ernie hangs out with me at the office when I work late. Hutch never had a problem with it."

"I guess I don't either," Evan said. "How's it going with the cell records?"

"Goff didn't tell you?" she asked.

"Haven't had a chance to talk with him much."

"Lucky you," she said. "The records from the cell company are a mess. We spent hours this morning sorting them, but before we could get down to actually seeing what we had, Tallahassee called. I've been on the phone with them since before you got back from Wewa."

"Tell me they got something good."

"Oh, yeah. They got something, alright. The gun you found is a positive match to the slug recovered at the scene. So, we have ourselves a murder weapon," Paula said. "The bad news is, the gun isn't traceable. The serial numbers can't be raised, just too much damage. It doesn't match the shell casings recovered from Ricky Nickell's property. And, the slug doesn't match any others in the data base."

"So, it's a dead end?" Evan asked, pulling out onto Monument.

"Not at all. That's the bad news. The good news is, whoever fired that gun left a piece of himself in it. Probably an inexperienced shooter. He held it wrong and the slide took a piece out of his hand when he fired."

"Slide bite," Evan said. His heart kicked it up a notch and he felt an involuntary smile trying to hijack his face. "Nice."

"This is several kinds of weird, if you ask me. The killer was very organized, deliberate. He left us almost nothing at the scene. But the gun was up a freaking tree and slide bite is a rookie mistake. Something doesn't add up."

Evan thought about this for a moment, as several huge raindrops fell from nowhere and beat on his car. A moment later, it really opened up. Evan was so grateful he wanted to stop the car and get out and dance in it.

"You're thinking two different people were involved?" he finally asked. "Maybe one set up the meet, but the murder was carried out by someone else?"

"Could be, I guess," Paula admitted, "or not. Hard to say, really. It's just that the facts we have aren't coming together for me yet."

"I hear you," Evan said. "Tell me this, will the techs up in Tallahassee be able to pull DNA?"

"Yeah, that's the other good news. The killer wiped the gun with bleach before tossing it, so nothing on the outside survived. But the slide grabbed some blood and a bit of skin, which were protected inside the gun. The techs are working on DNA as we speak. Fast-tracking it for us."

Evan let the smile take over. Slide bite, or tattooing, was an injury caused by an improper grip on a semi-auto pistol. It was a mistake few people made more than once. When the gun is fired, the slide slams backward several inches before falling into place again, loading a new round. If the shooter's grip is too high, the slide rips through the webbing between the thumb and forefinger, leaving two parallel slices. Not only does this trap DNA inside the weapon, it leaves the shooter with an easily recognizable, and difficult to conceal, injury.

Evan pulled into the Sheriff's office parking lot and saw Goff, in his rearview, doing the same. "Hey, Paula, we just pulled in. Why don't you go grab your dog and meet us back here? I want to get this oil off to Tallahassee tonight if it looks good."

"I don't mind spending the rest of the night working on the oil samples as long as I don't have to sort through anymore cell tower data today."

"I think that's a trade I can accept," Evan said. "Goff and I can handle the cell data."

"I have a feeling you'll be working it alone," Trigg said. "Just saying."

Evan parked, and suddenly everything fell quiet. He got out of the car and turned around, watched as a gray wall of rain made its way over the field behind the SO. Typical Florida rain, fickle as a cheerleader.

He looked across the lot to where Goff was getting out of his cruiser. "Not Goff's sort of detective work?" he asked.

"He had to wear his glasses when he was helping me earlier," she said. "I think it embarrassed him. Or gave him a headache."

"Probably both," Evan said. "Anyway, I appreciate you staying late. I think we're closing in on some answers."

"Yeah. No worries. We're just getting to the fun part."

TWENTY

TRIGG HAD BEEN RIGHT about Goff. He claimed he needed a break from close work after putting at least a dozen hours in reading bank statements and cell records. He was filing his report on the meeting with MacMac and going home, where Mrs. Skinny Old Man was preparing their regular Tuesday night chili burgers, and she wouldn't be excited about them overcooking. Evan probably could have pushed the issue, but he let it slide. He needed allies more than he needed help with the cell data.

Paula returned to the office with Ernie a little before five. She also brought coffees and grouper sandwiches from a place on Monument. Evan was so hungry he wanted to crawl into the bag with them, and he wondered what the procedure was for giving her a raise.

It took Evan until eight o'clock to wrangle the twenty-three pages of numbers from the cell phone provider into a cohesive picture. A total of eleven individual phone numbers pinged the Dead Lakes tower between the hours in question. Evan quickly identified Hutchens's personal cell and his work cell. He crossed those off the list, but did make a note of the time they went dead, 2:36 a.m.

A few hours later, through a slow and meticulous process, he had eliminated all but two cell numbers. One ending in 8930 and the other in 7345. This is what he had been looking for. One burner had been Hutch's. The other had been the killer's.

Evan leafed back through the pages, shuffled them into a different configuration, and cross-referenced these two numbers with the data he had compiled showing the movement of Hutchens's phones. The 8930 number pinged all the same towers, at matching times, as had Hutchens's other two phones. That left the 7345 number, the killer's number.

Just after 1:00 a.m. Friday, Hutchens's burner called the killer's burner. By tracking which towers each phone pinged, Evan saw that moments after this call, the killer had left white City and travelled to the Dead Lakes area. At this same time, Hutch travelled from Wewahitchka to Dead Lakes. Both phones showed up in the area within minutes of each other, about half past one. And both burners died at 2:36 a.m. – along with Hutch's home and work phones – when the killer tossed them into the lake.

He would need to request more pages from the cell provider. Now that he had the number of the killer's burner phone, there was a chance he could find out where it had been purchased, but he doubted that would lead to anything. It was beyond a long shot, but a necessary stone to flip for the sake of due diligence.

Evan rocked back in his chair, running his left hand through his hair and looking up at the ceiling. He had just begun wondering if he could get away with smoking in the sheriff's office – since it was after hours, and he was the sheriff – when something soft and wet dragged itself across his right hand. Evan froze, except for his eyes, which slid sideways, until they found the three-legged German shepherd that was licking his palm. Evan rocked back in his chair, running his left hand through his hair and looking up at the ceiling. He had just begun wondering if he could get away with smoking in the sheriff's office – since it was after hours, and he was the sheriff – when something soft and wet dragged itself across his right hand. Evan froze, except for his eyes, which slid sideways, until they found the three-legged German shepherd that was licking his palm. "Just stay away from the shoes," Evan muttered.

"Usually doesn't chew shoes," Paula said, leaning against his door frame. "Hats are more his thing. Hats and water bottles."

"My wife's cat's got a thing for shoes," Evan said, ruffling the hair between Ernie's ears. "Hannah got him about two weeks before her accident. I think he pisses in my shoes because he's mad she's not around."

"If that was true, he'd piss in *her* shoes, not yours," Paula said. "Maybe he's trying to mark you, you know? He lost her, so he's trying to make sure he doesn't lose you, too."

Evan considered her for a moment, then said, "I think he just likes pissing in shoes. You come up with anything on the oil?"

"It's close. I'd call it a match, but that's just me," she said. "The microscopic particulate is very similar in both samples. We'll need to get a sample straight out of the truck to be sure, send it up to Tallahassee, but I think what I have so far is a close enough match to get us a warrant."

"We've got the oil, and the tire track. I think it's reasonable to believe it was McMillian's truck there beside Hutchins's on the night of the murder. We've also got the questions about his status as a C.I, his affiliation with the Tens…his missing file. I think we need to bring him in, see what he has to say for himself."

"You want to do that tonight?"

"No, we know where he is. I need to wrap this up," Evan said, gesturing to the mess of papers on his desk, "and get search warrant requests typed up for Mac's truck. Are your samples ready to go to the lab?"

"It'll just take a minute or two, but there's no sense sending them until we have a clean sample from his truck.

Might as well wait until you pick him up tomorrow. I can get a cast of that tire to send up with the photos of the track, as well."

"Good point." Evan nodded. "Go ahead and call it a night. I have a feeling tomorrow is going to be interesting."

Evan sat on the sun deck, lights out, under a dark and heavy sky. The water and the occasional fish tapped lazily at his hull, sending gentle vibrations through the teak floor. The night air was fragrant, full of salt, and creosote from the dock's pilings. Evan inhaled deeply, and vowing to take the boat out soon, even if he just went out to the bay. An unlit cigarette rested in a clean ashtray on his rattan table. His mug sat beside it, empty except for a thin silt of turmeric and honey. He toyed with his zippo, absently walking it up his knuckles, then back down again.

Plutes lazed on a cooler by the door. Occasionally he would open an eye to a half slit, notice that Evan still existed, then close it again in intense disappointment.

One of the things Evan liked about the marina was that, as popular a hangout as it was, the Grill closed at nine on weekdays and eleven on the weekends. The place was quiet, save for occasional muffled voices from nearby boats and the creaking of fenders against the docks. High up on an aluminum mast, a pully clinked out a slow and monotonous metronome. But all these sounds seemed distant and thin, like the radio transmissions from a car in another lane.

The excitement of the day's discoveries had ebbed, overshadowed by a growing disquiet. Mac McMillian had not returned to his boat since Evan and Goff spoke with him that afternoon. His truck was not at the gym or the Thirsty Goat, where Mac tended to be whenever he wasn't in the marina.

Evan didn't think worry was appropriate. Not yet, anyway, but he had a little bit of worry on standby, just in case. It was unlikely that the Tallahassee Tens would make a move against the kid now. If they had intended to kill him, they would have done it already. Evan guessed there was a good possibility that MacMac would try to skip town, if he had, indeed, been involved in Hutchins's murder, but he felt almost certain that when the kid ran, he'd take his new boat, not his old truck. However, the truck had not returned. Nor had the kid. And the boat was still here.

Evan had a warrant to take oil samples from the truck, and plaster casts of the tire treads. This would essentially give him legal access to search the entire truck. He had enough probable cause to bring McMillian in for questioning, whether the kid wanted to cooperate or not. But neither the warrant nor the PC were of any use if the kid and the truck were gone. He would get a warrant for the boat if McMillian had not shown up by morning, but Evan figured if the scenario played out that way, it would be like strapping a life jacket on someone who drowned yesterday.

The Zippo missed a turn around Evan's bottom knuckle and dropped to the wood sole with a sharp *tack*. Plutes lifted his head, favoring Evan with a cat smirk. Evan scowled back. It was then that he heard an engine running and tires crunching on gritty pavement. He looked at his watch, nearly 1a.m. He turned to the side parking lot, which ran along the far dock, and saw a pair of headlights sweep across the water, then wink out. The sound of the engine died. Evan waited.

Hushed voices carried across the water, just above the other night noises. Evan slid open a drawer in the side table and pulled out a pair of compact binoculars. As he raised them to his eyes, someone appeared at the top of the gangplank. Not McMillian, Evan could see that right away. It was a young woman, one he didn't recognize, carrying a small purse in one hand and dragging a rolling carry-on bag in the other. Halfway down the ramp, she stopped and called back up to the parking lot, trying to yell and whisper at the same time.

Evan felt his pulse quicken. He stood and slipped his bare feet into his deck shoes. A second figure appeared at the top of the ramp, heavily burdened with baggage. It was MacMac. The young man had two large suitcases and a rolling trunk, in addition to his backpack. The tide was in, so the ramp's incline was not severe, and

MacMac was strong, but still he struggled, trying to hurry under the load.

"He's making a break for it, Plutes," Evan said.

Plutes looked at Evan for a moment, considered whether Evan's statement carried any relevance whatsoever, then closed his eyes and laid his head back down.

"Right," Evan said, then slipped his cell out of his pocket and hit speed dial. When dispatch answered, he gave a quick explanation of the situation and requested any available units to the marina. As he stepped off his boat onto the dock, the dispatcher let him know three units were in route, the closest about four minutes out.

MacMac would be out of the marina by then. Evan wasn't going to let it get that far. MacMac and the girl were arguing about something – she was moving too slow, he had left something in the truck, she didn't need whatever it was, yes she did, he'd buy her a new one – in their whisper-shouting. Both were still on the ramp and neither were looking his way. He eased along the dock, keeping the tops of the pilings between himself and MacMac, until he stood about ten feet from the foot of the gangplank. From here, he picked up the girl's name – Melly, or Molly, or Melee – something like that, and the source of their current conflict – a shopping bag containing something from Chanel that he had left in the truck.

They resolved the crisis, MacMac agreeing to run back to the truck as soon as she was aboard the boat, as long as she would get the engines fired up and the lines untied. Evan grinned at this. He had taken the liberty of reworking some of MacMac's knots. Melly would need a large knife to untie those lines anytime in the next hour.

Her heels continued down the ramp, accompanied by the thumping, rolling clatter of heavy luggage. She stepped off the ramp, turned right, and clicked down the dock toward Mac's boat, her carry-on rolling along behind with a *tack-tack-tack* as the wheels bumped onto each new plank.

Mac blundered off the ramp with even more clatter, nearly dropping one of the suitcases, muttering angrily under his breath. He set everything down, except the backpack, and began rearranging his load, trying to stack the cases on top of the rolling trunk.

"Give you a hand?" Evan asked, slipping out from behind the piling, just across the trunk from MacMac. His heart had settled into a quick steady hum, easy but ready, what Paula Trigg would call 'the fun part.'

Mac's head popped up, eyes wide. For an instant Evan was sure the kid was going to lunge at him, bounding right over the trunk. A simple off-lining maneuver on Evan's part would send the kid into the water before he knew what had happened to him, but it probably would have been smarter than what MacMac did instead.

Mac spun on his heal and fled, sprinting for his boat, still lugging one suitcase. "Run, Mallie!" he shouted.

Evan cocked his head. The blatant lack of insight on the part of some people never failed to amaze him. He moved around the abandoned luggage and jogged after MacMac. Four slips down, the engine coughed, bubbled, then growled to life.

MacMac was shouting "Go! Go! Go!" He leapt onto the boat and flew up the ladder to the bridge. "Get those lines loosed!"

The girl looked like she was trying to run in three directions at once, realizing he had left all her luggage on the dock and at a complete loss as to what to do with the mess Evan had made of the knots. The line was in her hands, her eyes were on her trunk, and her feet seemed to be running in place.

Just about the time Evan reached the boat, MacMac gunned the engine. The lines made a whip-crack *pop*, but held fast. The boat lurched backward about a yard and pitched hard to starboard. A shriek and a splash told Evan that Melly had just gone for an unscheduled swim.

"Gulf County Sheriff," Evan yelled as he approached, "Shut it down!"

The engine revved even higher, straining the lines. The rear cleat on the dock began twisting out of the treated timbers, threatening to let go at any minute. The boat rocked violently, sloshing and spraying foam. Evan feared Melly might be crushed between boat and dock, or shredded by the boat's propeller blades.

"Gulf County Sheriff! Shut it down!" he yelled again, but got the same result. The girl had disappeared. Evan hoped she had swum under the dock, but in the dark and churning water, there was no way to know. Evan's jog had accelerated to a full sprint by the time he reached the boat. He sprang across the three-foot gap between boat and dock without breaking stride.

Up on the bridge, MacMac felt Evan's impact. He looked back over his shoulder, saw Evan about to gain the ladder, and cranked the wheel in the opposite direction. Evan recognized his intent, set his feet in anticipation of the maneuver, but still fell to the deck as the boat canted to port and then slammed back into the dock.

Evan slid a foot or two, then hooked the bottom of the ladder with one hand. A second later, he was shuttling up the rungs.

MacMac grasped the wheel for dear life, almost as undone by the boat's lurching as Evan had been. The boat settled against its lines and MacMac gained his footing. As Evan's head cleared the top rung of the ladder, Mac launched a kick that would have impressed Pele… if it had connected.

Evan had expected the kick. It was MacMac's only obvious move and, frankly, Evan would have been disappointed if he hadn't tried it. He popped his head into view, then ducked again as Mac started his wind-up. As soon as the foot whistled through the spot where Evan's face had been, he sprang straight up and wrapped both arms around MacMac's leg. Evan dropped like a stone, his dead weight entirely dependent on MacMac's leg, jerking him off his perch. MacMac flailed for a handhold, found nothing, and fell with Evan. Half of MacMac – the lucky half – landed on Evan. The other half slammed into the deck, breaking things, like his nose and left wrist. A small handgun bounced out of his waistband and went skittering across the boards.

The bulk of the falling kid knocked Evan to the floor, as well, but he landed a bit more gracefully. He managed to regain his feet before MacMac understood what had happened. A second later Evan had the kid rolled onto his stomach and had a cuff on the right wrist. When he saw the state of the left wrist, he opted to latch the other bracelet to the bottom rung of the ladder. Mac-Mac's rolling eyes made it clear that any fight he might have had left had just been knocked out of him.

Evan hurried up the ladder and killed the engines, then scanned the green water for any signs of the girl. Down below, MacMac was groaning and cursing, but not in a way that suggested he would make any more trouble tonight. Evan spotted the girl he guessed was now MacMac's ex-girlfriend. She had managed to avoid dis-section-by-propeller by swimming under the dock and popping up on the other side. She looked pretty excited by the night's events. "You alright?" he called down to her.

He couldn't quite make out her response, but it didn't sound like something he was likely to repeat in mixed company. Evan took that as a good sign.

He realized he had been hearing sirens for the past couple minutes, and now the first of the three cruisers pulled into the lot, scattering gravel. He pulled his cell and redialed dispatch, filling them in on his situation. By the time his breathing had slowed, the marina parking lot had filled with emergency vehicles. Paramedics stabilized MacMac's nose and wrist, then transported him, under guard, to Sacred Heart for any aid someone felt like giving him.

The girl, Mellinda Betancourt, was the daughter of a wealthy couple on an eco-tour of the Dead Lakes. They'd only been in town for two days, so she clearly didn't have anything to do with the murder. She proved to be uninjured, though her shoes were a total loss. She babbled incessantly about lawsuits and brutality, but when her father arrived to pick her up, Mr. Betancourt simply thanked Evan for not shooting her and apologized for whatever part of this trouble his daughter may have caused. One of the deputies got her statement, and she was allowed to leave with Daddy. It had seemed pretty exciting to run off to the Bahamas with the blond guy from the bar, but Evan guessed it hadn't turned out as fun as she was hoping.

The medics checked Evan over, finding only minor scrapes and one large bruise, then left him alone. He pulled Sergeant Peters out of the crowd. The two walked back to Evan's boat, where Peters produced a notepad and Evan gave his statement, recounting the events from the time he heard Mac's truck in the lot until the backup units arrived. He told Peters that he would be at the office in the morning to interview MacMac, but that the kid was to have no other visitors. "I don't want him to say a word *to* anyone but me. And I don't want anyone saying a word *about* him to anyone but me. Got it?"

"That's exactly how we've always done it around here, boss," Peters nodded, though his smile suggested otherwise. "We'll keep a good eye on him 'till you come back tomorrow."

Evan bid him a good night and watched as the sergeant stepped onto the dock. He noticed that he hadn't seen Plutes since the excitement began. Evan found the cat in his stateroom. He had pulled Evan's slacks off the bed and wadded them into a cozy nest. He had then proceeded to coat the pants in short black hairs before curling up and going to sleep.

Evan changed into clean boxers, crawled into his own bed, then stared at the ceiling, waiting for sleep or daybreak to take him.

TWENTY-ONE

EVAN WOKE TOO EARLY to an odd and alarming scratching sound. His feet were on the floor with a quickness. The scratching now sounded like someone was cutting a Barbie doll's throat. The plastic bag he'd wrapped his last pair of dress shoes in. Evan reached over to his nightstand. He'd been waiting for this for days. He grabbed the air horn, then silently stepped over to the locker and jerked the door open. The cat looked up at Evan, the sound of urine hitting Italian leather making Evan want to weep. He let loose with the horn before Plutes could move.

The sound was so loud, and so brutal, that Evan wondered if he'd thought things through as well as he should have. But as Plutes bolted up the stairs, Evan laughed and followed in hot pursuit. "No, we won't be pissing in anyone's shoes anymore, pal!" Evan yelled as he made the salon. Plutes was nowhere in sight, which was where Evan liked him.

The thrill of victory was short-lived. A dull but emphatic ache announced itself across the top of his left shoulder, a souvenir of last night's exploits. Springing out of bed and bounding up the stairs hadn't helped. The pain began to crawl up the back of his neck into his scalp.

Evan paused to take stock. It was early. The sun was up, but just barely, its rays slicing at an acute angle through thin gaps in the curtains. A prime suspect in the only case that mattered sat in a cell. Evan was convinced Mac McMillian held the key to the sheriff's murder, but so far, he had been less than cooperative. Evan needed to be on top of his game today. That was going to be difficult now that his spine felt as limber as old beef jerky and his last pair of dress shoes was full of cat piss.

He washed down two Tylenol with his first cup of coffee, then chewed and swallowed some Ibuprofen for good measure.

The soggy shoe, and its drier mate, went into a trash bag for later disposal. Plutes had pissed precisely, filling the shoe but leaving no mess at all on the shelf. Evan showered, then selected a pair of black slacks and a white button down from his collection. They would look super with his Docksiders.

He ran through the case's idiosyncrasies as he drove to work, noting the certainties, the suppositions, and the outstanding unknowns. His light-colored shoes lurked just at the periphery of his vision, constantly distracting him, reminding him that he was slightly out of sync with his own world. He told himself it wouldn't matter what shoes he was wearing to interrogate MacMac, and by the time he arrived at the SO, he almost believed it.

He had a plan for the interrogation. He had facts that put MacMac in the swamp, with the sheriff, at the time of the murder. MacMac had been trying to sneak out of town, he had assaulted a law enforcement officer, and he had been carrying a concealed weapon without a permit. MacMac would talk. Evan expected he might even be able to file murder charges and call this case closed by the end of the day.

What he didn't expect was the parking lot-full of news vans when he pulled into the station. As he crossed the lot after parking, James Quillen hurried over to great him, dressed in his finest suit and smiling like a politician at a press conference. Then Evan remembered. He *was* a politician at a press conference. The local media were on scene to introduce the new sheriff to the people of Gulf County. Or, more accurately, they were here so that Quillen could introduce his selection for interim sheriff to the people of Gulf County. Several deputies and staffers were on the front steps, Goff among them.

Quillen's smile blazed as he reached Evan, but then faltered a bit when he caught site of Evan's shoes. Evan pretended not to notice and extended his hand.

DAWN LEE MCKENNA & AXEL BLACKWELL

"Good morning Commissioner," he said, evenly. "We're going to have to postpone this press conference."

Quillen grasped his hand, then pulled him in for an around-the-shoulder hug. This brought his mouth close enough to Evan's ear for him to whisper, "We don't postpone press conferences."

Evan pulled away. "Look, I have a major break in this case. I have a suspect in custody who can probably tell us—"

Quillen cut him off. "You see all those news vans over there? They are here to meet you."

"I've been sheriff all week, Quillen." Evan said. "That isn't news anymore."

Quillen recovered quickly. "Then we need to let them know we have a suspect in custody"

"No, at the moment I'm too busy doing my job," Evan said, brushing him away as he hit the sidewalk that led to the door. "But you're welcome to say whatever you like."

"As an elected official, you have a responsibility to your constituency."

"I wasn't elected, remember?"

"But it's a press conference," Quillen insisted, sounding baffled and more than a little furious. "You have to be there."

"Photoshop me in," Evan called back over his shoulder as he hit the top step.

Several deputies standing around the door had been watching the exchange. Goff gathered himself off the wall and opened the door for him. As he entered, Evan could see he had moved one or two notches closer to gaining their acceptance.

"Well," Goff said, staring across the lot to where Quillen stood smoldering, "there's a hen you can't unpluck."

Evan studied Mac McMillian through the one-way mirror before starting the interview. Mac sat in a steel chair. The splint on his left wrist was too big to accommodate a standard handcuff, so to manacle him to the eyebolt in the center of the table, the deputies had used a set of ankle chains. In addition to the splint, Mac's nose had an upside-down cross of white tape holding it in place. Faint reddish bruises curved beneath both of his eyes. Another set of bruises, three dime-sized circles, marred his jawline on the right side. It looked like knuckle prints, as if he had been punched.

"Notice anything?" Evan asked when Goff sauntered up beside hm.

"Looks grumpy," Goff said. "Probly miffed about his hairdo. A night in the holding cell tends to flatten it out."-

"Not sure if grumpy is the word I'd use," Evan said. "To me he looks scared, but not in a desperate way. He looks putout angry, not backed-into-a-corner angry."

"And," Goff added, "no slide bite."

"Well, we knew that yesterday," Evan said. "But the truck was there. I know it. I'm thinking there had to have been two people involved in this killing. At least two people, right? Whoever shot Hutchins hadn't had much practice with a pistol."

"I'd hazard a guess to that effect. He probably wasn't much of a baseball player, either."

Evan nodded his agreement. "So, whoever actually pulled the trigger didn't have much experience shooting people. But whoever planned the thing seems to have known exactly what he was doing."

"You got your smart one and your dumb one," Goff summarized.

"Exactly," Evan said. "And therein lies the problem. Mac doesn't have a slide bite, which means he's not the dumb one. But I'm having a real hard time seeing him as the smart one."

Goff pursed his lips, staring through the glass at the kid, then slowly nodded his agreement. "That'd be sadder'n hell."

Evan pushed through the door and Goff followed. MacMac scooted back in his chair and sat upright. Evan noticed the chair's odd tilt, and grinned. Its front two legs had been shortened, giving the seat a slight forward tilt. This made it difficult for the chair's occupant to find a comfortable sitting position, one of many little tricks used to keep a suspect off his toes. Another little trick, keeping the room temperature anywhere but comfortable, also seemed to be in effect. Mac's arms prickled with goose flesh.

"Good morning, Mr. McMillian," Evan said, taking his seat. "Would you like a glass of water, a cup of coffee before we get started?"

"How about turning off the air conditioner," he said. "My fingers are turning blue."

Evan smiled. "Oh, I think it feels nice. It's a hot one out there today. The sunrise this morning, man, let me tell you, it's going to be a beautiful day today."

"Yeah, yeah, I get it. It's nice outside but I'm stuck in here," Mac said. He tried to slouch back in his chair, but his butt slid forward on the slanted seat. The chains on his wrists wouldn't allow him to cross his arms, as he would have liked to. In the end, he opted for slouching there looking stupid.

"What do you want, man?" he asked, in exasperation. "Why am I here?"

"We've got a lot to talk about, Mr. McMillian," Evan said, his tone deliberate, considering. "You weren't willing to talk with us yesterday. Today, I'm hoping you'll be a bit more cooperative."

"I don't have to tell you anything"

"No. No, you don't *have to*," Evan said, "but, I think you're going to want to. I think you're going to see that talking to us is the only thing that makes sense for you. Right now, I can charge you with assault on a law enforcement officer, possession of an unregistered firearm, reckless endangerment…probably a few other things if I think about it for a bit. I can get you trespassed from the PSJ

Marina, maybe even get your charter license revoked. And that's just for last night's hijinks.

"But this interview is not about last night," Evan continued. "I'm willing to ignore everything that happened last night, if you're willing to talk to me about what happened last week."

"Last week?" Mac asked. "You mean Hutch getting killed? Man, I told you. That was the Tens!"

"Hold on," Evan said, "I'm not asking you who killed Sheriff Hutchins. Maybe we'll get to that later. That's not what I'm asking about right now." Evan sat back and watched Mac for a moment, letting the kid's wheels turn. "All I want to know from you right now is, who else drives your truck?"

MacMac stare was as blank as a dead television screen. He opened his mouth once, closed it, stared a moment longer, then finally said, "You mean the Ranger?"

"Yes, Mr. McMillian, the primer-red Ranger with the oversized bald tires," Evan said, evenly. "Other than yourself, who drives that truck?"

"Nobody drives my truck," Mac said, still sounding very confused. "I don't even drive it much. It's a…like a project, you know. Why are you asking about my truck?"

"So, nobody else ever drove that truck? Not one of your buddies?"

"No."

"Does anyone else have a key to your truck?" Evan asked. "Is it possible that someone borrowed it without your knowledge?"

"No. I have the only key. What is this about?"

"So, if I saw your truck parked somewhere, it would be reasonable for me to assume that it had been you who parked it there?"

Mac's eyes widened slightly. He again tried to sit back and was thwarted by the shackles and awkward chair. The skin on his arms still showed the effects of the cold room, but below the goose flesh, Evan also noticed more bruising than he had seen the night before.

Mac responded warily, "Where did you see my truck?"

"Wherever I saw it, you'd have to be close by, right? That's what you're telling us. Nobody else ever drove it. Nobody else has a key. That's what you just told us. So, if I see your truck parked anywhere, the only way it got there is if you put it there. Do I have that right?"

Mac nodded slowly, eyes shifting from Evan to Goff and back again. "Yeah," he said hesitantly, "I guess that'd be true...unless, you know, like someone stole it, or something."

"Mr. McMillian, did someone steal your truck?" Evan asked. "Do you have any reason to believe your truck was stolen at any time last week?"

Mac hesitated, fidgeted with his hands, then slowly shook his head.

"Nobody stole your truck? That's what you're telling us?"

"Nobody stole it," Mac said. "Not that I know of."

"So, I ask you again, if I saw your truck parked somewhere, the only possible way it could have gotten there is if you parked it there."

"Well, yeah, I guess," MacMac said.

Evan nodded, then shuffled some notes in his folder.

"Here's the deal, son," Goff said, in a long, slow drawl, "we're fairly certain you weren't the one who shot Hutch."

"Where did you get the gun?" Evan asked, before Mac had a chance to fully process what Goff had just said.

"I didn't do it, man! I didn't have nothing to do with that!" He raised his hand and tried to stand, but the chains held him.

"Sit down," Evan said. "The gun, Mr. McMillian. Where did it come from?"

MacMac's blank stare returned. He looked dazed.

Evan reached into the file box and pulled out an evidence bag containing the small pistol Mac had dropped the night before. "This gun, Mr. McMillian. Where did you get it?"

Recognition and fear spread in equal measures across MacMac's face. "Look, man, I just…I just got that for, like, protection, you know, self-defense. I didn't go looking for trouble. Those guys came to me. And when I realized what was going on, man, I did the right thing! I did what I was supposed to do. I told Hutch about it.

He asked me to keep tabs on them, and dude, I didn't want to do it, but Hutch talked me into it, so I did. And now I'm screwed!" He shook his head and thumped his hands on the table.

"That why he's dead?" Goff asked.

Mac started to answer in the affirmative, but caught himself. After a second he said, "I'd guess that's why, not because he screwed me over, but because he was messing with some bad dudes. I think the Tallahassee Ten found out he knew they were scouting down here, so they had him killed."

"And you were the one passing this info to Hutch?" Goff asked. "About them scouting the area? You think they found out that you were snitching on them to the sheriff, so they killed the sheriff, but they didn't do nothing to you?"

MacMac looked back and forth between the two men.

"That doesn't really make much sense to me," Evan said.

"It don't even make good nonsense," Goff said.

MacMac slid down his chair again, then straightened. He looked from side to side, eyes wide and watery. "Dude, I am telling you. That's why I had the gun, 'cause I was afraid of those guys coming after me. But man, I swear, I don't know what happened to Hutch. I didn't have nothing to do with that!"

"But your truck was there," Evan said, calmly. "And you already confirmed that if your truck was there, then you were there. Because you're the only one who ever drives your truck."

"What? What do you mean my truck was there?"

"The night Sheriff Hutchins was murdered, your truck was parked alongside his out at the Dead Lakes," Evan said. He leaned back and folded his arms, letting the words hang for a moment, then he continued, "Here's the deal, Mr. McMillian, like Sgt. Goff said, we don't believe you were the shooter, but we know you were involved. You know who the shooter was. You know why Hutchins was killed."

MacMac was shaking his head so violently his chains rattled. Evan continued, "You murder a sheriff in this state, you can pretty much guarantee you won't breathe free air for the rest of your life. The only sunshine you'll be seeing will be through bars. You're a young man, Mr. McMillian. You have a lot of years ahead of you. And from where I sit, it looks like you 're going to spend the rest of them using the crappy shampoo the state provides."

Mac threw his hands up, as far as the chains would go, and let out a frustrated sound that was somewhere between a scream and a growl. His head dropped into his hands and he tugged on his hair. "What do you want me to say? I don't know anything about Hutch getting killed! I wasn't there, I didn't do it! I don't know nothing about it!"

Evan waited until MacMac quieted. He flipped through a few more pages in his folder, then looked back up at the kid. "You want to tell us where you were last Thursday night?"

MacMac looked up, "Thursday?"

Evan nodded.

"Um…" MacMac looked at his hands, seemingly counting on his fingers. After a moment, he snapped them and sat up straighter. "I was out on the Gulf! I was out all night, didn't come back until breakfast."

"Did you have a charter?" Evan asked.

"No. But I was with someone. I was with a girl I picked up at the Goat."

"Ms. Bentencourt?" Goff asked.

"Ms… No, no, not that one, I just met Melly a couple days ago. This was Cindy…something, Cindy…shoot, she was from Panama City…I can't think of her last name."

"Do you have a phone number for Cindy," Evan asked, "or an email address?"

MacMac looked at his lap. "It was just a, just a thing, you know. A one-nighter. I don't have any way to contact her."

"And at what time did you and this mystery woman leave the marina?" Evan asked.

MacMac looked up. "It was about eleven o'clock, I guess," he said, a hint of hopefulness in his voice. "And we were gone all night. Didn't get back till breakfast."

"Ten fifty-six, to be exact," Evan said. "I took the liberty of viewing the marina's security footage this morning. You and a young lady – Cindy, presumably –

board your boat at Ten thirty-four. Then at Ten fifty-six, your boat is seen leaving the marina. You return again at nine twelve the next morning."

" See! See! I told you," MacMac was practically jumping up and down in his seat. "I was out on the water the whole night. There's no way I could have killed Hutch!"

"The problem is," Evan said, "it appears to clear you, but in reality, you still have plenty of time to dock your boat somewhere else, go kill the sheriff, then come back in the morning, looking like you've been on the water all night. Your girlfriend is unreachable, so there's no way for us to verify your story."

"Funny thing about that camera footage," Goff put in, "it shows the parking lot, where your truck oughtta be. But guess what? It ain't there. Now, why would you go and park your truck somewhere other than the marina parking lot?"

"My guess is," Evan said when MacMac didn't reply, "you parked your truck a mile or so down the coast – maybe at a private dock, maybe at a little waterfront joint that doesn't have security cameras – so that after putting your face on the security video at your marina, you could make your way over to this other dock, jump into your truck and drive out to Dead Lakes to meet with Sheriff Hutchins."

Mac had his head in his hands again and was shaking it slowly back and forth.

"Now," Evan continued, "like I said before, we don't believe it was you who shot him, but we know your truck was there, and you've made it very clear that nobody else drove your truck. You have an alibi, but it's as suspicious as it is flimsy. I think you know who killed Hutchins, and why. I think you need to start giving us some answers that make sense. Dig deep, Mr. McMillian. Think hard. You didn't shoot him. Do you really want to spend the rest of your life—"

MacMac popped upright and snapped his fingers again. "GPS! My GPS, man! I've got it wired right into my boat. That thing is always on, man. Check it out! Go check it out. You'll see. You'll see I left the marina and didn't dock again until morning. I swear, you'll see. We didn't go nowhere near—"

He stopped mid-sentence, index finger frozen in mid-point, eyes slowly growing wider until they looked about ready to pop out of his head.

The words came very slowly now, a reluctant realization. "My…truck. Thursday night. Thursday night my truck was…" MacMac looked to Goff, then to Evan, then down at his hands. "Thursday night my truck wasn't at the marina because it was in the shop! It was up in White City. I was getting a new lift kit installed. I, I got a receipt. I got a bank statement, shows the check I wrote. I didn't have my truck that whole weekend, man. You guys! Check the GPS! Check with…"

MacMac's excitement died faster than it had started. His face went white.

"Check with who, Mr. McMillian?" Evan asked, very calmly. "Who was working on your truck last Thursday?"

MacMac continued to stare at the two, looking shell-shocked.

"Now is not the time to be covering for your buddy," Goff said. "Whoever it is left you hangin' out to dry."

MacMac heaved a heavy sigh, "Tommy Morrow," he said, "Guy that fixes cars cheap out in White City. Tommy Morrow had it."

"Listen, Goff," Evan said as soon as they had stepped out of the interview room, "I don't want anyone else listening to that tape. And, I doubt I need to tell you this, but do not say a word about this to anybody."

"They won't hear it from me," Goff assured him. "You thinking Morrow's good for this?"

"His story never set well with me," Evan said. "I can't think of any legitimate reason why Hutchens would want to spring him early."

"Makes one wonder about the nature of their relationship," Goff mused.

Yes, it does," Evan said. "Add to that the fact the the killer's burner phone spent most of its time in White City, where Morrow lives, and the fact that Morrow was in possession of the truck that met with Hutchens…"

"And you got yourself a suspect," Goff finished for him.

Evan nodded. "I need you to round up a couple deputies and start running down loose ends. Send someone over to Thirsty Goat, see if they have surveillance video from last Thursday. Let's try to get an ID on Cindy."

Goff nodded, drawing a notepad and starting to scribble in it.

"Get a signed consent form from this kid to search his boat, specifically get that GPS downloaded onto one of our computers and see if we can verify his story. I need warrant requests drawn up for Tommy Morrow's bank records, and cell records. I'll also need warrants for his home and business, to verify he was working on Mac's truck."

"I'll get Crenshaw, Stephens, and Meyers on it," Goff said. "What else?"

Evan thought for a moment, then said, "Cell records. Let's get Tommy's personal cell number and cross reference it with the killer's burner phone, see if they match up. Also, go down and pull any evidence we have from Tommy's most recent arrest, and all the associated documents. We may find something of interest there."

"On it," Goff said. "What are you going to do?"

Evan studied his sergeant for a moment then asked, "Did you notice the bruising on Mac's jaw and forearms?"

"I did," Goff nodded. "I hear he took a tumble on his boat last night."

Evan pursed his lips. "I'm concerned that might not be the only tumble he took. Do you think he might have got roughed up a little by one of our guys after he was in custody?"

Goff's eyes narrowed. "Killing a sheriff ain't a very healthy habit. Not around here," he said, in slow, measured tones. "Nor is accusing folks of stuff you don't know nothin' about."

"You're telling me no one on our staff wanted to get a few licks in on Hutchins's killer?"

"I reckon just about all of us want a piece of whoever did it," Goff said. "But, that don't mean it's an impulse we're gonna act on. 'Sides, if any of us was going to do something to that kid, he'd be a hell of a lot more banged up than he is."

"You're not giving me a lot of confidence, Goff."

"Hate to be the one that's got to tell you this, boss, but we managed to get along all right for a lot of years before you showed up."

Evan sighed, looking through the one-way mirror at MacMac, then made up his mind. "Listen, Goff, this kid didn't kill Hutchins. After our little chat, I doubt he was involved at all."

Goff nodded.

"Make sure every deputy in the station knows that. I don't want to see as much as a single new scratch on that kid when I get back."

Goff's icy eyes held Evan's long enough for the interim sheriff to remember why folks sometimes called the older man "Frost." Finally, Goff said. "I'll see to it."

"Thank you," Evan said, evenly. "I have to step out for a few hours. Call me as soon as your guys turn up anything."

"What about goin' and pickin' up Tomorrow?"

"Let's get the warrants first," Evan said.

Goff nodded, but he didn't look happy. Evan thanked him, then headed for the door.

TWENTY-TWO

AS SOON AS EVAN'S PILOT was out of the Sheriff's Department parking lot, he dialed Wewahitchka Police Department, intending to ask for Chief Beckett. The greeting told him he could skip a step.

"This is Beck," his voice was smooth, with an inflection of either familiarity or contempt. Evan couldn't tell which.

"Chief Beckett, this is Evan Caldwell from…"

"Well, Sheriff Caldwell!" Beckett chuckled. "What a lovely surprise! I was just fantasizing about you."

Evan didn't bite. "I have a bit of business I need to take care of in White City. I could use some backup, preferably officers who were not particularly close to Hutchins."

Beckett chuckled again. "Well, Bigtime, I guess you called the right guy."

"I'm on my way up there now. Can I meet you somewhere?"

"Sure thing," Beckett said. "There's a country store on the corner of Highway 71 and Volunteer Avenue. I'll see you there."

When Evan arrived fifteen minutes later, Beckett was already waiting for him, even though his drive from Wewahitchka was twice the distance. Evan didn't bother to comment on this. Instead, he laid the file on the hood of Beckett's Monte Carlo and brought him up to speed on the case.

When he had finished, Beckett shook his head. "Tommy Morrow. Man. Never would have picked him for it."

"I don't have this locked down, yet," Evan said, "but the pieces are coming together. I was hoping to have a word with him, and maybe have someone with me who's a little more objective than my deputies seem to be at the moment."

"You've got some impetuous boys over there. I could see a couple of those guys losing their…what did you call it? Objectivity?" Beckett's broad grin spread across his face. "Best to call in someone who isn't too upset about a world without the Hutch."

"Something like that," Evan said.

"Well then, let's go have a chat with Tomorrow." Beckett said thumping Evan on the shoulder. "I'll have one of my officers meet us out there."

Beckett followed Evan out of the country store's lot, toward the edge of White City limits. It wasn't a long drive. On the way, Evan's phone rang. When he answered, Deputy Crenshaw's voice greeted him.

"MacMac's story checks out," Crenshaw said. Evan heard a seatbelt warning chime in the background, then a car door slamming. "I just finished up at his boat. The GPS shows he left the marina around eleven and didn't go anywhere near land until late morning. He's got a receipt from Tommy Morrow dated the Monday after Hutch was killed. I'm headed over to the Thirsty Goat now, to see what they have in the way of video from that night, but it looks like MacMac is in the clear."

"Yeah," Evan said, "I think that's going to turn out to be the case. Where are we on that cell data?"

"Meyers and Stephens are working on it. Don't know it they came up with anything yet," Crenshaw said. "Glad I didn't pull that duty. That's some tedious crap right there."

"Yeah, I hear you," Evan said. He was just pulling into the Morrow's property. At the far end of the drive, someone was hunkered under the hood of an old GMC, elbow-deep in the engine. "Thanks for the update. Have those guys call me as soon as they have anything."

"Will do," Crenshaw said, then hung up.

Beckett's black Monte Carlo slid up alongside Evan's SUV as he came to a stop. The two men stepped out of their vehicles and approached the mechanic. Tommy Morrow looked up from his work and forced a welcoming, though nervous, smile.

"Sheriff," he said, nodding, "Chief."

His hands were black with grease, but as Evan approached, Morrow slipped on a pair of leather work gloves.

Beckett stepped forward and thrust out his hand. "Tommy Morrow! How you doing, my man?"

Morrow instinctively accepted the Chief's hand. As soon as their hands were clasped, Beckett shook, then jerked the glove off.

"Hey!" Tommy shouted, and quickly covered his right hand with his left. But it was way too late for that. The two parallel slices that cut through the webbing between Tommy's thumb and forefinger were clearly evident, even under the thick layer of grease.

"Wow, Tommy," Beckett said. "That is a nasty cut. How'd you manage to do that?"

"Cooling fan," Tommy said, instantly. Then, in a better imitation of a natural response, he tried again, "One of those new cooling fans that kicks on automatically. I was messing with the radiator, fixing to pull it, and…"

Beckett was smiling. "Tommy, you've been turning wrenches since before you could walk. There ain't no way you forgot to disconnect a cooling fan before sticking your hand in it." He stared at Tommy, daring him to speak again. When he didn't, Beckett said, "You're a hell of a mechanic, Tommy, but you can't lie to save your life. Never could."

Tommy took a slow step backward, away from Beckett, and shot a glance over his shoulder to the door of his trailer. Evan had already moved up beside the kid while he was focused on Beckett.

"Don't try it, Tommy. You know I'm faster than you. And slim, here," he nodded at Evan, "he's got surfer legs, might be faster than the both of us."

"It…it was a cooling fan," Tommy tried again. "I swear. It kicked on…automatically. When I was fixing to pull the radiator…"

"On which vehicle?" Beckett asked.

Tommy was shaking his head, but didn't answer. A crunching of gravel alerted them to another vehicle arriving. Tommy's shoulders slumped. Evan chanced a quick glance and saw the black-and-white Wewahitchka police cruiser coming to a stop beside Beckett's Monte Carlo.

"Mr. Morrow," Evan spoke up, "last weekend, you installed a lift kit on a 1997 Ford Ranger owned by a Mr. Mac McMillian."

Tommy's face lost what little color it had left. His shoes began walking backward, seemingly without any input from their owner.

"You picked the vehicle up from the Port St. Joe Marina Thursday afternoon and returned it Monday afternoon. You were in sole possession of that vehicle during that time. Is that correct?"

Tommy's back peddling brought him to the open hood of the GMC. His butt bumped against it, stopping him. He put a hand into the engine compartment and came out with a large wrench. Evan dropped his hand to his service weapon, but didn't draw. Tommy didn't brandish the wrench as a weapon, but rather clutched it to his chest like a security blanket.

"Talk to us, Tommy," Beckett said, an almost friendly appeal. "Say something other than 'cooling fan.'"

Tommy just stared at the dirt between his feet, wringing both hands on the wrench and shaking his head. When he finally spoke, it wasn't to Evan or Beckett. "This ain't right," he muttered. "This ain't right. This ain't how it was supposed to happen."

"Mr. Morrow," Evan spoke with calm authority, "I am taking you into custody on suspicion of murder. We are going to ride up to Wewahitchka. You can tell us exactly what was supposed to happen and what went wrong."

"But, it wasn't murder. I didn't murder nobody," Tommy said, bringing his eyes up to Evan's. "It wasn't supposed to go this way."

"I can see that, Tommy," Evan said, nodding. "Why don't you put that wrench down. We'll get you cleaned up and see how much of this mess we can straighten out."

Tommy shook his head, slowly, and dropped the wrench on the GMC's bumper, continuing to deny he had murdered anybody. Evan continued to disbelieve him. He also couldn't help feeling that he wished someone else had been their guy. He didn't have a specific reason for that, just a vague sadness.

On Beckett's orders, the uniformed officer worked with Tommy to get the worst of the grease off his hands and arms, then got him secured in handcuffs and situated in the back of the cruiser.

As they drove north on Highway 71 to Wewahitchka, Evan called his office and asked to speak with either Meyers or Stephens, the two deputies who had been assigned to sort through the cell data. Meyers picked up the phone.

"We haven't quite finished yet," Meyers said, "but we already have more than enough to nail this kid to the wall."

"Spell it out for me," Evan said.

"Tommy's cell phone pings all the same towers, at the same times, as the burner phone we recovered from the lake. We're working through the rest of the data, eliminating all the other numbers, which will take a few more hours, but this is a slam dunk. He's had that phone with him at all times for at least two weeks before the murder."

"What about the night of the murder?" Evan asked.

"Yep, all day, until about twelve-thirty that night," Meyers said. "The burner gets a call. Ten minutes later, when it pings, it's hitting different towers than Tommy's cell. Tommy's is still in White City, while the burner is moving north toward Dead Lakes."

Evan thanked Meyers and let him go. He took a deep breath, held it for a moment, then exhaled slowly. He had no doubt that Tommy had shot Hutchins, it was the only way to interpret the evidence they had collected thus far, but he could not see Tommy at the center of this crime. Someone else had been pulling Tommy's strings. That was the only way this made sense. But who?

Tommy might tell them, but just as likely, he wouldn't. If someone had been persuasive enough to convince him to murder a county sheriff, they would likely succeed at persuading him to keep his mouth shut. Evan was surprised Tommy hadn't been their second body.

He was still wrestling these thoughts when he pulled into the Wewa Police Station. Evan felt a twinge of panic when the patrol car bypassed the parking lot and instead drove around behind the station. He had visions of Tommy disappearing, through one nefarious scheme or another. He put his car in reverse, intending to back out and follow the cruiser, but then he saw the sign marked 'Sally Port' pointing to the rear of the building. He realized the officer was just following standard procedure for dropping off a prisoner.

Beckett parked beside him and shot him a broad grin. Evan rolled his window down and Beckett did the same.

"Damn, Bigtime, you nailed that one." Beckett said. "Took you long enough, though."

Evan nodded and said, "He's just part of this. Probably not the biggest part."

"Well, I may be just a small-town cop, but even I could'a told you that," Beckett said, still grinning. "Let's go see what we can shake out of him."

Beckett led Evan through a police station that was compact but functional. At the rear of the building was a single holding cell just large enough to accommodate a cot and a commode. Evan guessed the cell had never held anyone more interesting than the town drunk. The officer who had driven Tommy to the station was in the process of collecting and cataloging his personal items as Evan and Beckett approached.

"You got somewhere private we can talk to him?" Evan asked.

Beckett nodded, then called over to the officer, "You can finish booking him in a minute, Chet. We need a word with him first." He looked at Evan. "We don't have much of an interview room, but it'll do."

He and Evan walked Tommy down a short hall and to a room that was barely large enough to fit the three of them, a small square table, and two chairs. Beckett sat Tommy down in one of them, and indicated that Evan should take the other. He leaned up against the wall between them.

"This is looking pretty dismal for you, Tommy," Evan said. He leaned forward, elbows on the table, hands clasped. "What I've got so far, you're looking at spending the rest of your life behind bars. The people of this state have very little pity for a man who murders an officer of the law."

Tommy met Evan's gaze for a moment, then dropped his eyes to the floor.

"Here's the thing," Evan continued. "I don't think you acted alone. I think someone else put you up to this, planned it out for you. You tell me who you were working with, help me understand what led up to this, why you decided to murder the sheriff, and maybe we can do something to help you out."

"I didn't murder nobody," Tommy said.

"Tommy," Evan said, "we know you were there that night. We can place MacMac's truck at the scene, and at the time, of the murder, and you were the only one with access to that truck. We can connect you to one of the burner phones used to set up the meet."

Tommy was shaking his head, still looking at the floor.

"And we know it was you who pulled the trigger. When you shot Hutchens, the slide tore a chunk of skin off the back of your hand. That chunk of skin was still inside the gun when we recovered it. It'll take about a week for us to get a DNA profile from that sample, but you and I already know whose DNA it is, don't we?"

Tommy looked up from the floor, just for a second, then looked back down. "I guess so," he whispered.

"Help us understand, Tommy," Evan said. "Help us see the bigger picture. Hutchens wasn't involved in your original arrest. He helped you get out of prison early. What was going on between you two? Why would you want to shoot him?"

Tommy shook his head. "I didn't."

"Didn't shoot him or didn't *want* to shoot him?"

The door opened, and a young officer with shockingly red hair came in with three bottles of water. He looked at Beckett.

"Give 'em here, Pruitt."

The young officer handed Beckett the bottles, nodded at his boss, and left. Evan waited while Beckett took the cap off of one and held it out to Tommy. Tommy reached up with both hands and took it.

"Oh, them's ice cold," Tommy said, sounding like a little kid with a popsicle. It made Evan sad. "Thanks, Chief."

Evan took a second bottle from Beckett, but didn't open it. He set it down on the table and watched as Tommy drained half of his, a small stream of it cutting a track through the grime on Tommy's chin. He waited until Tommy had put the bottle down before he continued.

"Tommy, talk to me about that night. What made you decide to shoot Hutch?"

Tommy just shook his head and shrugged. "I don't know…" he mumbled.

"See, Tommy, I don't believe that," Evan said, gently. "You put Hutchins down on his knees and shot him in the back of the head. You don't do something like that without a reason."

Tommy said nothing.

"According to what Caldwell here got from the cell phone records, Hutch called you." Beckett said. Evan was surprised by his voice. It was completely devoid of the flippant sarcasm Evan had come to expect from him. "Hutch asked you to meet him, right? Why? What was it he wanted to meet with you about?"

"I…I can't tell you that," Tommy said to his water.

"Son," Beckett said, "it can't get much worse for you than it already is. You understand that, right? No matter what you tell us now."

"I gave my word," Tommy said.

Evan and Beckett exchanged a look.

"You don't want to go back on a promise, but you've got no qualms about blowing half of Hutch's face off?" Beckett asked. "Those are some squirrely scruples, kid. Did the other guy help you out any more than Hutch did?"

Tommy grimaced, but said nothing.

"Gave your word to who, Tommy?" Evan asked, but got no response.

"I ain't saying nothin' else," Tommy said.

"When you left your place to meet Hutch," Beckett asked, "were you already planning on killing him? Or did something happen at the meeting?"

"I said, I ain't saying nothin' else," Tommy growled. "Don't ask me nothing else, cause I ain't answering."

Evan sat up and sighed. Beckett was about to speak, but Evan gave a slight wave, stopping him. He let the silence settle, then said, "No more questions, Tommy. For now, anyway. But I'm going to say a few words, and

I'd like you to think about what I'm going to say, because this will determine how you will spend the remaining years of your life."

Tommy spread his hands, still shaking his head and looking down. "Go ahead and say your words," he said. "Don't need my permission. Ain't nothing I can do to stop you, anyway."

"We know you put Hutchins on his knees and executed him with a single shot to the back of the head. We can prove this in court. If you're lucky, you'll be sentenced to life in prison. If not, you'll get the death penalty. This is Florida, Tommy. Florida executes. You know that, right?"

Tommy looked up at Evan, his expression a mixture of fear and sadness. Evan felt like he should apologize for reminding the kid of how bad things really were.

"Tommy, think this through with me. We know what you did. We also know you didn't do it on your own. Somebody put you up to it, right? Somebody helped you plan this out. You say you gave your word not to tell. I get that, I do, but whoever it was that helped you plan this, I bet he gave you *his* word, too, didn't he? Said that if you did everything just right you couldn't get caught?"

Tommy looked up quickly, and Evan knew he was right.

"Well, he lied to you, didn't he? Here you are, headed for Bradford County. I want you to think about that.

Think about giving up the rest of your life to protect the person who had you kill a man that tried to help you."

"That ain't who I'm protecting," Tommy said. "You guys don't know what you're talking about."

"Somebody put a fair amount of planning into killing Hutch," Beckett said. "That same somebody conned you into pulling the trigger. And now that somebody's just gonna let you pay the whole bill."

Tommy looked from Beckett to Evan, then stared at his water like he wanted another drink but didn't think he deserved it.

"It's okay, let him think for now," Evan said, standing. "But Tommy, you need to really think about what's happening here. By refusing to talk to us, you're not protecting anybody. Not really. We will figure this out eventually, one way or the other. But if you talk to us, if you lay it all out, maybe we can help you. Maybe get you a lighter sentence, give you the chance to get out of there before you turn eighty."

Tommy looked up at him, and his look reminded Evan of half the kids he knew in foster care. The scared ones.

"Have Beckett call me if you decide you want my help," Evan said.

Beckett called his officer in and instructed him to finish booking Tommy, then followed Evan out to the front of the station.

Evan had a cigarette lit before he'd cleared the door. He stopped on the front steps and Beckett nodded at his smoke. "Get one of those from you, Big Time?"

Evan held out the pack, and Beckett slid one out, used his own Bic to light it, then blew out a big plume of smoke.

"That kid's the sorriest thing," Beckett said finally.

"You think of anybody he thinks he owes more than he did the sheriff?"

Beckett shook his head. "I don't really know the kid that well. They're from over around Crawford-ville, Wakulla, someplace over there. Moved here after Tommy's mother died. I think Tommy was around eight, something like that. The old man was a first class jerk. Nobody liked him, nobody mourned him."

"What happened to him?"

"Drove his Tahoe into the rear end of a semi carry-ing a load of pigs," Beckett said. "Pigs were uninjured."

"You think he's thinking?" Evan asked.

"Thinking's not Tommy's strong suit," Beckett said, "And I'm saying that to be mean. He needs a lawyer that'll get him evaluated, see if maybe he can get some leni-ency for him. Life sentence. Somebody played the kid."

"You're sure you can keep him safe here, until we transfer him somewhere?"

"Yeah, nobody's gonna touch him," Beckett said.

"It's not just for his sake," Evan said. "He pulled the trigger. But I want the guy that pulled Tommy's trigger."

Beckett dropped his butt and held out his hand. "Kid's good here."

Evan shook it, thinking that sympathy for a cop killer was a strange thing for the two of them to bond over. If not bond, at least set aside their mutual dislike for a moment.

He squashed out his cigarette, poked it into the ash can nobody seemed to use, and headed for his car.

TWENTY-THREE

WHEN EVAN WALKED BACK into the SO, he felt like a pimp that had just crashed a church picnic. Not one person spoke to him as he made his way down the hall toward Hutchins' office, but everybody managed to give him one look or another, none of them friendly. When he turned into Vi's office, she looked up at him over her beak and her bi-focals, and pursed her lips.

"I'm impressed," she said without humor.

"Why's that?" Evan asked wearily.

"You made it all the way back here with all of your vertebra intact."

"I take it they're upset that I didn't let the SO make the arrest."

"Of course."

"You know, if the grid collapses and all of the cell towers go silent, none of you in this county will miss a thing."

"Your flippancy is not at all endearing, Lieutenant."

"Nothing about me is endearing, Vi." Evan sighed as he slipped off his blazer. "Look, I don't even want this job, and you know it better than anyone. But I can't do it without at least one person in my corner."

Vi took her glasses from their perch and let them drop against her chest. "There are no corners in this room, Mr. Caldwell," she said. "My office is round by necessity. I can't do my job, either, if I can't remain neutral. That is to say, I don't need you to plead your case with me. Just do your job with integrity and try not to make everyone else hate you."

Evan nodded, too emotionally worn to do much else.

"The warrants you requested are on your desk," she added.

"Which desk?"

"The one where I'm supposed to put things for the sheriff's perusal," she snapped, and put her glasses back on.

"Thank you," Evan said as he headed for Hutchins' office.

"Please be advised," she said to her computer monitor. "I don't believe for one moment that Sheriff Hutchins ever laid a hand on his wife. Neither does anyone else." Evan stopped with his hand on the doorknob, and she looked back at him. He was too far to be sure, but he swore her eyes were watering. "I would have been the first one to beat him senseless."

He nodded, then went inside the office he didn't want to occupy.

·•✳•·

An hour later, Evan asked Vi to get Goff for him. After a few minutes, Goff opened the door and came in, carrying a Styrofoam cup of coffee.

"Are you speaking to me?" Evan asked him.

"Well, I haven't said anything *yet*," the man answered, and sat down in the chair in front of Evan's desk.

"You know what I mean," Evan said.

"Look, I can see both sides," Goff said. "A lot of them were real close to Hutch. They think they oughta been allowed to see this thing through."

"I understand that," Evan said. "But their personal feelings could blow the whole case, get it thrown out before it has a chance."

"On account of Mac being banged up and all," Goff said. Evan shrugged. "MacMac mouthed off to the wrong cell mate, tried to be a big man. It's on the video from last night. Evan sighed. Goff threw him a triumphant half-grin. "Guess you stepped in somethin', Caldwell. Got some bias on your shoe."

Evan nodded. "I guess it runs both ways."

"So, what'd you need from me?"

"I've got trouble with these cell phone records," Evan answered, poking at the stack of papers in front of him.

"What kind of trouble?" Goff asked, before filtering some black coffee through his moustache.

"I've been looking at these things for two days," Evan said. "The thing that's bothering me is I can't find a connection to a third party. We've got two burner phones, one used by Hutchins, one used by Morrow. We know somebody else had to have put Tommy up to this, Tommy nearly admitted as much. But if there was a third person, he doesn't show up on any of the cell records. The two burners only ever called each other, and I can't find any calls to Morrow's or Hutchins' personal lines that could have been from a third burner."

"You know, back before phones, people still managed to conspire," Goff said.

"And I'm sure you still managed to catch them," Evan said.

One side of Goff's mustache lifted. His eyes twinkled just a bit as he leaned back in his chair.

"All I'm getting at is maybe they didn't talk by phone."

"Let me ask you, Goff, if you had been the brains behind this, would you have the confidence in Morrow to send him out to kill Hutchins in the first place, and then to keep his mouth shut about it afterward?"

"Well you know what they say about two men keeping a secret."

"Exactly," Evan nodded. "So, why didn't he kill Morrow after Morrow killed Hutchins?"

"They must be close," Goff said. "Family, maybe?"

"Could be…" Evan considered, but it just didn't sit right.

A knock at the door interrupted his thoughts. Before he could answer, James Quillen swung the door open and made his entrance into the sheriff's office. Evan stood. A second later, Goff lowered the front two legs of his chair and got to his feet as well.

"Commissioner," Evan greeted him.

"Sheriff," Quillen said, showing all his pretty teeth. "I hope I'm not interrupting anything."

"I was just leaving," Goff said. Evan hadn't noticed him moving, but Goff had slipped past Quillen and was almost out the door already.

"Hold up, Goff," Evan said. "I still need your help."

Goff looked underwhelmed, but leaned against the wall and took a sip of his coffee.

"I hear you have a suspect in custody," Quillen said. "Got a confession and everything, according to the gossip."

"A partial confession," Evan admitted. "We're still working to get the rest of it. I am not quite ready to announce anything publicly."

"Oh, no, of course not," Quillen chuckled. "Still gotta tie up all those pesky lose ends and what-have-yous, eh?"

"Something like that," Evan said.

"Well, I don't mean to take up too much of your time. I just dropped by to congratulate you on bringing this case to a close so quickly. This has been a very tragic and traumatic loss to our community. I know your diligent efforts will help restore the county's faith in its elected officials. I wanted to be the first to thank you, in person, for your dedication and professionalism."

"I appreciate that," Evan said. He studied Quillen for a minute then said, "While you're here, let me ask you a question. Something has been bothering me about this case."

"What's on your mind?" Quillen asked.

"Mac McMillian has been a key player in this case. In fact, he was our prime suspect for a few hours," Evan said.

Quillen continued to smile at Evan, but said nothing.

"It turns out, he had been acting as a confidential informant for Hutchins." Evan said. "Were you aware of this?"

"Well, sure," Quillen said. "As commissioner, I regularly receive briefings from the sheriff as to his doings. I believe McMillian's name came up once or twice. Why do you ask?"

"His file is missing," Evan said. "The folder is still in the drawer, but all the contents are gone. I'm assuming Hutch took them out of the office, maybe in connection with the meeting the night he died. You don't happen to have it, do you?"

Quillen looked confused. "Why would I?"

"Well, sir, I reviewed the surveillance video from the station's cameras," Evan said. "From the time Hutchins was killed until the time I discovered McMillian's file missing, and aside from Vi, you are the only other person to be in this office alone. I thought maybe, since Hutch was reporting to you on it, that you might have needed the file."

There was a space of about five yards between the two men, but it seemed like it took Evan's words several minutes to cross that distance. Quillen stood frozen, his face unreadable. Evan had time for an image to pop into his mind – an old grandfather clock, ticking away the seconds. Then, the upturned corner of Quillen's lip twitched even higher, and he responded.

"There were actually two individuals who had access to that file, Sheriff Caldwell. One of them is so well liked and trusted by the good people of this county that he has been elected to the county commission eleven times. The other one just drifted into town a few months ago. If there are any questions about stolen evidence or other unsavory behavior, which of those two men is more likely to be suspected of misconduct?"

"I didn't say anything about misconduct, sir."

"Well, your tone implied it."

"My tone implied that it's been a rough week and I could use that file," Evan said. "Nothing else."

"I know you have a lot on your mind just now, so we'll let it slide." Quillen said this without his smile faltering in the least. Before Evan could respond, Quillen said, "Again, congratulations on a well-run investigation. I will see myself out." Then he turned to the door and left.

Evan looked at Goff, who shrugged. "You ever rub anybody the *right* way?" the old man asked.

Evan was coming up with a quip when his intercom buzzed.

"Yeah," he said as he depressed the button.

"This is Vi," said Walter Cronkite.

"Yes, Vi."

"Chief Beckett is on the line for you."

Evan connected the call. "What's up?"

"You might as well come on back out here," Beckett said.

"Why?"

"Tommy's politely requested two things: a PB&J, and another talk with you."

"That was fast," Evan said.

"I'd hurry before he changes his mind," Beckett said.

Evan hung up on him, grabbed his cell, a pen and his smokes from his desk, and hurried out to Vi's office. She looked up at him as he stopped short by her desk. If there hadn't been carpet, Goff would have slammed into him.

"I need a peanut butter and jelly sandwich," he said.

Ten minutes later, a waxed paper parcel in hand, Evan strode down the hall with Goff on his heels.

"Goff, I need you to take that search warrant and a couple of deputies and get on over to Morrow's house," he said over his shoulder.

"On it," Goff answered. He stopped short behind Evan again as Evan came to a stop in front of the main staff area, where half a dozen deputies either sat at their desks or stood at the coffee counter.

"Listen up!" Evan said loudly. Everyone stopped and gave him their reluctant attention. "I apologize for assuming that someone here had roughed up a prisoner. I apologize that the sheriff is dead. I apologize that I got shoved into his job, and I apologize that I'm from Miami."

Evan looked at each man in turn before going on. "I don't care about being the damn sheriff. I'm just trying to do my job. I don't have the luxury of quitting rather than taking Hutch's place. I have…responsibilities and I need my paycheck, just like the rest of you."

A couple of guys shrugged, one nodded, but in a noncommittal way. Peters, who was standing by the coffee machine with his arms across his chest gave out a grunt. "Well, I reckon I *would* have beat his ass, but it was the Master Chef finals and I had to get home," he said.

Evan tried not to smile, but did so anyway. "Well, I'd appreciate it if my apology spread as fast as everything else around here," he said, and headed for the front doors.

TWENTY-FOUR

OFFICER PRUITT MET EVAN in the lobby of the police station, then led him back to Beckett's office. The Chief had his black Justin ropers propped on his desk, next to two plates of peach pie.

"I had Becky fix a plate for you, too, Bigtime," Beckett said. "I don't often do that."

"Are we celebrating?" Evan asked.

"Not yet," Beckett said. "Let's see what the kid has to say, first." He swung his feet down off the desk and led Evan to the interview room. Another officer was standing against one wall, swiping at his phone. Tommy was staring at the wall until they entered, then looked over at them as Evan closed the door.

"Thanks, Jake, you can go," Beckett said to the officer.

Evan waited until the door closed again, then held out the wax paper package to Tommy. "I brought you your sandwich, Tommy," he said.

"Oh, thank you," Tommy said, taking it in both hands. He put it down on the table, and Evan reached over.

"Let me unwrap that for you." He opened up the wax paper, smoothed it out, then sat down across from Tommy.

The desperation that had colored Tommy's face earlier was gone, replaced by a calm resolve. On the table between them sat a tape deck that looked like it had been manufactured in the early 80's, and probably ran on D cells. Beckett punched a button and slid it to the side.

"You were right, what you said before. You were right about that. It just took me a little while to realize it," Tommy said, and then took a bite of his sandwich before he continued. "Strawberry. He made me promise not to tell what happened. He said if I told anyone, it would all be for nothing. But, he also swore to me, he swore there was no way I'd get blamed for this. He said he'd thought it all out and no matter what, I couldn't get caught. "

"He played you, Tommy," Evan said. "No matter what else may be true about this situation, that's what matters now. Your partner in this set you up to take the fall. You don't owe him anything. You help us nail him and I will do everything in my power to help you."

Tommy shook his head. "No, man, you don't get it," he said. "You can't nail him, because he's dead."

Evan shot a look over to Beckett, who just raised an eyebrow and shrugged.

To Tommy, Evan said, "I'm sorry, I'm not sure I understand."

But in the back of his mind, he was suddenly worried that maybe he understood a little too well. Tommy and Hutchins were the only two people they'd tied to this case.

"I told you I didn't murder nobody," Tommy said after swallowing another huge bite. "It wasn't murder, it was suicide. I mean, sure, I pulled the trigger, but he wanted me to, begged me to. That's why he got me released early. It was part of our deal."

Evan narrowed his eyes, searching Tommy for any tell or hint that the kid was fabricating. He could find none. Behind Tommy, Beckett mouthed the words, "What the hell?" Evan gave him a slight but bewildered shake of the head.

Evan took a deep breath and let Tommy's words sink in. He sat back in his chair, let the breath out, then pulled a note pad from his jacket pocket. "How about you start at the beginning, Tommy. It sounds like there's a lot of story we need to hear."

Tommy nodded. "I guess you would piece enough of it together, you know, over time, so that it wouldn't matter if I told you or not. It all made sense when Hutch told me. I mean, not at first. At first, it was just nuts, you know, I thought he was messing with me. You know how cops are," Tommy laughed. It was a self-deprecating, sad sound.

"But then he told me what he would do for me, and how we would do it, and why he wanted it done, and it all kinda just made sense. I mean, he was, like, an authority figure. He was coach and sheriff. We always did what Hutch told us to, you know, growing up. So, when he comes and tells me he can get me out of jail and keep my brother in college and all I gotta do is… well, he didn't spell it out at first, not the whole thing, you know, until I was already caught up in it, and then it was too late. I was committed, you know, past the point of no return, or whatever."

"Hutchins told you 'all you gotta do…' was what?" Evan asked.

"He said, he told me there was this real bad guy, this guy that did terrible things and he needed to be put down, right, like vigilante justice type stuff, like super hero type stuff. That's the way he sold it, see. He said there was this real bad dude. Somebody needed to kill him, but Hutch said he couldn't do it, said it was complicated. But he said I would be able to get close to the bad guy and put him down and no one would ever suspect me. And the world would be a better place once this bad dude was dead."

Evan felt slightly nauseous. He wanted a smoke.

"Anyhow, I drove out there that night when he called, just like he told me, but when I got there it was just me and him," Tommy said. "He was standing by his truck, just leaning on it. And when I asked him where the other guy was, he said there wasn't no other guy."

"Damn," Evan heard Beckett whisper, but he didn't take his eyes off of Tommy.

"He took out this pair of gloves and give 'em to me, and then he handed me this gun wrapped up in a towel. And he said I had to shoot him."

Evan let out a slow, even breath. "Did he say why?"

"Cause he couldn't stop beatin' up his wife," Tommy said slowly. "He said he tried, tried real hard, but he couldn't quit it. He said he loved her an' knew it was all wrong, but he just couldn't quit." An uncharacteristic hardness settled over the kid. Evan thought it made him somehow ugly, the way a friendly dog will sometimes turn ugly if it's on its own too long. "And he knew how I felt about my momma."

Tommy swallowed hard. His eyes moistened and he blinked the tears away.

"What about your mother, Tommy?"

"He knew I felt real bad cause I didn't do somethin' to stop it," Tommy said. "He knew it scared me to death when my daddy beat on her. And one night he beat on her, and me and my brother hid on the back porch, just listening. And when I got up lookin' for my breakfast the next morning, she was just layin' there dead in her bed."

Evan glanced up at Beckett, but Beckett's eyes were on Tommy, his face unreadable.

"I was real scared at first," Tommy said. "When Hutch gave me that gun I was shakin' so bad and I said I couldn't do it, couldn't do it at all, but he said if he did it himself his wife wouldn't get no money from the sheriffs, and she deserved to get that money. He said she deserved a lot more, but it was all he could give her."

Tommy looked down at the second half of his sandwich, but he didn't feel like eating it anymore. Then he looked back up at Evan.

"But then he told me that it was my big chance," he said.

"To what? Help your brother?"

"To make it up. To do the right thing. He said I might not of helped my momma, but I could redeem myself. I could be a man and do the right thing."

Evan sighed, looked down at his note pad. He hadn't taken a single note. "So then what happened?" he asked.

"He got down on his knees. Down there in the dirt, and he was prayin'. I was still real scared, and I didn't want to hurt him. I didn't. But I let him pray a while, and I thought about how scared I had been when daddy was beating up momma. And I thought about how scared she must have been, and how she looked when we found her. And then I shot that gun." He sat up straighter in his chair, pushed his skinny little shoulders back. "I shot that gun and I got redeemed."

Silence settled over the room, slowly, the way silence settles over the night after a gun has gone off. The echoes of Tommy's story hovered around the room like a conversation between ghosts.

Eventually, Evan said, "Tommy, we're gonna take a little break." He looked up at Beckett. "I need a cigarette."

Beckett nodded and headed for the door.

"You shouldn't smoke, Sheriff," Tommy said, shaking his head. "Ain't any good to anybody, those things."

Evan nodded as he slipped out the door.

TWENTY-FIVE

BECKETT ASKED THE RED-HAIRED officer to go back in and mind Tommy Morrow, then he and Evan stepped outside. They smoked in silence for at least two minutes before Evan spoke.

"Hutchins manipulated that kid," he said.

"You brought that boy out to my station for a little 'objectivity,' remember?" Beckett said. "Let me offer some of that to you now. Tommy Morrow put a .45 caliber handgun to a man's head, a sheriff's head, and pulled the trigger, knowing full-well what he was doing. At that point, the 'why' ceases to matter. You have him for murder in the first, and it's going to be real hard for him or anyone else, to argue that down to manslaughter, or self-defense, or anything else. Really, this is murder of a law enforcement officer *and* conspiracy. That kid's dead in the water."

"I already get all that," Evan said, lighting another cigarette.

"You even *hint* at suicide and it'd be like drop-kicking a hornet's nest into a bus-full of preschoolers. It won't be line of duty anymore. Not only that, but Hutch committed conspiracy. Since he hired some poor kid to blow his brains out instead of doing it himself, Marlene's not even gonna get the life insurance."

Evan slowly exhaled. Something slimy was creeping up his spine. "What are you getting at, Beckett?"

"Marlene getting screwed, this kid getting the death penalty, that doesn't help anybody."

"It's not about helping or not helping, it's about the law."

"Don't preach to me, Hollywood. I've been enforcing the law since before you lost your virginity," Beckett snapped. "But what does humiliating Marlene accomplish for the law? Her being broke as hell after all the crap she took? I hated that man, but this might be the one damn thing he did that I can almost respect."

Evan swallowed and looked away, stared at the boarded-up feed store across the street.

"Look, Caldwell, I know where you're coming from, and believe it or not, I'm not much for bending the law as it suits me, either," Beckett said. "But if we can get that kid to change his story a bit, leave the suicide thing, the abuse, out of it, he might be able to live to see forty, Marlene might get to live the rest of her days with some kind of peace, and your little sheriff's office over there gets to keep its pride."

"I don't care about pride," Evan said.

"It's not about you," Beckett said. He lit another cigarette himself. "Let me ask you something. Who benefits from knowing what we just heard?"

Evan cut his eyes at Beckett. "We have an obligation to do our jobs. Tommy killed Hutch, whether we wish that was true or not."

"And he's going to prison for the rest of his life for it," Beckett said. "Does he need to get the penalty for it for the debt to be paid? The kid's not right in the head, man! He thinks he did something good."

Evan shook his head. "I need to go for a walk," he said, and headed off across the parking lot toward nothing in particular.

·•✳•·

Forty minutes later, Evan peeked through the little window in the door of the interview room. Tommy was sitting there with a plastic pint bottle of milk in front of him. Across the table, the redheaded cop was scribbling on a piece of paper. It looked like a game of hangman.

Evan moved on down the hall and walked into Beckett's office. Beckett was sitting at his desk, staring at the wall. He looked ten years older than when Evan had left. Evan closed the door behind him.

"I know," Beckett said quietly. "We can't sell it. Tommy can't sell it."

"No," Evan said. "Maybe he could once, for an official statement. But he's…like you said, he's like a kid. He wanted to tell the truth. He might want to tell it again, and then we're both in prison, and he and Marlene are right where they already were."

Beckett stared at the pencil he was flicking back and forth. "Hutch's death is gonna be for nothing. This kid's life is gonna be for nothing. And Marlene's gonna be poor and pitied."

"Yes," Evan said.

Three days later, Evan finally had some time off. Two whole days, like regular people. He'd spent the first day and a half fishing off the pier and buying two more pairs of dress shoes and a plastic tote with locking lid to store them in. He'd visited Hannah, gone to the farmer's market, and anything else he could think of that needed to be done and might also help him bide his time while he processed his changing perceptions of his former boss, Chief Nathan Beckett, and the differences between morality and ethics.

As far as Hutch went, there was revulsion there, but like Beckett had said, a small, grudging respect as well. Hutch had been wrong to use that poor kid to do what he couldn't do himself. But maybe he'd really thought it was the only way to save his wife.

Beckett, well, Evan didn't know if he'd ever like the man, but he wasn't so sure he had him pegged, either.

As for Tommy and Marlene, Evan suspected he'd wonder for a while if he'd done the right thing. Or if he could have done the right thing a little better. He'd been sitting on the sun deck for almost two hours mulling that one over, and he was no closer to knowing the answer, or sticking to just one.

Plutes, sitting over on top of the cooler, didn't care whether Evan found any resolution or not. Evan drained the last of his golden milk, and set it down just as his cell rang. Evan picked it up and recognized Shayne's phone number. His wife's boyfriend.

He called every few weeks, just to check in, and Evan was still of a mind to tolerate it, though he wasn't sure why. Penance?

He connected the call. "Hello, Shayne."

"Uh, hey, Evan," the other man said.

Evan pictured him on the other end, with his sun-bleached hair and his professor glasses, and his sympathetic eyes. Evan hated him.

When Shayne asked, Evan reported that Hannah was doing well, but doing the same, which really wasn't the same thing at all. No, there were no changes. No, Evan didn't need anything for her.

They were all set to say goodbye when Shayne popped it out like an afterthought, which it probably was. "Oh, hey. How's Plutes?"

That took Evan a second. "Plutes?"

"Yeah, the cat. My cat, how is he?"

Evan looked over at Plutes, who was polishing his armor, and wanted to punt him over the side. "This is your cat?"

Shayne hesitated. "Well, uh. Yeah. Yeah, I couldn't keep him in my new place, no pets, you know? So… well, Hannah took him." He waited for Evan to say something, but Evan didn't. "So, I guess he's still there, huh?"

"Yeah, he's still here," Evan said.

Evan sat there for a minute after they'd ended the call, staring at nothing off in the distance. Then he looked over at the cat.

"Well, what do you know, Plutes? He didn't want you, and she didn't want me."

Plutes looked at him for a couple of blinks, then his head started jerking forward. Evan stared at him, thinking he looked like he was doing an impression of Don Knotts bobbing for apples, but then something that looked like a wet, black caterpillar fell to the deck with a soft *plop*. Evan and the cat both looked at it for a second, then the cat jumped down without a sound and walked inside.

Evan sat there for a few minutes, wondering if he could pay The Muffin Girl to run over there and take care of it for him, maybe take the cat with her when she left.

Then he went inside to get a pair of gloves and some paper towels.

THE END

THANK YOU FOR READING
DEAD RECKONING

WANT TO KNOW when the next book in the Still Waters Suspense Series is released? Sign up here to be put on our mailing list. We won't bug you, but we will give you a heads up as soon as each new book hits the shelves.

You can also read **Dawn Lee McKenna's** bestselling *Forgotten Coast Florida Suspense Series* here

AMAZON.COM/GP/PRODUCT/B01N36XL4S

and follow her Facebook fan page.

FB.COM/DAWN-LEE-MCKENNA-1470505269903994

You can pick up **Axel Blackwell's** critically acclaimed books, *Sisters of Sorrow* and *Timeweaver's Wager* here:

AMAZON.COM/AXEL-BLACKWELL/E/B00W0I2UO4

And keep up with his solo releases by following his Facebook fan page here.

FB.COM/PROFILE.PHP?ID=100004365286512

You can also fine his website here.

AXBLACKWELL.WIXSITE.COM/AUTHOR

If you have a minute, we'd really appreciate you using it to leave an honest review for other Amazon readers.

ACKNOWLEDGMENTS

THE AUTHORS WISH to thank their long-suffering families for making the writing of this book possible. We'd also like to thank book designer Colleen Sheehan of **WDRBookDesign.com** for her beautiful formatting and design, Debbie Maxwell Allen for her keen editing, and Shayne Rutherford of **WickedGoodBookCovers. com** for her inspired cover design. We can't leave out the best group of authors we could ever hope to call friends. AC, thank you for the laughs, the support, the shared learning, and the GIFs.

ABOUT THE
AUTHORS

DAWN LEE MCKENNA is the author of the novel *See You*, and the bestselling *Forgotten Coast Florida Suspense* series. A native of Florida, she now lives in northeastern Tennessee with her five children and one domineering cat.

AXEL BLACKWELL grew up in one of those small Indiana towns where the only fun is the kind you make yourself. Many ghost and UFO sightings in central Indiana between 1985 and 1990 can be attributed to Axel and his brothers attempting to escape boredom. Axel now lives with his family and an assortment of animals in the Pacific Northwest.

48919366R00179

Made in the USA
Middletown, DE
30 September 2017